A STATE OF MIND

for Eavan Boland and Eavan Casey, with love

A STATE OF MIND

Kevin Casey

THE LILLIPUT PRESS
DUBLIN

First published 2009 by
THE LILLIPUT PRESS
62–63 Sitric Road, Arbour Hill
Dublin 7, Ireland
www.lilliputpress.ie

Chapter 1, in a slightly different form, first appeared in *Krino 7*

ISBN 978 1 84351 153 3

1 3 5 7 9 10 8 6 4 2

A CIP record for this title is available
from The British Library.

Set in 11 on 15pt Ehrhardt by Marsha Swan
Printed in England by Athenaeum Press Ltd, Tyne and Wear

A STATE OF MIND

ONE

THIS IS AN ATTEMPT to record the events of last summer. I want to understand what happened. I am tired of bewilderment and sadness and the faint unease with which I awake each morning, as if from a disturbing dream. If I describe my feelings, I will, perhaps, learn to understand them. In the fiction I have written, I sometimes stumbled with surprise on a hidden truth, a sudden awareness of a character's possible motivation, something that I did not realize I knew. I would push on with the plot in the manner planned, always hoping for the unexpected moment, the reward for a month's labour. I start this record with the same hope of discovery, writing in this small red notebook, awkwardly, like a child.

I love words. I love their shape, their sound, the precision of their meaning, yet somehow, four or five years ago, I lost confidence in my ability to use them. Day after day I would stare at the blue lines in my notebook, the blank sheet of paper in my typewriter. Nothing could have been worse. My craft crumbled, my confidence waned. I felt defeated and incomplete. My books went on selling but I felt estranged from them. The bright covers of paperback editions rebuked me. I was no longer the man who had written them. My publishers, believing that I was working on an ambitious project, sent me encouraging letters which made me feel even more fraudulent. I went less and less into my study. I drank more but managed to give up cigarettes.

I pretended to my wife and daughter that I was not worried, but they would occasionally express their concern. I wondered if I should return to journalism. I thought of ideas for plots. I lived a life of rural leisure and private desperation.

The house that my books had bought for us was situated in that part of County Wicklow favoured by foreign writers who wish to avail of Ireland's tax-free concessions. It has a stolid, middle-class charm that has appealed to us from the start. A drive leads from the roadway upwards through a small and sloping paddock towards a Gothic portico that a previous owner, a merchant in the village of Ashford, had added to proclaim his prestige. One should, I suppose, have set about demolishing this gesture, to reveal the more spare and telling lines that the original builder had devised but somehow the self-important imperfection of those pillars is like a character defect that makes a friend all the more endearing.

Behind the portico there was a house that one could come to admire and even grow to love, angular and self-confident, a proclamation of windows and chimneys that, in their parody of the mountains that rose above them, benign and enduring and safe, echoed an owner's hope of longevity. I had become fascinated by the title deeds. My solicitor, a friend since schooldays, had set about the minor task of detecting the name of the man who had built the house. He was, it appears, the second son of the local landlord. The series of social awkwardnesses and progressions by which this modest lodge, overlooking a pond and a river and a series of unchallenging peaks, had become more imposing and assertive could be understood through a study of the changing ownership since then.

We had bought it from the widow of a Dublin barrister. When all her furniture had been taken away in vans, the interior looked subdued and shabby but after a few months' work and the installation of our own things it became friendly and filled with light.

There is a large hallway with a parquet floor and a narrow welcoming fireplace. Much-admired mahogany doors with plain brass fittings lead into a sitting room, a dining room and the study in which I am writing these words. A passage leads to the kitchen and to a former scullery, now converted into a breakfast room. Upstairs, there are five bedrooms and two bathrooms. I suppose that I am describing all this bourgeois respectability because I am proud of it. It proves that I was once a writer, that I knew something about plots and about characters, that I had something to say. I can touch the walls of this house and for a few seconds, at least, my success is tangible.

I could not have afforded this leisurely lifestyle on my salary as a journalist. The five or six books I wrote so effortlessly redefined me and my way of life. The first success was unexpected and, because of that, all the more exciting, like a new sexual experience involving facets of the personality that have previously remained detached. Good reviews, the first film offer, the first foreign translations, the first interview on television – it was a world of heightened consciousness which seemed to interleaf fantasy and reality even more adroitly than I could do in my books. I was, for a while, a minor celebrity, a creature of the media, quoted and corruptible. I look back at that time with some amusement, missing only the quiet hours that I spent working on the next book.

When I left journalism, after practising the trade for almost twenty years, my colleagues presented me with an inscribed silver salver. I have it here on my desk. There was a reception in the local pub at which most of us got very drunk.

I must confess that my memories of the occasion are blurred but I know that as the evening went on the opinions being expressed by a number of the guests were radically different from the sentiments inscribed on the salver. This hurt me, for I had taken pride in my persistence and accuracy as a journalist. For two years I had acted as Northern Ireland correspondent and the pieces I had filed from there were often praised and were not without some influence. I was a professional and I expected to be assessed professionally. 'You were always a hack,' Brady the chief sub-editor said to me that evening, 'so it'll be no problem to you to go on churning out hack fiction.' Everyone standing near to us had laughed. I felt both hurt and oddly isolated, knowing, rationally, that he was motivated by jealousy at my success, yet wounded, emotionally, because I was made to feel different and friendless. Brady and I had never been particularly close but neither had we had any disagreement. I had to conclude that he was articulating an official viewpoint and that those who publicly wished me well may have been saying something different in private. It occurred to me then that I had little gift for friendship. There was something about my manner or my personality that discouraged intimacy. I had a tendency to invent myself for others, presenting them with that aspect of my character with which, instinctively, I assumed they would feel most comfortable. This tendency allowed me to have a wide circle of acquaintances, all of whom impinged on my life on different levels and in different ways but none of whom could be described as a friend. My only close relationships are with my wife and daughter.

Wife and daughter: this might be the title of some forgotten Victorian novel or one of those exquisitely subtle but almost unreadable books by Ivy Compton-Burnett. My home is feminist, a tiny matriarchy built on the new and alert aspirations of intelligent women. I sometimes feel awkward, like an old colonizer who is back, blundering through the landscapes of oppression in what is now a newly independent nation. There is no one here with whom to share the crude race memories of the oppressor. It is the future that is pointed to, not the past. When my daughter leaves these peaceful rooms, she will have to conquer the world.

Wife and daughter: Laura and Rachael. The names now assume a kind of Biblical authority. Some months ago Rachael asked us, for the first time, how we had chosen her name from all the others that would have been at least as appropriate. To our surprise, we could not remember. It had no particular logic, it commemorated no ancestor; we must simply have liked it. This is the way I have given names to the characters in my books but it seemed a little sad that the identity of a real and much-loved person should have been arrived at almost casually. Yet lives are made as casually as that in couplings, happy and thoughtless, and in this island of ours they are also taken away with perhaps even less premeditation. I must admit that it is only since I have had a child of my own, a life that would not have existed if I had not felt some passion or commitment or, at the very least, some lust, that I have become sensitive to the personal domestic tragedy of little deaths. One can use words like soldier, terrorist, gunman, Catholic, Protestant, innocent victim. These words and phrases preclude important daily rituals and needs: the kiss, the pay-packet, the smile of approval, the good school report. It must be terrible to look down on the shattered body of a loved one, to see the blood oozing and the bone exposed by the impact of a planted bomb. How could one accept the finality of that act of violence? There were moments last summer when I worried about the safety of my family and I remember the feeling of rage, rising like lust, difficult to control.

When I first saw Rachael, her little body was dark and streaked with blood. I was reminded of African tribal markings, as if she had come from the womb already initiated into some secret ritual. Laura was laughing, her face glistening with sweat as the nurse lifted the new and separate life and the first sound that the baby made was more like a cough than a cry. That was fifteen years ago but the emotions created by the event spread out from the table, filled the harshly lit and antiseptic delivery room and they come back to me now as if just experienced. I can remember the smell of the moment of birth, the urgings towards exertion as if it were an athletic event, and Laura's anxious eyes. She held my hand, gripping it as a climber might, holding on for life. I felt closer to her than in the lovemaking that had created the baby, joyous though that had been. She was vulnerable and courageous and even pain could not take away her pride. She settled into the exercises that

11

she had practised, holding my hand and ignoring the strange if not unfriendly faces of white-coated men and women who would pause to take a look and then move to the door of another cubicle.

Last summer, when I feared that they were threatened by a force that I could not understand, I thought a lot about those hours in Holles Street Hospital. And, as if seeking for some pattern of logic in a sequence of unconnected events, I also thought about our first meeting. To what extent can the accuracy of my recall be trusted? I do not think of myself as having a particularly good memory but the necessities of journalism trained me to create pegs and pointers for important events, so I believe that I am a reliable witness to some, at least, of the events in my past. I envy painters who can find greater truths by distancing the image from the object but I must rely on literal accuracy with the mundane aid of sounds, smells and snatches of music.

A collection of schoolgirls, boisterous rather than lyrical, were singing Christmas carols to the accompaniment of some guitars, a whistle or two and the rattle of collection boxes as I walked down Grafton Street to the Bailey to meet a girl with whom I dearly wished to have sex. It never happened. She was an American, the daughter of a Chicago businessman, and she reminded me of a woman in a Sargent portrait, unsure yet full of tension and of grace. In the yeasty warmth of the bar she introduced me to her flatmate. 'This is Laura,' she said and out of the anonymity of the crowd a girl smiled at me, lips parting slowly to reveal strong white teeth. That smile, familiar now, but exciting, even exotic, then, was like the gift of a password to a new way of life. She was wearing something ordinary – denim jeans and probably a denim jacket – and although she was pretty, even beautiful, there was no logical reason why it should have seemed to me that everything in my past had been a preparation for this special moment. I looked at her and tried to think of something adequate to say. I noted her small skull and the dark hair parted rather severely in the middle and her prominent eyebrows and the long lashes and the grey-green loveliness of her eyes. Her nose had a sensuous sweep, despite a slight fleshiness. I liked the way that she smiled and her determined chin and her air of calmness appealed to me as if it had been devised for my benefit. 'It's so nice to meet you,' I said, and she laughed.

It all started from there; out of the trivial we create the tabernacle of our feelings. An English-born radiographer, the daughter of emigrant Irish parents, became a part of everything that I was and that I wanted to be.

TWO

THIS MORNING, when I woke and pulled the curtains on the window of our bedroom, the scene that I witnessed had a beauty of such intensity that it caught me by surprise. There are numerous landscapes by minor Victorian painters that can prompt a similar emotion: small frozen stillnesses, precisions of clouds and trees and tranquil, grazing cattle, glimpses of escape from reality. These other worlds can haunt us with their promises of peace.

When I opened the window, the air was already warm and resinous. Magpies clattered in a neighbouring wood, angry at some intrusion. The mountains were benign and one-dimensional, the fields mottled with subtleties of greenness. A rook moved slowly against the translucent sky.

I turned from the window and looked around the room, chilled by a memory of impending loss. I wanted to construct some lasting edifice to the concept of family, to create a bond of enduring strength with the two women in this house. Laura was asleep and breathing peacefully, but her face had a troubled expression as if she were contemplating, in the awkward logic of a dream, some newly perceived threat. Her eyelids flickered and the fingers of her left hand pulled restlessly at the sheet. A strand of hair had fallen across her high and unlined forehead and, as she moved her head, as if dissenting from the dream, there appeared to be some bruise-like smudges beneath her eyes. She shifted her position; the soft outline of a breast was detectable under the rumpled sheet and suddenly, involuntarily, she swallowed, her throat constricting, the lean line of her jaw momentarily tightening, a curve of defeat or depression lowering the usual tilt of her lips. I watched her, anxious to interpret these moments of utterly private reappraisal, stirred by the shape of her body, imagining the texture of her skin beneath my fingers, wanting her. We had made love so often, there was little novelty or surprise left in the act but there was always reassurance. Our passion may have assumed a certain ritualistic progression based on so many years' awareness of individual preference, but beyond that elaboration we had retained some spontaneous urgency. We needed the sudden intimacy of release, the tastes, the sounds, the involuntary bodily movements that redefined us to each other. We belonged together. We had combined to form a family.

The concept of family meant little enough to me until Rachael almost died. Its three syllables encompassed the memories of a lost boyhood in County Meath rather than a manner of comprehending and redeeming middle age. Families stretched backwards in faded photographs; they were a benign coven of black-skirted, large-bosomed maternal ancestors with severe hairstyles, keen eyes, broad mouths and the same pieces of jewellery unageing against wrinkled necks. Families were redolent of dust. They were familiar names chipped into damp gravestones, they were ornaments bought while abroad.

When Rachael wasn't yet two years old I was invited to Iowa City to take part in a conference on contemporary writing. The three of us travelled together and everything was going well until, on the fifth day, I went to wake Rachael and saw immediately that she was unwell. She was holding her head oddly and there was foam at the corners of her mouth. I remember longing for her to smile, to come out from behind some pretence, but she stared up at me, her lovely eyes the colour of sucked butterscotch and there was no sign of recognition, no welcome for the start of a new day. She had kicked back the blankets and there were sweat marks on the sheet. From the apartment next door I could hear the familiar urgent sound of water sizzling in a shower. The voice of a radio announcer injected some drama into the news. For a few moments I was locked into inaction, staring down at her staring up at me, her little hands clenched into fat fists, her breathing fracturing the air between us with its harshness. The yellow-walled room, bare except for the cot and a few of our empty suitcases, was already fluid in the distinct and magical early morning light of Midwestern America. The panic I felt was a mixture of fear and cowardice. I wished I could have been somewhere else, that this precious life depended on a person of greater resourcefulness. I simply did not know what to do. Iowa City had been comprehensible and welcoming for days but was now an alien place. There was no one to call on the telephone, no authoritative relative to consult. There was just the three of us.

Laura, aware of an abnormal silence, came hurrying into the room.

'What's wrong?'

'I don't know. I just found her like this.'

'Her neck is stiff,' Laura said. 'I think there's a risk it's meningitis.'

'But people die of meningitis!'

'We can't lose another minute.'

After that it was all rush and flurry. One of us remembered that the conference folder contained a list of useful addresses. We had not had to consult it before. The time in Iowa City had been full and interesting and happy. Now Rachael's illness made all that seem unreal. The list, when I found it, included the name of a doctor. The street on which he had his surgery was close to our apartment. Holding Rachael tightly and anonymously, like an imperfectly wrapped piece of shopping, I ran along the length of leaf-strewn North Dodge towards the downtown area, aware that Laura was running just behind me. We must have looked like a crazed couple from an amateur movie or from a country in which some atrocity was happening. I remember a woman frowning at us and pulling her small, ugly dog nearer to the safety of her legs. We passed the corpse of a squirrel on the sidewalk, its worn teeth revealed in a grimace of rage or of pain. If she dies, I thought, if she dies, if she dies ... unable to complete that unthinkable proposition. Laura was crying, big, public, uncharacteristic tears.

The doctor was decisive. I remember him with gratitude, his early-morning manner disappearing beneath sudden professional alertness. In a small, underfurnished room, functional and cold as a photographer's studio, he went about his arcane tasks. 'The neck', he said, 'isn't good. You're lucky in one way. The best man you could go to is at Mercy Hospital. I'll call him for you now.'

She lay looking up at us with a kind of exhausted trust, seeming even more diminished by examination. 'Meningitis,' he said into the phone, pronouncing the word as casually as a familiar endearment. 'They're coming over to you now.'

I knew where Mercy Hospital was. Only two or three days before I had read the words on the commemorative stone outside the main entrance. The site had been chosen by a small band of Irish Sisters of Mercy who had come, on a mission, to follow the logic of their vocations in this obscure corner of the Midwest. I was intrigued by their journey, wondering what they had made of the still discernible wagon tracks in the hard, black Iowa earth, the corn, the hogs, the respectable Lutheran ethos. I imagine those women, to whom we may owe the life of our daughter, as arriving from Chicago, early in the morning, on the Rock Island Line, stepping nervously from the carriage with their cheap Irish suitcases clutched tightly. Dressed in black, like my maternal ancestors, they must have busied themselves amongst the poor, speaking in accents as unfamiliar as the manner of their movements, hiding their emotions as adroitly as they disguised the curves of their bodies, so that androgynous and strange as a new species, they created the building into which we ran.

The next days blur in my memory like something that one has overheard but not experienced. I remember the doctor reading the results of a lumbar puncture.

'There sure are a lot of pus cells in there.'

Laura borrowed a medical dictionary from the university library and we read and reread the miserable details. I remember kneeling in the wax-scented hospital oratory, making an attempt at prayer. Rachael lay still in a small room with a clear ceiling. They had shaved one side of her head and inserted a tube through which the antibiotic dripped. There was a small television set in the corner of the room. She stared without interest at cartoon characters or doleful Captain Kangaroo.

The meningitis did not respond to ampicillin. I was not there for the convulsion which lasted for a little more than four minutes. When Laura described it to me, we were sitting in a café just off Market Street; over the amplification system The Commodores were singing 'Three Times a Lady'. I would avoid the sentimentality of that detail if the memory were not so vivid. We gripped each other's hands and made unconvincing attempts at reassurance. In those trite surroundings, with the easy emotion of the music, we were forced to consider the possibility of Rachael's death; memories of creaking swings in Happy Hollow Park and the hot sound of crickets and the long, lovely Midwestern twilights and the trips by bus to the liquor store out near to the K Mart and the Interstate and the Saturday afternoons spent watching the Hawkeyes playing at Kennick Stadium, all frozen into some metaphor of grief. They changed the drip to chloramycetin and slowly, like an image emerging in a darkroom, Rachael was transformed from the uncertain colour of sickness and came out from behind the mask of a medical condition to become a familiar person, alert and with curious eyes.

I remember the doctor taking a phial from the pocket of his white coat. We stared suspiciously at the spinal fluid as if it had the properties of a crystal ball. 'It's like water,' he said. 'Your worries are over.' We took Rachael back to the apartment and after a few days we began to relax again and think about the importance of family.

I kissed Laura very gently on her hot, dry cheek, inhaling as if in a effort to experience the mysterious essence of her sleep. Her eyelids flickered and her lips parted but her expression remained troubled. Sometimes, recently, when we cling to each other in the act of love, I have detected a resistance, a holding back of some part of the assent that I have taken for granted for so long. My betrayal has wounded some element of her spontaneity.

She woke and stared at me as if puzzled that I was there. 'I love you,' I said, reaching to touch her cheek. 'I've been watching you for ages. Were you dreaming?'

'I forget. I don't think so.'

She stretched her arms. 'I had a lovely sleep. Is Rachael awake yet?'

'I haven't seen her. It's a really nice day. What time do you have to be at the airport?'

'Not until three. And I have everything packed.'

I longed to make love to her then, to bring her an intensity of reassurance that was beyond resisting, but the moment was too inhibiting. I felt awkward and intrusive and knew that I detected a slight impatience that I had woken her and expected conversation.

Her mouth had an early-morning softness when I leaned down and kissed her, and I loved the taste of her tongue and the way that her fingers arced around the back of my neck. 'Will you miss me?' she asked, pulling back a little so that she could watch my expression and for a moment I could see her father's face behind the prominence of her cheekbones and her inquisitorial eyes.

'Of course I will,' I said. 'Everything's different.'

'I didn't mean that. I just wanted to know that you'd miss me.'

'I miss you now.'

'Me too. I'm so glad that we have each other.'

I pulled her close to me, kissed the top of her head, moved my hands across her shoulder-blades into the soft hollow of her back. Her hair smelled of some herbal shampoo that Rachael might have given her as a gift and I noticed with a faint stirring of unease the first intrusive flecks of grey. I moved my hands down her body; then we heard Rachael outside. She knocked and came in, as I stood up quickly, and she approved of our closeness with a superior smile. I have never spoken to her with candour about the events of last summer and don't know exactly what Laura might have told her. She is a bright and enquiring girl; it would be foolish to imagine that all the muted conflict left her totally unmarked. She stood near to the doorway with that mixture of awkwardness and grace that is the paradox of adolescence. In her faded blue jeans and white tee-shirt, her long hair falling casually across her face, she was unrecognizable as the baby we had brought back from Iowa, alive. She had grown into an entity that could no longer be easily defined, indicating some part of our future and the complex unfolding of our past. I looked at her, loved her, and wondered what to say.

'You're up early.'

'Well it's such a nice morning.'

'Are you looking forward to the flight?'

'More or less.'

'I'm going to miss you both.'

'You could still change your mind,' Laura said. 'My parents would be delighted.'

'No. I'm determined to work. It's gone on for too long. I've just got to get a book underway. Apart from anything else, we need the money.'

'Are we poor?' Rachael asked.

'Not exactly poor but what's in the bank won't last forever. We'd really be scuppered if Mum didn't work. But I have an idea for a book that I think might be good.'

'I'm sure it will be,' Rachael said with the loyalty known to children who prefer not to confront disappointment. 'May I read what you've written when we get back?'

'You know I don't like that. I get superstitious.'

'We'll be rooting for you,' Laura said and I wanted to take her into my arms. Rachael, sitting on the bed, was like a pencil sketch of the woman behind her with features that were a gifted if smudged impression of the original. They were both looking at me as if expecting me to define some area of accord. There were moments when they were as indivisible as panels of a diptych.

'I'll really miss you,' I said to them. 'I'll go and get some coffee now.'

I enjoy driving on the narrow, unexpected Wicklow roads. Suddenly, through a gate that is the only break in a long line of thick yet intricate hedges, there is a view of fields plunging towards the suburbs of the city. The V8 Discovery smoothens even the deepest potholes. It is the toy that has brought the greatest amount of innocent pleasure into my middle years. Today, the roads were dusty and clouds of almost transparent midges came like heat against the windscreen. We listened to a Gershwin tape and Laura reminded me of things that needed to be done, domestic details that are a part of one's subconscious response to the routines of the day. When we came to the crossroads near to the disused Church of Ireland that features in all direction maps to our home, I turned left and realized only then that I was avoiding going past what I still thought of as Cromer's house. This route added about a mile to our journey, but neither Laura nor Rachael made any comment. I felt oppressed by their tactfulness but realize now that they may not even have noticed. These roads replicate themselves but, for me, the stretch in front of Cromer's house had assumed all the authority of a historical landmark. By avoiding it I acknowledged, if only to myself, its enduring importance. It was impossible to expunge it from the memories of last summer. I knew the house too intimately, the creak of its floorboards, the way the branch of a flowering cherry tree scraped against the landing window. I knew the view from that window, the distant prospect of our own house standing grey and grave against the mountains.

When we got to the airport, the elaborate swoops and flourishes of Gershwin's music bonded us together. I left them at the Departures Terminal and found a parking space. As I went back to the Terminal, I experienced a sudden craving for the comfort and companionship of a cigarette but I resisted it and the craving passed.

They had already gone through the departure gates. I bought a morning paper, then drove back here and started work on this journal.

THREE

I SLEPT BADLY last night. The empty house was unfamiliar, even eerie. Lying awake, I found myself wondering what would happen if I died. How long would it take before some concerned stranger would break the glass in a window and come cautiously up the stairs to discover, with barely concealed distaste, the body in the bed? This level of morbidity is uncharacteristic but I could not push it away. I felt self-pity like the onset of an illness, as I lay there, lonely in the darkness, a potentially comic figure, open to the many indignities that attend on paranoia.

There was something unnerving about the torpidity of the night. I switched on the bedside lamp but could still imagine darkness rubbing up against the window like a cat. I thought I heard footsteps and waited anxiously for other sounds but there was nothing except for my own breathing and that most mournful of country intrusions, the distant braying of a donkey.

I went downstairs and poured myself a whiskey, then went into the study to find something to read. The notebook in which I am now writing was open on my desk. I looked along the shelves of books and was calmed by their generous presence. For as long as I can remember, they have given me pleasure. They are as intimate as pieces of my own experience. I believe I can remember the exact circumstances in which many of them were purchased. Idly, I took down a copy of Cromer's autobiography. He had given it to me and written in it 'This precocious memoir, with much affection and admiration from your friend William Cromer'. I brought it upstairs. I suppose that I wanted to recapture his tone of voice. I got back into bed, and began to re-read it with considerable apprehension.

Does anyone else remember the phenomenon of the Angry Young Men? The phrase sounds as dated as much of their work and as facile as the attempts that journalists made to gather such disparate voices into a group. In the decades before them, the English novel was largely a chronicle of middle-class life. Then, towards the end of the nineteen fifties, the working-class hero became a fashionable figure, endowed with brash, personal freedom, great sexual vigour, a hatred of cant and of the rigorously protected machinations of the British class system. This new hero refused to accept boundaries, so he appealed to timid readers. He was a romantic, sentimental, but not unattractive creation and for a decade or so the prevailing voices in fiction spoke with the honest accents of the North of England. Sometime in the nineteen seventies, for reasons that would repay both critical and political attention, the fashion changed and the working-class hero, with all his rages, hangovers and attractions to destructive sex, was seen to be a bore. Cromer's most recent novel, a picaresque account of a young man let loose in Europe, causing chaos at soccer matches and in clubs, acting out a nationalism that would be alien at home, was given only the briefest of mentions in the Sunday newspapers. That neglect would have been impossible to predict at the start of his career when his first novel, *Anything You Want*, enjoyed remarkable success. It was typical of the new genre but a good deal more expertly written than most. 'Raw, incisive and often very funny' was a much-used quotation from the review in the *New Statesman*. It appeared that Cromer had discovered both a voice and a perspective that would reveal new worlds.

It occurs to me just now that Cromer and his contemporaries were oddly misogynistic. In book after book the hero regards women as a threat to freedom, the antithesis of his individuality. In the company of other men they could be themselves but they knew that women were waiting for any sign, however small, of weakness. Women wanted to ensnare and enslave them with absurd needs and many pregnancies, a desire to reduce great worlds of possibility to the dimensions of terraced houses and small suburban homes.

When *Anything You Want* was published, Cromer was twenty-six. His childhood, if his memoir is to be believed, was shaped by the frequent absences of a weak and ineffectual father and the presence of a mother who was inordinately ambitious for her puny only son. Through him she lived the life that had passed her by in the drab humiliation of domestic service. They discovered books together and went secretly to the local repertory theatre. Together, as if bound by some illicit aim, they plotted ways in which Cromer could get to a provincial university; he endured grim schooldays and general unpopularity in pursuit of this uncommon dream. At the age of eighteen, when he walked into the large and ill-designed entry hall of the university, he was without friends and already resentful about the difficulties of the journey he had made.

The next few years changed him and extirpated his mother's influence. As he grew away from her, in a world of radical student politics, she became a sad and bitter figure who, for the second time in her life, had committed herself to the wrong man. Cromer describes in his memoir, and in several of his novels, the attempts, on his infrequent weekends at home, to regain some easy communication. They ended, always, in failure, tears and acts of emotional recrimination. His independence affronted his mother. She was ashamed of his politics. He failed to do her proud in the eyes of her neighbours. Above all, she deplored his guiltless sexual promiscuity. When he married an actress who was to become famous, his mother attended the ceremony and sat stony-faced beside his father, who was drunk. She took no pleasure in his literary success. She had craved respectability; he had brought her nothing but a certain notoriety.

The memoir ends with Cromer's first visit to America. In the last chapter, I recognize, without difficulty, the man I knew. His book is on the best-seller list, his wife has a good role in a British play about to succeed on Broadway, yet there is a hint of fear in the writing, a certain tension in the tone, as if he were already aware that brashness is an insufficient guarantee of continuing success. There are some brooding pages in which he attempts to analyze the nature of his gifts or comprehend the necessity to invent a fictive self. His political awareness leads him to describe the novel as a palliative. He longs to change society, yet knows that he is achieving less than a competent social worker. He wants to be a man of action but his talent depends on introspection. It is a conflict that he can never resolve.

Our neighbour, the novelist Barbara Worthing, was the first to tell me that Cromer was coming to live in the locality. I remember being interested in the news. Little enough that happened in the neighbourhood provided much stimulation. We were in the lounge of the pub where, every day, between half past four and seven, Barbara put away an awesome quantity of large gins and tonics. This was years ago. Since I was not working, I often joined her there for the pleasure of her sharply observed gossip. She was typical of the English writers who had been attracted to the area, wealthy and unserious, the authors of over-researched thrillers or of sagas about ambitious women who pay the price for having reached the top. Barbara was cheerfully dismissive of her own historical novels, which sold in large numbers in many countries. 'Crap, darling, absolute crap! I hardly even know how I write them. I sometimes think that the word-processor has a mind of its own.'

Cheerfulness characterized her. She got drunk slowly and happily. Her only moments of asperity were reserved for her young to middle-aged lovers who appeared on the scene at unpredictable intervals looking and sounding oddly alike, chosen to some formula and rejected for some inadequacy within a matter of weeks.

'He's bought that house down at the corner. The one they've been working on.'

'It was once a rectory,' I said. 'It has lots of potential.'

'Well let's hope he enlivens the place. Do you know if he's married? Isn't he married to that actress, what do you call her?'

'I think there've been one or two Mrs Cromers since then.'

'Well, he's rather handsome, isn't he? Or was, if his photographs are anything to go by. Maybe he's ravaged like the rest of us by now. He'll be company for you, darling. The two of you can have terribly important literary discussions.'

I remember feeling obscurely offended by this remark, as if she were relegating me to the role of local bore, the man who buttonholes you in the corner with deadly serious conversational intent. I liked to think of myself as being more vital than that, yet was not unaware of a certain tendency towards the ponderous in my social manner.

'I wonder if he has children,' I said, attempting to hide my feelings. 'It would be nice if there was someone who could be friends with Rachael.'

'He probably has an entire quiver full of them. Wild, insufferable children and a mistress with big tits and an enviable arse who'll attempt to make the rest of us feel terribly tiresome.'

I bought her a drink. A special supply of Beefeater's was maintained for her exclusive use. Then we talked idly about local happenings and the idiosyncrasies of other writers whom we knew. The details have blurred but I'm sure that my recall of our conversation about Cromer is exact. I suppose that I have looked back and thought about it often in the past two years, attributing significance to the relatively unimportant, seeking additional meanings. We both got drunk that evening but I'm fairly certain that Cromer's name wasn't mentioned again.

He arrived two or three weeks later while we were visiting Laura's parents in their home in a village outside Southampton. Being there was a little like finding oneself in a discarded world. People talked calmly and affectionately and with unfailing good manners in rooms filled with polished furniture, flowers and nautical memorabilia. An elderly cook made good, if rather plain, meals in a kitchen with windows that overlooked a croquet lawn. Neighbours trimmed their hedges, often into elaborate shapes, hosed their lawns and were friendly and unassertive. They voted Tory as they always had done and valued the continuum of their days. Despite the hospitality, which was formal but almost warm, I never really felt comfortable there. I was always on the point of turning speculation into argument or of having too much to drink. Laura was different. She would revert without difficulty to a childhood world of security and routine, surrendering her independence to the fuss that her mother made of her and to her father's self-deprecatory but firmly held opinions. Rachael didn't seem to mind this change but it would create, in me, an uneasy mixture of love and irritation, appreciative of her family's good qualities but anxious to reassert the more acceptable checks and balances of our own life. It could all be something of a strain, so I tend to remember the relief of coming home more acutely than any other aspect of our holiday.

Perhaps I am investing this particular homecoming with a surfeit of emblematic content but it is very vivid in my memory. Dublin was festive, its streets filled with visitors, its old buildings blue-grey against a faded sky. Hundreds of amateur painters were displaying their works on the railings around St Stephen's Green and all those landscapes and seascapes and portraits seemed to combine into a large mosaic of Irish life. When we drove out of the city, the prospect of mountains and winding roads was wonderfully familiar. I felt grateful to be home.

'Look,' Rachael said suddenly, 'someone's moved into the Old Rectory. They must be having a party.'

There were eight or ten cars parked along the narrow road in front of the house. I recognized Barbara Worthing's customized Morris Minor.

'Of course,' I said, slowing down out of curiosity. 'I heard that William Cromer had bought it.'

'Cromer,' Laura said. 'He was really famous once, wasn't he? I remember reading one of his books. Daddy didn't approve!'

'He's out of fashion now,' I said, 'but he's still quite well known.'

'That was Barbara's car, wasn't it? I wonder if they're friends.'

Laura didn't like Barbara; she mostly offered her little more than tolerance. She found her uncomfortable and a little vulgar yet, sometimes, at parties, they would be attracted to each other's company and appear to enjoy themselves.

'I don't think so. In fact I know they aren't. It was she who told me that he had bought the place and was having it decorated but she never mentioned that she knew him.'

'I wonder if he has kids,' Rachael said.

She missed the friendships and intrigues of her boarding school and was often lonely during the holidays. We would drive her to the city or to towns in other counties so that she could spend time with her friends but that kind of prearrangement lacked the intimacy of easy companionship. Both Laura and I felt guilty about this; it was the major negative in our choice of a place to live.

'Let's hope so,' I said, 'but the chances of their being of the right age is a little remote. Still, we'll soon find out.'

'I'm already missing Granny and Papa.'

'We must write to them,' Laura said dutifully, 'and thank them for being so nice to us.'

'I can see our house!' Rachael said.

She had being making this exact comment at the exact spot on the road for many years, when the gable end of the house became suddenly visible between the trees.

'It looks lovely,' she said. 'I'm glad we're home.'

The remainder of the summer stretched peacefully ahead. I'm sure that I was hoping to begin some work. The act of taking our suitcases from the car resembled some ceremony of a new beginning, carrying offerings into rooms that had grown a little strange in the few weeks of our absence. We spoke in slightly hushed voices at first as if to propitiate a ghost.

This had been a good day's work, more than I have attempted or achieved for a number of years. It would have been better if the work had been creative rather than the recounting of memories in a journal but I am satisfied by the sight of words on pages. Earlier, I spoke to Laura and to Rachael on the phone. They sounded well. They said that they miss me. I certainly miss them. The house is still but perhaps the intensity of this atmosphere has helped my concentration.

Now that I have finished working for the day and the surface of the desk is tidy, I begin to fear the slow passage of the hours that lie ahead. I don't want to drift back towards morbidity. I want to preserve the source of energy that I was able to draw on today. I will go down to our local pub, which is called Kennedy's, although it is owned by a morose man named Moore, have something to eat and talk for a while to whomever happens to be there. An hour or two of companionship will certainly be relaxing. I can also look around with a newly interested eye for some details that I may need to use in the next section of this journal.

FOUR

ON THE DAY AFTER we returned from England, I drove down
to Kennedy's for a drink. The lounge has been created from the
three or four downstairs rooms of what had once been a family
home, so it is low-ceilinged and contains many quiet corners as
well as an L-shaped area where the counter is and where a turf fire
burns, during autumn and winter days, in an ugly, yellow-tiled fireplace. The walls are covered with a surprisingly large collection of
framed photographs of local interest: victorious football teams and
the winners of sheep and pony shows and pilgrims to a nearby holy
well. There is a dartboard in the corner farthest from the door. The
local team has an invincible reputation; tarnished trophies are lined
up on a high shelf. Small octagonal tables are arranged in no particular order and there are artificial plants in the dusty windows.

The young locals drink in the bar; they can sometimes be
heard but not seen. Their elders have proprietorial rights to the
tables nearest the fireplace. They have shown consistent tolerance
to the five or six writers and their families who have settled in the
area. Over the years I have witnessed some minor outbursts of
temper or some clashes of personality but these were never the
result of a simple divide or of an inbuilt hostility between the old
and the new.

Mr Moore's greeting was characteristic.

'You'll be wanting a Powers?'

His conversation, although probably intended as friendly, always succeeded in making anything that required some action on his part sound like an intolerable imposition.

'Yes thanks.'

'And I suppose you'll want water with it?'

He was a large man with a bald head of almost fluorescent brightness. It was difficult not to stare at this expanse of highly polished skin which seemed to glow in the generally gloomy light of the lounge. He was probably sixty years old and had never married. Once, when he was asked about this, I heard him explaining that he preferred greyhounds. This, inevitably, led to some ribald speculation. I have no idea whether he was serious or not.

'I haven't seen you this long while,' he said.

'No, I haven't been here. We were visiting my in-laws in England.'

He considered this explanation for some moments before nodding in acceptance.

'I hope your lady wife is well.'

'She is indeed. Are there any sandwiches left?'

'Ham.'

'I'll try one of them.'

'There's a new one of you lot above in the Old Rectory. Do you know him?'

'No, but I know who you mean. I heard that he had bought it.'

'That's him over there.'

He nodded towards a table in the corner where a man whom I couldn't see very well was holding a pipe and drinking a glass of red wine. The bottle was on the table.

'The best in the house,' Mr Moore said with mysterious disapproval. 'Côtes du Rhône, if you don't mind. No vin ordinaire for that boyo.'

The man shifted in his chair and some light from a window

made his features a little more clear. I was surprised by his appearance. He looked more like a schoolteacher than the author of the novels and short stories I had read. There was something about the way he was sitting that suggested a kind of fussy authority. This was incongruous when one remembered the anarchic intention of much of his work.

'You're sure that's who he is?'

'Well, that's who he says he is anyway. Your friend Miss Worthing told me all about him,' he added with exaggerated patience, as if he were explaining some point of logic to a not very intelligent child. 'They're the best of friends.'

I looked at my watch.

'She'll be here in an hour or so,' I said. 'I suppose I should go over and welcome him to the locality.'

'I suppose you should. He's not often by himself. He's got a ...' Mr Moore paused as if overwhelmed by the need to be tactful, '... a girlfriend, if you don't mind. A German lady.'

'Really?' I said, wanting to know more. 'Have they settled in well?'

He stared at me as if I had blundered into something that was well outside the bounds of acceptable conversation. He indicated additional disapproval by looping his fat thumbs behind his braces and clearing his throat noisily.

'They have a great welcome for themselves,' he said.

I carried my drink over to the corner where Cromer was sitting. He was reading the *Irish Times*.

'I don't want to interrupt you,' I said, 'but I'd like to welcome you to the neighbourhood. My name is John Hughes.'

He stood up quickly and rather awkwardly, the newspaper falling to the floor. We shook hands.

'I know all about you from Barbara Worthing,' he said. 'You've been away. I actually called around to your house to invite you to a drinks party we were having but it was evident that there was no one there. Won't you join me?'

33

As we sat down, Mr Moore came across carrying a slightly jaded-looking ham sandwich on a plate. He left it on the table without saying anything and walked heavily back to the counter.

'Mine host isn't exactly a barrel of laughs,' Cromer said, 'but he certainly can't be accused of trying too hard. His is a subtle art.'

His accent had lost all traces of the North of England; it had neutralized into a mildly theatrical drawl. Sitting beside him, I could observe that he was less of the schoolteacher than he had looked at a distance. I was reminded more of an actor who specializes in eccentric character parts. I could imagine him as the cuckolded husband in a bedroom farce or as a clergyman talking benign nonsense in a comedy. I still had some difficulty reconciling this persona with the vigour and frequent anger of his prose. I had not then read his book of memoirs but knew enough about his life to recognize that he had assumed protective coloration.

We talked about the neighbourhood; he was both inquisitive and well informed. We discussed the violence in Northern Ireland and I found that, like many other concerned English people to whom I had spoken, he knew little enough about the history and reality of the conflict. He believed that the withdrawal of British troops would lead to a speedy and satisfactory solution.

'People would have to come to their senses,' he said emphatically, waving his empty pipe. 'The Catholic and Protestant working classes would see how much they have in common. They've both been the victims of cynical economic manipulation.'

I had reported from Belfast for two years and knew the depth of this fallacy but didn't want to get into an argument so early in our acquaintanceship. I contented myself with saying that the problem was a good deal more complex than that.

'But isn't that just like you Irish! You've always complicated matters that, to a rational mind, can be seen as relatively simple.'

That rankled; I felt patronized and defensive but decided to remain cool rather than appear to engage in some symbolic re-enactment of ancient conflicts.

'We'll talk about it some day when we both have much more time.'

'I'd like that,' he said. I must have betrayed some irritation for he sounded conciliatory. 'I've never even been to Belfast, so of course I'm talking off the top of my head. You must tell me the books I should read.'

'I'll loan you some.'

'All my own books are in tea chests. We've scarcely started to unpack. As soon as we do you must come and have dinner with us. Here's Ingrid now,' he added as a tall woman walked towards our table. Her handshake, when he introduced us, was warm, her stare frankly appraising. She had very large, very clear blue-grey eyes. When I look back on that first meeting, it is her eyes that I remember most vividly.

She sat beside Cromer and kissed him on the mouth in a manner that transcended the affectionate and was unmistakably sexual. This was so sudden and so surprising that I found myself looking away, as if there were something interesting to be seen in a corner of the familiar lounge.

Mr Moore came over to us, emanating disapproval.

'I suppose you'll want another round,' he said to me, picking up the empty wine bottle and staring at it. I ordered a whiskey for myself, a vodka and tonic for Ingrid, a brandy for Cromer. This transaction allowed me to watch her and form more impressions. She was in her late twenties or early thirties and had a swirl of faded blonde hair falling casually across her tall forehead. Her skin was almost unlined but a faint white scar stretched from her prominent right cheekbone to the corner of her mouth. She had very even teeth and a narrow but determined chin. She kissed Cromer again, more casually, then leaned back in her seat.

'Oh lovely,' she said. 'I always enjoy the first drink of the day.'

Her English, despite a pronounced German accent, was fluent. She wore her plain white blouse and tight black leggings with an ease and a lack of concern that suggested the pleasure she might take in nakedness.

'Do you like it here?' I asked her when she noticed that I was staring at her.

'This pub? It's fine. Not for food. But it's fine.'

Cromer excused himself and walked a little unsteadily to the toilets.

'Have you been in Ireland before?'

'Never. I come from Frankfurt,' she said, as if pre-empting the next question I might ask, 'but I've been living in London for the past five or six years. Two of them with Bill.'

'It's nice here,' I said feeling both nervous and awkward. 'It's a lovely part of the country, yet it's very close to the city.'

'And it's close to London as well. That's important to me.'

'You'll commute?'

'When I have to. I design for the theatre.'

She offered me a cigarette and I noticed that she had lovely hands, long, tapering fingers with smooth, almost oval nails.

'Your wife? Is she a writer also?'

'No. She's a radiographer. She works in a hospital in Dublin.'

'How interesting. Have you children?'

'A teenage daughter.'

'Bill has two teenage sons but they live with their mother.'

'Rachael will be disappointed.'

'I like the name Rachael,' she said, then blew a perfect smoke ring.

'That's clever,' I said.

'I can do it whenever I like,' she said, staring across at me. Her eyes seemed to be even larger. Cromer came back and she put her hand on his knee. I envied him. The action seemed to proclaim the lasting excitement of their relationship. I felt sedentary and boring, a man with a predictable future of more or less acceptable decline.

'John has a teenage daughter called Rachael.'

'A teenage daughter called Rachael must be a great blessing,' Cromer said. 'Barbara mentioned her to me. I have sons myself but, to be frank, they fall short of the exotic.'

36

'My daughter was hoping that there'd be some new young people in the area,' I said.

'We'll do what we can,' Cromer said, and Ingrid smiled. Their complicity made me feel crass and intrusive. 'But seriously, the boys will be visiting here and will be delighted to meet her.'

'Laura is English,' I said, anxious to fill a space in the conversation. 'I was telling Ingrid that she works as a radiographer.'

I was aware that I was saying Ingrid's name for the first time and wondered why this seemed to be of such importance.

'She was born in a small town outside Southampton.'

'What an extraordinary coincidence,' Cromer said. 'My first wife has recently taken up residence in Southampton. The place is obviously about to become fashionable.'

'You're getting drunk, Bill,' Ingrid said without accusation.

'Drunk? I'm not getting drunk.'

'Yes you are. It's too early in the day,' she said more seriously, hinting at some turbulence.

'Henpecked,' Cromer said to me. 'I'm dreadfully henpecked by this good woman. It appeals to some masochistic aspect of my personality. Obviously the Germans have a special aptitude for it.'

'What would you do without me?' Ingrid said softly. As she leaned forward to extinguish her cigarette, I noticed that she had a very small red and blue butterfly tattooed on her right shoulder. I longed to touch it, imagining that it would be a little coarse against the smoothness of her skin.

'Well, look who's here!' Cromer said as Barbara joined us. It was interesting to see the way Ingrid reacted. Although effusive in her greeting, she became a little more watchful, a little more proprietorial of her central position in the group. Barbara was nearly sixty, but she could still be regarded as competition and Cromer certainly appeared pleased to see her. He ordered a round of drinks from Mr Moore's niece, a tall, sad girl called Lily, then questioned Barbara about her shopping expedition to Dublin as if she had been to some remote place, searching for exotic trophies.

Ingrid watched, smiling but still; she might have been deciphering some coded subtext in an anecdote about a department store. I was fascinated by her controlled force and by the elegance of her pose. The fingers of her left hand were spread wide on the worn leather of the seat, her head thrust forward, watching Barbara with total concentration. I wondered, for a moment, what I was doing in this group. I would not want to be a part of it on any regular basis, but I knew how much I wanted to see Ingrid again. Cromer, sitting there ignoring her, had insights that I longed to share: stories about her childhood, the things she liked and feared, the way she behaved in bed. I attempted to imagine those hypnotic eyes focusing on the face of an expectant lover as her body unleashed waves of passion. Then I noticed that Cromer was staring at me.

'You've been daydreaming,' he said. 'Tell us about it.'

'My mind was blank.'

I knew that I sounded churlish and resentful.

'Darling,' Barbara said, leaning towards me with a display of mock concern. 'I don't think that I've ever seen you looking quite so glum.'

'I'm sorry,' I said, 'I think that I might be coming down with a cold or something. I'm determined to take an early night.'

'We've got to leave now,' Ingrid said decisively. 'We're going to the theatre this evening. Our first time to see the Abbey Theatre.'

'Do we have to?' Cromer said irritably. 'There's a match on television.'

'Yes, we have to. You can video it.'

'It's never the same.'

'I've never understood the appeal of football,' Barbara said, 'except as an act of male bonding. I think it must appeal to men who are basically afraid of women.'

I felt more and more detached from the conversation. I looked at Ingrid and wondered how she had disturbed me so easily out of some emotional rut.

'Are you designing anything at the moment?' I asked her.

'Yes I am. A revival of a play by David Storey. Bill remembers the opening night. I've made some sketches but there's a long way to go. The director has his own ideas. We've got to discuss it. But it's a good play. I think it will turn out well. Then there's an offer from Japan.'

'Really? Would you go there?' I asked, strangely disappointed at the thought of her being somewhere else.

'I'd go anywhere if it's the right place.'

She smiled at me as she reached for Cromer's hand. 'Off we go.'

'Am I to be left all alone?' Barbara asked. 'Does no one care if I'm ravished by the landlord?'

Mr Moore was sitting on a stool beside the counter, reading the *Evening Herald*. He looked across at us and yawned.

'That's a risk you must take,' I said.

'It's just as well I brought a book.'

I said goodbye to Ingrid and Cromer in the carpark. She had an arm around his waist; his right hand was on her shoulder. Knowing about the tattoo was like an intimacy.

'We must meet again soon,' she said as I turned away, rather than watch them walk together to their car.

Although two years have passed since that afternoon, I still remember it with some pain. It marks the exact occasion on which the seeds of disloyalty were sown. I went home dissatisfied and noticed, with impatience, that Laura, who had been working in the hospital since early morning, was tired and irritable. I told her about Cromer, but didn't mention Ingrid. I think I was afraid that I would reveal the extent of the impression she had made on me. She was a stranger, yet in less than half an hour she had undermined some certainties. She had done this without the slightest effort or without knowing that she was doing it. That made it even more disconcerting. In starting a process, in making the next betrayal almost inevitable, she could be said to have created, however unknowingly, the chaos of the summer. I realize that this sounds passive. There were other choices I could have made, other instincts I could have followed. These understandings depend on hindsight. At the time I seemed to be accepting a logic far too powerful to resist. This embarrasses me now, but I have other confessions to make that are much, much worse.

FIVE

CROMER AND I became friends. At first, we would meet in Kennedy's. Ingrid was seldom there; she was working on the Storey revival in London. I introduced him to Laura, who liked him, and to some of the locals, who were polite but reserved. As I got to know him better, I became aware of the hurt that was almost hidden by his flamboyance. He believed that his achievement had been minimized, that the literary establishment had accepted him only while an interest in provincial realism prevailed, had regarded him as a token working-class radical and then dismissed him when the fashion changed. He believed that his books were well outside the limited category in which they had been praised and that he was writing more ambitiously than ever. I put this information together like the pieces of a puzzle. He was invariably oblique in his references to writing; sometimes he was boastful, at other times self-deprecatory, and neither manner was entirely plausible. It was from his comments on other writers and his references to individual critics and the politics of publishing that I gathered most information. The knowledge that less talented writers had greater reputations was a constant irritant to him.

'I read the books they're praising,' he said to me once. 'There seems to be no possible connection between the reviews and those effete little texts. What the hell are they talking about? Has everyone gone mad?'

His work was better known in the United States and in Eastern Europe than in his own country.

'What sense does that make?' he asked me one afternoon in Kennedy's. We were drinking wine and waiting for Barbara to join us. 'What's happened to the English novel? Where has all that energy gone? It's nothing now but word games and private jokes.'

I could hardly ever get him to speak about Ingrid in any detail. I was avid for information and would bring up her name whenever possible.

'Does Ingrid read much? She really has exceptionally good English.'

'She reads nothing. Nobody who has anything to do with the theatre can read. I learned that bleak truth when I was married to the great white hope of the English theatre. At the time she was having some of her greatest successes in Chichester, she read nothing but *Woman* and *Woman's Own*, and those with some difficulty.'

'Ingrid's career seems to have taken off.'

'I suppose so,' he said, without much evident interest. 'I wrote a play once but almost nobody liked it. Oddly enough, they liked my screenplays.'

We talked about Irish history and subsequently he read all the books I recommended to him. It was weeks before he told me that he had worried for more than a year before deciding to live in Ireland.

'A neighbour of mine had served as an officer in Enniskillen. Don't get me wrong. I'm anything but a lover of the officer classes but he wasn't the very worst. He was quite emphatic that no Englishman would be safe in any part of this country. Even here, in this pub, when I'm on my own, I sometimes wonder what the young chaps in the bar are really thinking. After all, I am the traditional enemy.'

'A similar factor doesn't seem to interfere with the course of Anglo-German relationships.'

'That's simply a debating point. I've read enough to know that the feeling is visceral here. But I've been assured over and over again that it's largely unexpressed. We must go together to Belfast. It's absurd that one of the most infamous cities in the world is so near to us and yet I've never been there. I think I'd like to write a piece about it. And you must know your way around.'

Sometimes we went for long walks, trudging through silent woods or climbing the nearest and least daunting of the mountains. From its rocky summit, we could see a great expanse of small, irregularly shaped fields and two or three villages joined by the same narrow glint of roadway and the metallic glitter of the Irish Sea. He had little feeling for nature and was often disconcerted by the silences and distances we would encounter.

'It's obvious that you miss the city. Why didn't you buy a house in Dublin?'

'Because living in the country is a posh thing to do,' he said in a rare and unexpected moment of vulnerability.

'But who are you impressing?'

'If you had seen our street where I grew up,' he said, 'you wouldn't even consider asking that question. I'm impressing myself.'

One afternoon, our walk took us to a turn in a river where an old man was fishing. I recognized him and could see that he recognized me. He was the last man in the county whom I would have chosen to introduce to Cromer. He was an old Republican called O'Dalaigh who, almost seventy years before, was supposed to have shot three members of the British forces during an ambush at a crossroads near to where we were. This was his local claim to fame and he had lived his life in a kind of fierce loyalty to the act, rejecting the validity of successive Irish governments, insisting that all the things generally regarded as progress were nothing but a national betrayal. In the years that I had spent in the locality, I had noted how the manner in which he was regarded had undergone subtle changes. His reputation could be read like a barograph; it plotted the unsteady line of local political reaction. The few of his contemporaries who were still alive regarded O'Dalaigh with a mixture of envy and disdain. They would like to have had the local renown, the row of medals, the something big to remember, but they rejected his contentious dismissal of their lives as collaborationist and his unshifting definition of loyalty to a cause. The young people, at different times and in reaction to news from the North, thought that he was either a touchstone or an embarrassment, a great Irishman or an unregenerate old fool.

'It's yourself,' he called to me, in a voice that still had some vigour, although he looked almost impossibly ancient, his withered neck stretching out lizard-like from the too-large collar of his shirt. He habitually wore an old green tweed suit, shapeless and threadbare.

'Any luck?' I asked, although his bag was open on the riverbank and obviously empty.

'Not a bloody bite. The day is too bright and I brought the wrong bait with me.' He was staring at Cromer. 'I won't give it too much more of my time.'

'Have you met William Cromer? He's living in the Old Rectory.'

'Nice to meet you,' Cromer said. 'I've done a spot of fishing myself.'

O'Dalaigh ignored him and Cromer's affability wilted with surprise.

'This river isn't what it once was. I remember when you could drink out of it. Now there's pollution somewhere upstream.'

As O'Dalaigh spoke he grew angry, a patch of vivid red appearing on each cheekbone, old veins standing out and straining against the ash-grey skin of his neck. In a way that is difficult to define, the depth of his anger appeared to rejuvenate him. He became more active in movement, less burdened with age. He reeled in his line and cast it awkwardly into the middle of the river.

'Isn't most rural pollution the result of improperly stored slurry?' Cromer asked him.

O'Dalaigh stared at him.

'You seem to know a hell of a lot about this country,' he said. 'Have you lived here long?'

Cromer must have recognized that the question was both hostile and disingenuous, but he pressed on politely.

'Only some weeks. My observation is based on the English experience.'

'Oh, the English experience!' O'Dalaigh said, reeling in his line. 'You're bringing us the benefit of the English experience so that we can learn from it and profit from it like we did in the old days.'

Cromer looked at me for some sign of support.

'Bill's a writer,' I said to O'Dalaigh, without much hope that this would make any difference.

'If there's one thing this country doesn't need now it's writers,' O'Dalaigh said. 'The place is full of them and they're not worth tuppence, the lot of them.'

'That's a bit harsh,' I said, wishing we hadn't run into him.

'Harsh! It's no more than the truth. I'm a man who knows what he's talking about.'

'We'd better not interrupt your fishing any more.'

'Not a bit of it,' O'Dalaigh said meaninglessly. 'Not a bit of it.'

'Who on earth was that?' Cromer asked as we walked along the narrow, muddy path beside the river. He sounded agitated and when he stopped to light his pipe, his hands were trembling.

'A dinosaur,' I said. 'One of the last survivors of the War of Independence living in this part of the county. He's done nothing for almost seventy years except live off the fact that he took part in an ambush near here. He's never accepted the legitimacy of the State.'

I was attempting to make the encounter seem unimportant but the old man's malevolence appeared to follow us.

'And there's one more thing. His grandson is your postman.'

'I think he hated me.'

'Not you personally.'

'It felt like it to me.'

'He's an old fool.'

'It's everything I was warned about before coming here.'

'Don't get it out of proportion. He's the equivalent of some terrible old blimp in a military club ranting on about the Jerries.'

'Is he influential in the neighbourhood?'

'No!'

'I know that you're going to say I imagined it, but in Kennedy's a few days ago I saw two young chaps looking at me and muttering something that obviously wasn't friendly.'

'You're imagining it.'

'Barbara agrees with you. And she doesn't exactly make any effort to be inconspicuous.'

We left the road and walked up the sloping fields towards my house. I had become a little oppressed by his company but invited him in for a drink. Laura was at work; Rachael was visiting friends. He looked at the books in my study as I poured him a brandy.

'*My Fight for Irish Freedom*', he said, 'by Dan Breen. That sounds vaguely familiar, although I know I haven't read it.'

'It's totally unreliable,' I said, 'but it still provides some insight into the O'Dalaighs of this world.'

'May I borrow it?'

'Of course.'

'I like this room,' he said, looking around. 'As soon as Ingrid gets back we're asking Laura and you around for dinner. She's a very good cook.'

'I'll look forward to that.'

I attempted to sound matter of fact about it but the mention of her name had brought images of her frank sexuality into the room. Thinking about her had made me uneasy about the reality of my own life. Everything appeared to be less substantial than it had been. I could picture her body with agonizing exactitude; the long lean thighs, the swell of her breasts, the richness of her eyes. I can appreciate now that I had depersonalized her into being a sex object. In all my imaginings, we were together in bed. I think I believed that if we made love it would be unlike any other time with anybody else and that I would write again and my life would be more vital. It is a formidable list of consequences to attribute to the power of lust. I was aware of the disloyalty of my attitude, especially when Laura and I made love and I would attempt to imagine that it was Ingrid I was entering and then feel disappointed at the familiarity of the act. This process meant that I depersonalized Laura also, destroying the real act with the imagined, ignoring the depth of our feelings. It was a time of considerable unhappiness, for all of which I blame myself. I was reckless, obsessive and uncaring.

'Will Ingrid be home soon?'

'In a week or two, I think.'

It infuriated me that he could sound so casual about her. How could he tolerate not having her beside him in their bed?

'You're a friend of David Storey?'

'Not a friend, exactly, but we knew each other some years back. I really liked his first novel. Sport is such a big part of so many people's lives, especially in England, but it hadn't been written about all that much. They were interesting years. Did you know that I wrote a book of memoirs, a kind of precocious autobiography?'

'I've never read it.'

'It came out years ago. I was still in my twenties. Can you remember what it was like to be in your twenties? Anyway, it's just been reprinted in paperback. I'll give you a copy.'

'I look forward to reading it.'

'I haven't read it myself for years. I think I'd be terrified by the confrontation with my younger self. Would he despise me now? There were such limitless possibilities then. What would the I of the memoir make of this boring old fart? "From Angry Young Man to Boring Old Fart". I see that as a graceful curve.' He laughed. 'Bastard,' he said.

We had another drink.

'You have a good way of life,' he said.

'Do you think so?' I said, surprised. 'Sometimes I think that I've let myself get into a rut.'

'That's easily rectified. Start doing things differently.'

He was sitting close to the window, staring out at the damp fields through which we had walked and the distant bulk of the mountains. Laura's car turned into the drive.

'I must be going,' he said, standing up abruptly. 'I've imposed on you for far too long.'

'Why don't you stay and join us for dinner?'

'No, I've work to do. And Ingrid filled the freezer with nice stuff that I've just got to pop into the oven.'

He kissed Laura when she came into the room and told her in detail about O'Dalaigh.

'Do I know him?' she asked, turning to me. 'Yes, I think I do. An unprepossessing little guy.'

'That's him!' Cromer said.

I walked with him to the gate, then Laura and I chatted for a while before preparing the evening meal.

'You look tired,' I said to her.

'It was a very long day.'

'When Ingrid gets back, they'll invite us to dinner.'

'That could be pleasant. He's a nice man isn't he? Not at all what I'd expected.'

'How do you mean?'

'I had expected someone tougher. Is that terrible?'

'No,' I said. I know what you mean. The words angry young man suggest that.'

'Exactly.'

'But it's interesting to know them.'

SIX

SOME TIME LATER, Cromer telephoned Laura and invited us to dinner on the following Saturday. I looked forward to it with an intensity that was almost painful and found it difficult to suppress my excitement when Laura told me.

'He says that Ingrid is a very good cook,' I said, taking some pleasure in pronouncing her name.

'Do men still say that kind of thing about their partners?' Laura said. 'I must say that you surprise me.'

I felt deflated but determined to avoid the argument that I suspected could be just seconds away.

'It will be fun to see what they've done with the house,' I said. 'I suppose that it's going to be a little theatrical. Barbara said that they've spent a fortune.'

'Barbara will be there?' Laura asked, without enthusiasm.

'I suppose she will.'

'With the latest boy wonder?'

'Who else?'

'Still it's nice to be going out,' she said in a conciliatory tone that she could produce like an award for good behaviour. We had made love earlier and I had been especially careful to let nothing intervene. It had been good, even if my passion had been the result of some effort, and I thought that we had reassured each other. But now, driving the short distance to Cromer's, the thought that I would soon be seeing Ingrid was more important than any other consideration. I longed to be beside her, to share some intimacy with her, to impress myself upon her mind.

I parked outside The Old Rectory. Barbara's car was there and an old silver Jaguar I had not seen before.

'Do I look all right?' Laura asked, fiddling with the rear-view mirror. Despite my impatience to go into the house, I thought she looked beautiful. She was wearing a loose black dress with a neckline that pointed like a provocative arrow of fair skin to the space between her breasts.

'You're looking beautiful,' I said. 'I'm very proud of you.' She smiled shyly and I held her hand as we walked up to the front door. Cromer opened it and spread his arms in an expansive welcome.

'Down from the hills,' he said, 'and looking so tremendously bon ton!' He kissed Laura. 'I'm ravished!' He was wearing a green velvet suit and a yellow shirt and looked like the illustration of an Edwardian rake in some book I had once read.

'Come in, come in, you're both most welcome!'

The hallway was dramatic: dark-blue wallpaper, white woodwork, a collection of theatrical masks. The stairs, which were carpeted in blue, went steeply upwards towards an octagonal window that appeared to incorporate a design by Beardsley. I had just finished reading the book of memoirs that Cromer had given me and was struck by the contrast between this flamboyant setting and the grim, small brown and green kitchen that he remembered from his childhood. Each morning, his mother had scoured the tiled floor; the sweet scent of cheap soap had remained hanging in the air, a lasting impression of poverty.

'I like your house already,' I said, wondering when Ingrid would come out from one of the rooms. 'I've never actually been here before but I always assumed that it was dull in the old days. There was something distinctly fustian about the old rector when he was alive.'

'He left us a mature garden,' Cromer said, 'and, more importantly, a sundial. It reads *Horas non numero nisi serenas*. I intend adopting that as my new philosophy of life.'

'It's scarcely appropriate for a novelist.'

'For my philosophy of life! My art will continue to investigate the presence of shadows.'

He directed us into a room at the back of the house. From its open French windows I could see the roof of our house and the familiar shape of the mountains. The room was decorated in white and green; despite the warmth of the evening there was a log fire burning. A number of surrealist landscapes, instantly disturbing in the over-intensity of their observation, were hanging on the walls and I was aware of white armchairs and photographs in ornate silver frames on small tables. Ingrid was not there. Barbara stood up, kissed Laura and introduced us to a young man called Aidan, who smiled sheepishly, uncomfortable in a suit that looked as if it was being worn for the first time. He looked away from us when she described him as 'my latest discovery'. A grey-haired man in his late sixties, dressed too youthfully in a red shirt and tight black jeans, was standing by the fireplace. Cromer introduced us to him.

'Walter Ritchie, my solicitor. And this is Sally, his lovely wife.'

An elderly lady, sitting in a chair near to the window, nodded with the jerky intensity of a mechanical toy. She was wearing a brown tweed suit and seemed to have emerged from an era quite different from the image being projected by her husband. He looked sullenly towards her as if to indicate that he was completely aware of their incongruity.

'Walter and Sally are staying with us for a few days,' Cromer said. 'They've never been in Ireland before and are relieved that we aren't all shooting each other.'

'It's ever so peaceful here,' Sally said. 'It's not at all like I imagined. I was in two minds about coming here at all. Are we doing the right thing? I said to Walter.'

'Ingrid won't be long,' Cromer said. 'She's doing last-minute bits and pieces in the kitchen. Let me see to the drinks.'

As he poured out our gins and tonics, we talked, with difficulty, to the Ritchies. She smiled a lot; he made little effort to join in the conversation except to contradict her with unusual vehemence when she expressed the opinion that Wicklow reminded her of parts of Scotland.

'There's no comparison whatsoever,' he said. 'Open your bloody eyes! Scotland has grandeur! All that you've got here is a collection of bloody hills!'

She smiled as if she were agreeing with him.

'What was the name of that place where we stayed a few years ago? The place where the Dutch fishermen were?'

'That's nothing to do with it!' he said angrily. 'We're talking originality. We're talking about the impact of a landscape on the soul! You're wrong and you must realize that you're wrong and that's all to be said about it.'

Sally smiled at Laura, her fingers playing with the string of large pearls that she wore.

'I'll think of it in a minute,' she said. 'The hotel was painted black and white and was very close to a waterfall. You could hear the sound of it all night. It kept me awake at first but then I got accustomed to it.'

I muttered an excuse and went over to Barbara and Aidan. He was sitting on the floor beside her chair; her hand was resting on his head. I guessed that he couldn't be more than twenty-five. He stood up, brushing something from the seat of his trousers.

'I don't mean to interrupt,' I said, 'but I find the Ritchies a little unrewarding.'

'Unrewarding!' Barbara said. 'The fellow is quite mad!'

'Are you talking about me?' Cromer asked, bringing me a drink.

'Your lawyer over there.'

'He doesn't travel well,' Cromer said, 'but he certainly knows his law. He handled my divorces.'

'The fact that he appears to have married his mother,' Barbara said, 'does him very little credit.'

'There's less of an age difference than you might think,' Cromer said.

Aidan smiled uneasily but Cromer didn't seem to care.

'She thought that I was Barbara's son!' Aidan said. 'How ridiculous can anyone get!'

'They're holidaying in Ireland so I had to make some effort,' Cromer said. 'Ingrid isn't exactly delighted at the prospect.'

I saw that Laura was looking over at us accusingly.

'For one thing,' Ritchie was saying loudly, 'it's a totally different climate. And for another, you're talking through your arse.'

'I'd better rescue Laura,' I said.

Then Ingrid came into the room. She was wearing a long, white caftan on which a recurrent geometric pattern was embroidered in silver threads. Although it disguised the outline of her body, the effect was entirely feminine; the garment appeared to shimmer provocatively as she walked across the room to greet Laura. Then she came over to me and kissed me on both cheeks. Her lips were warm and dry. She was wearing a perfume that contained some hint of the East and when she stepped back from me, her eyes seemed even larger than I had remembered.

'It's so wonderful to see you both here,' she said. 'Has Bill been looking after you?'

'Very well,' I said, holding up my glass. The cubes of ice tinkled as I indicated this manifestation of hospitality.

She smiled.

'You're looking beautiful,' I said, hoping that Barbara would not hear but of course she did.

'I don't remember getting a compliment from you,' Barbara said to me.

'You don't need to be told, Barbara,' Ingrid said. 'It's people like me who need the reassurance.'

'That's very gallant of you, Ingrid,' Barbara said. It was obvious from their archly adversarial tones that there was some quarrel between them.

'Anyway,' Ingrid said, 'you've got this nice young man to pay you compliments. I'm afraid that I've forgotten your name.'

'Aidan,' Aidan said unhappily.

'Of course! I'll remember it from now on.'

'Did the play go well?' I asked, hungry for her attention. Cromer was talking to Laura and the Ritchies were ignoring each other.

'Yes, very well, thank you.'

Barbara and Aidan were whispering to each other. For a few moments it was as if we were alone together.

'It got good reviews but I don't think that it's going to have a very long run. But everyone is happy and my set is a success. I have some photographs of it somewhere.'

'I'd love to see them.'

'You're interested in theatre?'

'Very.'

'That's great. Do you think I was rude to Barbara?'

'No. Do you often cross swords with each other?'

She stared at me and I realized that she was unfamiliar with the expression. Her foreignness made her vulnerable and even more desirable.

'I think I can guess what you mean,' she said. 'You mean send little darts? Yes, she annoyed me to begin with. She would talk mostly to Bill and ignore me.'

'That was unwise.'

'Wasn't it?' she said laughing. 'Do you think that she even realized that I would notice or care? That my only role in Bill's life was to perform in the bedroom like one of her silly little boys? Where does she get them and what do you suppose they do together? I suppose she gives them money.'

'I've never really thought about it,' I said. 'They've always just been there.'

'Does your wife approve of her?'

Her large eyes seemed to glitter with some inner force as she interrogated me.

'Approve isn't really the word,' I said, 'but they're civil to each other.'

'Are they? How boring!'

'Laura is quite shy,' I said defensively, looking across the room. She was standing beside Cromer, with a polite expression on her face, listening to something that Mrs Ritchie was saying. Ritchie had turned his back on them and was examining one of the paintings. A log crackled noisily and shifted in the fireplace.

'The fire was Bill's idea,' Ingrid said. 'He insisted on it even though it's such a warm night. He wanted to show off the fireplace. It's original.'

'I know. You've done a wonderful job on the house.'

'You must give credit to Bill as well. He had many ideas and some of them were very good.'

I was saddened by her loyalty. I wanted her to hint at some dark area of discontent so that I could get to work on it and maximize it, fomenting disloyalty. I wanted her to treat me as someone other than a friendly neighbour or an acquaintance of Cromer's.

'Do you miss life in London?' I asked, hoping she would say that she did.

'Yes and no. It's nice to be there and then it's nice to be at home. I don't think that I'd want to be in either place for every week of the year.'

'I'd love to see those photographs some time,' I said because I could think of nothing else to say.

'Yes of course. I'll show them to you after dinner. That reminds me: we should go in soon.'

'Do you need any help?'

'Not at all. Darling!' she called to Cromer. 'We should go in now.'

The dining room was formal and cool, with pale-blue walls and a circular mahogany table. It was not what I had expected. I was accustomed to local parties at which food, although appreciated, was largely an excuse for heavy drinking and an increasingly malicious exchange of gossip. At these dinners, a typical meal would be spaghetti bolognaise served with a salad and garlic bread. These would be consumed from a plate balanced on one's knee wherever one happened to be sitting. The formal display of crystal and of silver, of tall red candles that Cromer was lighting and of china that appeared to be both old and translucent was so unexpected that I stood there staring at it as if I had come to worship at a shrine. Laura, standing beside me, obviously shared in my surprise.

'Let's sit down,' Cromer said. 'I'll put you there, Walter, beside Barbara. Aidan, you sit beside Sally.'

Sitting between Barbara and Sally I felt somewhat claustrophobic.

'This is awfully posh,' Barbara whispered. 'I had expected something much more Germanic, hadn't you? Sausages and sauerkraut and that sort of thing.'

'They've gone to a great deal of trouble,' I said. 'We're all going to have to raise our standards. No more pasta and plonk. This is the rising tide that will lift all our sauce boats.'

'We're not going to be short of a drink anyway,' she said, nodding towards a display of bottles and decanters on a sideboard. 'Frankly I could do with a large Scotch at this minute.'

'You mustn't be naughty, Barbara,' I said. 'They're nice people and they're making a very real effort to integrate with the rest of us.'

'I certainly noticed that you and Ingrid had plenty to say to each other.'

'Just small talk.'

'Really! Look at Aidan! He looks as if he's just about to choke in his collar. What on earth can that old trout be saying to him? Do you suppose she's talking dirty?'

Sally appeared to be reciting poetry to a mute and disconcerted Aidan. I leaned a little to my right in an effort to hear what she was saying but she was speaking very quietly and I could hear only the monotone of her voice going on and on relentlessly. Ritchie was talking to Laura; he looked a little mollified, a little less red about the face, less ready to take offence.

'Have you known Aidan for long?' I asked.

'Yes,' she said. 'For several weeks. He works in a bookshop in Dublin. Don't you think he's rather cute?'

'He's not quite my type, Barbara, but how nice that you share an interest in literature!'

'He's got a nice bum. And he's a willing learner. I'm an excellent teacher.'

Cromer and Ingrid came into the room, each carrying a tray. There was something theatrical about their entrance as if it had been planned to make a precise impression. In some odd way I resented them.

'I hope that everyone likes soup,' Ingrid said. 'It's a great favourite of mine. Watercress and potato.'

'Delicious,' Laura said and there was a general babble of assent as Ingrid passed around the bowls and Cromer poured out glasses of very good dry sherry. Ritchie, unexpectedly, proposed a toast.

'To our charming hostess and host! May they have many prosperous and productive years in this house!'

'Do you think that he intends to be risqué?' Barbara whispered to me.

I ignored her and attempted to make conversation with Sally as we ate the excellent soup. It took me several minutes and many perfunctory answers before I realized that she was resisting any intrusion on her conversation with Aidan.

'Your friend certainly has a way with the ladies,' I said to Barbara.

'Aidan!' she said. 'Are you flirting again?'

He blushed like a schoolboy, the red rising from his neck and blotching across his forehead.

'Sally's been telling me about her family,' he said.

'How very interesting for you!' Barbara said.

'Yes it is,' he said uncertainly. They're all so … different from each other.'

'Isn't that fortunate?' Barbara said, smiling.

Sally didn't react to this.

'Ben always wanted to do something with his hands,' I heard her say.

'Ben sounds like my kind of man,' Barbara said to me.

'It's not that he isn't clever. He is! He's as bright as a button but he has very special hands.'

'I wonder if he ever felt tempted to put them around her fat neck?' Barbara whispered.

I was watching Ingrid eat, noticing, for the first time, her broad strong wrists and the precision with which she used her spoon. She brushed at the corner of her mouth with a napkin, became aware that I was staring at her and smiled.

'That was delicious,' I said.

'You liked it? Good.'

'You must tell us how to make it,' Barbara said.

I was becoming tired of her irony and felt protective towards Ingrid in a way that I had to disguise. There were moments during the meal when I feared that my interest must be obvious. As she collected the soup bowls, I asked her again if I could be of any help.

'If you'd like to pour the wine,' she said. 'Bill will be with me in the kitchen.'

I felt, absurdly, that I had been privileged to have been allocated a role, as if this had brought me closer to her. I went to the sideboard where there were two large decanters filled with red wine. I took one of them and poured some into Sally's glass.

'He was only eight at the time,' she was saying to Aidan,' but already his teachers were saying he was unusually gifted.'

I moved on to Barbara. It was like changing stations on the radio. She was leaning towards Ritchie, who was staring at her as if he were unfamiliar with the language she was using.

'I suppose that as a solicitor you must spend most of your time with lowlifes? Hookers and pimps. Have you ever considered writing a novel?'

'Would Madame like some wine?' I asked Laura.

'This is all a bit of a strain,' she said quietly, reaching for her glass.

'Our friend?' I asked, nodding towards Ritchie, who was still listening to Barbara.

'All of them. I wish that I was at home in bed. With you,' she added as I touched her bare shoulder. The familiar texture of her skin beneath my fingers was warmly sensual but I was thinking of Ingrid, wondering what it would be like to touch her, fondle her, feel her respond to my desire. I felt a little guilty for experiencing feelings that were so unacceptably priapic, knowing that it demeans the one who is desired but yet this longing was all that I knew about Ingrid and it was precious. Could any of this have been conveyed to Laura through my faithless fingers? She moved forward as if to escape from my touch and pretended to be rearranging cutlery. I finished pouring the wine and left the decanter beside Cromer's plate. He came out of the kitchen, carrying a silver tray, and the smell of roast lamb and herbs drifted across the table as if a window had just been opened onto a new and exotic landscape.

I attempted not to look at Ingrid as she put dishes of potatoes and carrots onto the table but when I glanced at her she was looking at me, perhaps accidentally. I was startled and she must have noticed that but she looked away, continuing to perform her duties, like a good host.

Cromer carved the lamb, much more expertly than I could have done. I felt alienated from the occasion as if I were looking in from outside, witnessing strangers participating in some inexplicable ritual. This feeling lasted for several minutes. I had experienced similar detachments before, moments when the familiar had become puzzling and my presence was like an imposition on the progress of other people's lives.

Barbara passed me a plate of roast lamb. I passed it on to Sally.

'Oh how lovely!' she said. 'If there's one thing I like it's roast lamb with all the trimmings.'

Aidan was talking to Laura. The feeling of detachment was receding and I became suddenly aware of how loudly everyone was speaking.

'I hope that you're writing,' Barbara said to me unexpectedly.

'You know that I'm not! I just can't find the confidence to start.'

'Balls! Just get on with it. Maybe you're simply lazy.'

'Barbara, I want to do good work.'

'You've already done that.'

'Well, I hope so,' I said, mollified. 'But you make it sound like something that's totally in my control.'

'But it is!'

'I can hardly remember what it's like to write! Where do the ideas come from? Did you ever have the odd sensation that everything was totally unreal? The opposite of déjà vu?'

'No,' Barbara said, looking irritated. 'That's the opposite of fiction. Making facts false.'

Ingrid was serving vegetables. As she leaned between us, I imagined that I could feel her breast against my shoulder but when I looked I saw that it was her upper arm. I served myself potatoes and thanked her formally. The wine, a Nuits St Georges, was rich and earthy. I felt suddenly uneasy with Barbara. I had described my feelings more accurately than I had intended and was already apprehensive about what she would make of them at other dinner parties. I was aware that she could choose to reduce me to a comic anecdote. It suddenly occurred to me that Aidan and I were the only Irish people in the room. This realization, coming at a moment when I resented Barbara, may indicate some kind of racial hostility. It made me alert, as if ready to defend myself from attack or justify my nationality. Ritchie was talking to Laura about Irish politics in a loud and overbearing tone.

'If the ordinary tax-payer, the ordinary decent British man and woman knew how much it was costing to keep the troops there,' he was saying, 'there'd be a revolt. People simply don't know the truth of the situation. It's a bloody disgrace!'

Laura's face was frozen into a mask of non-reaction. Ingrid was talking to Barbara about a fashion designer who was reputed to be moving into the area. Cromer had asked Aidan about the books that were currently selling well and he had responded with a predictable litany of mediocre titles.

'Delicious lamb,' I said to Sally.

'I was just going to say the very same thing. Isn't everything delicious? You wouldn't do so well in a hotel!'

'Do you like to cook?'

'I'm what you'd call a good basic cook. English cooking. You know what I mean? No fuss. The best food in the world.'

I didn't so I said, rather stupidly, 'Your husband is interested in politics?'

'Had you noticed? Politics. The law. Golf. He's a man of the world.'

I noticed that she had excluded herself and her children from his range of interests and felt some admiration for her commitment to the truth. Other people's relationships can have sad resonances and hints of empty places. It was difficult not to speculate, particularly after a certain amount of drink, on the reality of the sex lives of people to whom one is speaking. Ritchie and Sally were a particular challenge. Her bland and comfortable body, swathed in expensive, matronly clothes, must know the peppery persistence of Ritchie's lusts. It was difficult, although not entirely unpleasurable, to imagine her naked, pink and ample against the sheets, stretching lazily and with good humour, her legs moving slowly apart as Ritchie loomed impatiently above her, waiting to be hard enough, insisting that she could be doing more. It would happen only occasionally; it would be over quickly; she would be better than he at hiding her disappointment.

I was pleased with this imagined exegesis of their relationship. I almost murmured some words of sympathy but she was looking away. I knew that I had invented her but there was something creative as well as puerile about the process. I could now write anything that I wanted about her.

She turned to me and asked 'Do you play golf?'

'Not any more,' I said, looking at her with a new interest. 'I played it as a boy during long summers home from boarding school. But it ended up boring me.'

'I'm not at all surprised,' she said. 'I never understood the attraction myself.'

The plates were being collected. Cromer was talking loudly about his relationship with John Braine.

'No one could even start to understand the meaning of the word difficult until they spent an evening with poor John.'

'Is he talking about the man who wrote *Room at the Top*?' Sally asked.

'One and the same.'

'I liked that book. Very true to life. I'm told that you've written some books yourself. I must look for them in the library.'

'I'm not sure that you'd care for them.'

'Oh I'm sure I would! I like talking to you, so why wouldn't I enjoy reading you?'

Cromer filled our glasses; I felt that he had taken over my duties.

'I hope that you're both enjoying yourselves.'

'I'm just waiting for a chance to compliment your lovely girl-friend,' Sally said. 'The meal is perfection.'

'I was in charge of the vegetables,' Cromer said. 'Roast potatoes are my speciality!'

'The potatoes were particularly good,' Sally said, taking him seriously, as if he had been soliciting compliments. Perhaps he had. I stared at him, attempting to decide, then looked at Ingrid, aware that I had resisted that temptation for a while. She was relaxing, her left arm, long and lovely, hooked around the back of her chair, her eyes concentrating on a spot somewhere above and behind Barbara's head. I had never seen the angle of her jaw so precisely outlined or noticed that she had a mole, small and orange-brown on the right side of her neck. I longed to touch it. She was wearing a number of rings, one of which reflected candlelight as if emitting energy. Her earrings were silver, octagonal studs. She looked across at me.

'What are you thinking about?' she asked so directly and unexpectedly that I felt something like the suddenly remembered embarrassments of schooldays. Everyone else seemed to be listening and I couldn't think of anything to say. I sensed an element of mockery in her smile; she raised her eyebrows with false encouragement, willing me to answer. I glanced away from her and saw that Laura looked surprised. In the few seconds that followed I believed that my most private feelings were on display for the amusement or annoyance of everyone else at the table. I looked back at her. Her expression had not changed but the moment suddenly seemed to lose its significance and become trivial. Most of us, after all, were by now a little drunk.

'I was a thousand miles away,' I said, relying on the crutch of a cliché. 'I'm sorry if I've been rude. It's just,' I added, without any logic, 'that I enjoyed the meal so much.'

'You looked pleased to be at that place a thousand miles away,' Ingrid said. 'Is it anywhere that we know?'

Her persistence appeared to be malicious but I no longer felt inadequate to the challenge.

'Nowhere that you know,' I said. 'Just some Proustian associations.'

She laughed, mocking me, wanting to provoke me into some indiscretion. Was my desire for her so obvious, so easily detected at a glance and so comic? She leaned towards me so that I was aware again of how her eyes glittered like the rings on her fingers.

'What was the madeleine?' she asked.

'Why are you so interested, Ingrid?' I said, enjoying saying her name and knowing, at precisely that moment, that we were going to have an affair. The others were talking again and I felt less inhibited, although I worried about the expression that I had noticed on Laura's face.

'I must control my thoughts in future,' I said, 'when I'm lucky enough to be in your house.'

'Will that be a terrible strain?'

'Not if it brings me to your attention.'

She laughed.

'Did you feel that I was neglecting you? Surely not.'

'Is this a private duel,' Barbara said, 'or can anyone join in?'

'The more the merrier,' I said, although I wished that I could continue talking to Ingrid as if we were alone. 'Do you ever daydream, Barbara?'

'What an intrusive question!'

'It's what we were talking about. Ingrid caught me day-dreaming.'

'Is that what you were doing? I'd never have guessed! Well, I suppose I'm a professional supplier of daydreams really.'

Cromer was passing around a cheeseboard.

'What are you three up to?' he asked and I waited for Ingrid to say something disconcerting but she just smiled.

'I'm longing for a cigar,' Cromer said. 'Do you think it's too early?'

'Give it a few more minutes, darling, then nobody will mind.'

'Filthy habit,' Ritchie said. 'Absolutely bloody filthy. Nobody smokes in my house. Why haven't you given up? You know that you're killing yourself!'

'He did,' Ingrid said. 'Years ago. But, let's face it, there are worse habits.'

'Not very many,' Ritchie said challengingly. 'I simply have to question the intelligence of anybody who still smokes.'

He was the first of us to be evidently drunk.

'You gave them up a while ago, didn't you?' Cromer said to me.

'With considerable difficulty.'

'He smoked forty a day,' Laura said. 'If not more.'

'Good man!' Ritchie said. 'And I bet that you don't regret it! You're not slow-poisoning yourself like others I could name.'

'You mustn't go on about it any more,' Ingrid said. 'Bill is so looking forward to a cigar!'

'The least I could do as your lawyer is to give you good advice.'

'It's the first time that you've ever given it free,' Cromer said, 'or will you be sending an account?'

'Some people may enjoy inhaling other people's exhaled smoke,' Ritchie said, 'but I'm not one of them.'

'You're going to make it quite impossible for me to light up,' Cromer said, 'which is really mean.'

'Good. That was the general idea!'

'I'll just have to go somewhere else to enjoy it.'

'Don't you pay any attention to him,' Sally said calmly to Cromer. 'You smoke wherever you want to. Imagine telling you what you can or can't do in your own house!'

'Nothing prevents me from giving good advice,' Ritchie said.

I began to get impatient at the silliness of it all, missing the contact with Ingrid.

'I think that Barbara writes wonderfully,' I heard Aidan say. He was talking to Laura. She was smiling and looking interested. Perhaps she appreciated his demonstration of loyalty. He may even have meant it.

'I just know that people really feel better about themselves when they've read her books.'

'Aidan!' Barbara said, 'you're a sweet boy but you really mustn't speak that way about me. People will start to talk!'

I noticed how old the backs of her hands looked, the veins pressing prominently against swollen skin, folds of flesh heavy at the wrists. She was, I suppose, a gallant figure in her own way, fighting the fight against age and taking a stand.

Cromer had handed me a large glass of brandy. Ingrid looked

65

at me demurely, then smiled, as if we were conspirators. This appealed to me greatly. Then Sally said something to me and talked at me relentlessly until it was time to leave the table.

Back in the living room, Cromer was being jocular and expansive. He was talking to Laura. I noticed how good she looked and wondered if he desired her.

Ingrid touched me on the arm.

'Come into the kitchen,' she said, 'I've got something to show you.'

I followed her into a pine-panelled kitchen that was tidier than seemed possible. A dishwasher was humming away in one corner. Only the empty wine bottles on the table indicated that a meal had just been served.

'It was a wonderful meal,' I said.

'Thank you.'

'Ingrid,' I said suddenly, 'if I told you that I think I'm becoming obsessed with you, what would you think?'

'I'd think that you're drunk! And you are, aren't you? We all are a little!'

'I may be but I'm perfectly serious.'

'I don't even know what you mean by obsessed.'

'That I think about you all the time.'

'But that's just silly.'

'I don't think so.'

'Do you think it's fair to behave like this in Bill's house?' she said and the essential decency of the question embarrassed me.

'I'm sorry.'

'I only wanted to show you my designs.'

'I'd still love to see them. Is there any chance?'

She opened a cupboard and took out some rolls of paper and some photographs.

'These are the roughs,' she said, unrolling the sheets of paper and spreading them on the table. I realized that I was looking at them upside down. I moved around to her side of the table.

The drawings were charcoal sketches of plans and elevations of a stage. The lines were broad and confident against the light blue graph paper; some had been partially erased. They showed a complete interior on several levels; the various playing areas were indicated by a code that was detailed on one of the pages. It was a little like looking at the plans for an elaborate doll's house or the exploded view of a building with a use that was outside one's experience. As she went through the mechanics of the design, I was a little disappointed by its practicality. I had expected something that would transcend the ordinary, something that would capture the excitement that she embodied for me. She was engrossed in explaining the drawings, as if selling them to me, using a finger to trace the movements of characters, explaining how lighting could be used to create an illusion of space and of how reality could be suggested by the use of a small number of props.

'This worked really well,' she said and her enthusiasm was so real that I was infected by it and felt mean about my earlier reaction.

The photographs, taken from the auditorium, showed the stage lit up, looking like a giant puzzle.

'A shadow moved there,' she said, 'and the audience knew that it had become a completely different room.'

'I love hearing about it.'

She folded the drawings and gathered the photographs together. I moved closer to her and kissed her on the mouth. She tasted of wine and cigarettes. She stood absolutely still, her eyes closed, the photographs in her hand and I was aware of her breathing, a light but insistent sound. Then, without opening her eyes, as she tilted back her head and our tongues rolled together, I heard the door opening and Cromer saying 'Here we go!'

We started back from each other and looked towards the door. He was entering the kitchen backwards, pushing the door open with his shoulders, a large tray with coffee cups and saucers in his hands. I experienced a feeling of intense relief, a feeling more intimate and more resonant than the kiss. Then he turned and looked at us, without suspicion, and said 'So here you are!' as he placed the tray on the table.

'I was showing my designs to John.'

'Aren't they something else?' Cromer said. 'I'd sit down and write a play if I thought that I could attract a designer like you.'

'But you have attracted a designer like me!' Ingrid said with a degree of self-possession that surprised me. My hands were trembling with the relief that a confrontation had been avoided. I knew that my position was ignoble, that I had abused both trust and hospitality, but I didn't care. I had declared myself and, although the kiss had been oddly unexciting, I had at least experienced some hint of response in the probing of her tongue.

She went into the living room without looking at me and I was left there with Cromer, a deflating experience.

'She's talented, isn't she?' he said without obvious enthusiasm. 'I read a letter from the director. He's either in love with her or he genuinely believes she's good.'

'Or both?'

'Perhaps. Look, don't think that you've got to stay in here. I've just come in to have a cigar. If I smoked it inside, my legal adviser would probably suffer thrombosis.'

'He's a man of definite views.'

'Isn't he? I suppose that it's been hell for Sally but who knows? Behind all that homespun there may lurk a piranha.'

'That seems very improbable.'

'I don't know. There's a kind of Englishwoman that you may not be familiar with. I've known one or two Sallies in my day. I almost married one until I experienced the teeth. You're lucky to have such a stable marriage. Laura is a tower of strength.'

I forced myself to look at him, to see if this was sarcastic or confrontational, but he was lighting a cigar with an intensity of concentration that appeared innocent. The tobacco was sweet-smelling and the smoke swirled around his head like a theatrical effect that might have been devised by Ingrid.

'Yes,' I said, unable to think of anything else to say. I had never before kissed a woman while she was involved with another man. It was a new form of betrayal. As a boy, at school, I remember how impressed I had been by the sound and force of the ninth commandment. 'Thou shalt not covet thy neighbour's wife'. The word 'covet' appealed to me. It seemed to encompass the nature of my desire. Now that I had tasted her tongue and felt some diminution in the resistance expressed by her body, I certainly coveted her. I was almost tempted to tell him this. By the way, Bill, I covet your woman. Okay? These things happen.

'Have another brandy,' he said. 'There's a bottle somewhere. Is that it over there?'

'Thanks. You've done an amazing job,' I said, 'on the house.'

'Do you think so? I hope that it works out. I like living here more than anywhere I've been for the past dozen years. And, let's face it, the tax concession makes a huge difference to one's income.'

'I remember,' I said, with a bitterness that I hoped was not entirely apparent, 'when I was making enough for it to make a difference to me.'

I drank some brandy; it felt hot against the back of my throat and a trickle ran down my chin. It annoyed me that Cromer was evidently more sober than I was. In some odd way, this annoyance seemed to alleviate my guilt. I watched him smoking his cigar, apparently contented, unaware that he was talking to someone who was prepared to be his worst enemy. The sound of conversation from next door suggested a greater number of people than were actually there. I could distinguish Ritchie's petulant voice, 'taxpayer ... gigantic ... Labour government ...' and I knew that I had to go and see if Laura was happy or if she wanted to go home. I excused myself to Cromer. 'But of course,' he said, 'why should you be lurking here in the servants' quarters? If you see Ingrid, tell her that I'll be there in a matter of moments.'

I went into the living room. Laura and Barbara were sitting together on a sofa. They were both holding glasses of wine and appeared to be interested in each other's conversation. I went over to them.

'Go away!' Barbara said.

'You don't think that we should go?' I said to Laura.

'Not at all! It's far too early.'

She was a modest drinker but I could see that she had decided to enjoy herself.

'Barbara's just been telling me about those Americans over near Ashford,' she said. 'They make the rest of us seem really dull.'

'They write non-fiction,' I said. 'Dense, largely undigested stuff. They turn on their word-processors in the morning and by early afternoon the screens are full of what passes for fact.'

'Nevertheless,' Barbara said, 'everyone says they're brilliant in bed.'

I looked across the room. Ingrid was speaking to Aidan. As I watched, she touched his arm lightly to emphasize some point and I felt a stab of jealousy, more intense than I would have believed possible, a feeling of isolation and defeat so total that I wondered if I could cope with it.

'Are you all right?' Laura asked me with some concern, the banter gone from her voice. I was ashamed at how obvious my feelings must have been.

'Yes, I'm fine,' I said. 'A goose must have walked across my grave.'

That odd expression, retrieved from some part of my childhood – was it my grandmother who had used it? – surprised me for I had given it no forethought. Both women looked at me, puzzled, then, as if embarrassed, continued with their conversation. I looked across the room again. Ingrid was listening to Aidan and appeared to be absorbed by what he was saying, her head to one side and, as I watched, she laughed as if in appreciation of his intelligence or his wit. He was closer to her in age than I was and was more handsome and I may have underestimated the extent of his appeal. Perhaps he had a boyish charm that would attract a maternal instinct or was there some suggestion of a concealed vigour that would hint at previously unattainable heights of physical satisfaction? I stood there, sodden with self-pity and dislike of him.

'Penny for your thoughts,' Sally said to me.

'You'd be wasting your money,' I said.

'She is lovely, isn't she?' she said, nodding towards Ingrid. 'So full of energy.'

'I was just wondering what they could be talking about,' I said, hoping that a note of defensiveness would not be too evident in my voice.

'Mothers,' Sally said emphatically. 'They're talking about mothers. I earwigged for a while. I heard her telling him that her own mother died three years ago from some awful inoperable cancer.'

'But she was laughing?'

'Why not?'

'What's funny about dead mothers?'

'Wouldn't anyone seek some light relief to make the thing bearable?'

'You're right, of course.'

Ritchie came over to us.

'I'm absolutely exhausted,' he said. 'I wish I could bloody well go to bed.'

'Well you can't,' Sally said decisively.

'That's the worst of staying with people. I've said it before. You abandon the right to put on your coat and go home.'

'I'm sure we'll be leaving soon,' I said, 'and Barbara and Aidan will probably want to go as well.'

'Don't get me wrong,' Ritchie said. 'You can stay here all night as far as I'm concerned. I just want to go to bed. I'm an early riser as a general rule, so I like to settle down early.'

'They say that a regular life keeps you young,' Sally said vaguely, although she must have noticed that her husband looked old and haggard. I wondered how I looked to Aidan.

'Where's Bill got to?' Ritchie asked, peering around the room.

'I wonder if I could just go upstairs without anyone noticing.'

'You can't do that, dear,' Sally said with surprising firmness. 'Once you've put your hand on the plough there's no looking back.'

'What the bloody hell are you talking about?' Ritchie said angrily. 'What have ploughs got to do with it? I just want to go to bed.'

'Excuse me,' I said, oppressed by them, 'I'll just see if Bill is in the kitchen.'

He wasn't but there was a haze of cigar smoke in the air. The brandy bottle from which I had poured my drink was open on the table. I poured a little more into my almost-empty glass and was just about to go back into the living room when I heard a loud knocking on the back door. I hesitated, then went to see who was there.

I opened a door that led into a small back porch. A number of plants were flourishing in pots hanging from the ceiling; the area smelled slightly of decay. That is a distinct memory. I also remember seeing the dark outlines of two men through the glass panels of the back door. The door was locked but there was a large key hanging from a hook on the right. I opened the door with some difficulty and cool night air came like a haunting into the room. It was very dark outside, although some stars were visible and the lighted rectangles of the dining-room windows were imprinted on the grass.

'Mr Cromer?' one of the men said. 'We saw you through the window. We didn't want to disturb your nice little party, so we thought we'd just have a few quiet words with you here.'

He was middle-aged and stocky and spoke with a pronounced Dublin accent. There was nothing else memorable about him except, perhaps, the elaborate politeness of his tone.

'Listen,' I said, or something like that, attempting to regain sobriety, 'it's very late ...'

I had intended to explain that I wasn't Cromer but the words didn't come out correctly.

'We know that,' the second man said, 'but this will only take a few minutes of your time.'

He was younger and spoke with an accent from some part of

Belfast. I seem to remember a leanness about him as if he were actually hungry.

'You've settled down very well here, Mr Cromer,' the first man said. 'You're snug as a bug, aren't you, with your little bit of Ireland all to yourself? You're a very rich man, aren't you, Mr Cromer, so I'm sure that you feel it's a little bit unfair that you aren't paying any tax here? I'm Irish and I'm not well off but I'm paying tax. It doesn't really make sense, does it?'

'Listen,' I said again 'you're making a mistake.'

'Oh it's no mistake, Mr Cromer,' the second man said. He was more forceful. I felt that his tone of voice was just about to break into aggression. He was the kind of man who might easily be armed. He would certainly not be interested in debate. 'We're just asking you to think about what we're saying. When you think about it, you're going to agree with us.'

'We know that you're a decent kind of fellow,' the first man said. 'You've written about the class war, haven't you, Mr Cromer? There's not much sign of it going on here but you're obviously a man with a conscience.'

'Since you're not actually paying tax, there are other ways that you can help the class war.' The Belfast accent teased at the vowels. 'The Republican movement represents working-class people in their struggle against British imperialism. You probably know all about this but maybe it hadn't occurred to you that you could help. If you were to make a contribution to assist that struggle, it would be greatly appreciated.'

I had guessed at the reason for their visit only moments before the proposition was made. I stood there, looking out at them, feeling foolish.

'Do you follow our drift, Mr Cromer?' the first man said. 'It's only a suggestion but you might like to think about it. If you did the right thing, you could be absolutely certain that nobody would ever give you any bother here.'

'Since you made all your money from writing, we thought that you might like to support a magazine. There's a really good one in Belfast called *The Voice of Tone*. It comes out every two months but it badly needs funds. A donation of fifteen thousand pounds would make a huge difference to it.'

'Fifteen thousand pounds,' I heard myself saying, as if I were weighing up the value of some offer.

'That's right, Mr Cromer. We'd be happy with that. All you have to do is send it to the editor. In complete confidence, as the saying goes.'

'That's about it, Mr Cromer,' the first man said. 'It's been a great pleasure talking to you.'

They turned and walked away into the darkness. Why didn't I follow them, argue, protest about the mistake they had made? I was drunk and tired and surprised and even frightened by the abruptness of the invasion. It had happened too suddenly to be comprehensible; it had many of the elements of a physical attack.

I locked the door and sat down at the kitchen table to consider what had happened. My glass was there beside the bottle. The next thing I remembered was Laura was shaking me by the shoulder.

'You've been asleep,' she said.

'No, I haven't.'

'Yes you were! I've just woken you up.'

'I must have nodded off for a second. I just sat down.'

'You've been in here for ages.'

'Only for a few minutes.'

'It's time we went home,' she said. 'I'll drive. I'm not as far gone as you.'

I wanted to tell her about the men but I hesitated. It suddenly seemed a little unreal, like something that I had dreamed.

I went to the door of the porch and opened it. It was almost as I remembered, except that there were fewer plants and the key was hanging on the left rather than the right of the door. These were details of little enough significance, I thought, noticing a definite smell of decay.

'What on earth are you doing?' Laura asked impatiently.

'Just checking on something. Something that I want to be sure about.'

It occurred to me that the door of the porch might have been open earlier when I was talking to Cromer and that I might have observed the plants and the key at that time. They didn't really prove anything.

'It's time you were in bed,' Laura said. 'Everyone's getting ready to leave.'

'Have the Ritchies gone to bed yet?'

'Not yet,' she said, laughing. 'What an odd little man!'

We went into the living room. The others were standing near the door that opened out into the hall. Aidan was drunk and talking loudly to Sally, fractured nonsense that caused her to look at him with some alarm. I decided to say nothing to Cromer until I had thought about it and convinced myself that I was not making a mistake. I wondered how Ingrid would behave towards me in front of the others. This was a sobering thought. I looked at her, feeling the force of her beauty despite my embarrassment.

'I can't tell you how much we both enjoyed ourselves,' Laura said to her. 'Everything was just lovely.'

'The best thing was that both of you could come,' Ingrid said, not looking at me, kissing Laura on the cheek.

'Absolutely,' Cromer said. 'Absolutely. We must all do it again soon.'

'I'm going upstairs now,' Ritchie said. 'Don't worry about me in the morning.'

We went into the hall and I experienced a kind of bleakness. I knew that Ingrid's dislike or even her coolness would be enough to make me feel miserable all summer. I almost went back to apologize or to work out some kind of compromise, but she was talking to Barbara.

Laura drove home slowly, the dipped headlights sweeping across the hedges and picking out a startled fox that stood, rigid, for some seconds, ears pricked, one paw held in the air, before disappearing into the darkness.

It is almost three weeks since I have intervened in this narrative. Laura and Rachael will be home in six days. These have been good weeks, more or less. I have settled down each morning to a work routine that proceeded without any significant disturbance. I have been to Dublin three or four times, visiting bookshops and the National Gallery, bumping into acquaintances, buying new note-books. Mostly I have been here in this silent house, thinking about what I have written and what I might write the next day.

My account of that dinner party has been as accurate as I can make it. It was a turning point of last summer. In many ways it defined the entire shape of the months ahead but I must avoid any tendency to describe hints as certainties. Details bother and preoccupy me: the key, the plants, the possibility that I may have fallen asleep if only for a few seconds, and dreamed. I have hinted at these doubts in the narrative. Only the two men could confirm the accuracy of my memory and it is unlikely that they will ever do so. I remember one as faceless and one as a familiar type, but what use is that? There is nothing about their accents, gestures or into-nations to isolate them from other people and make them more real. If it were a dream, would they not have been more grotesque or nightmarish or odd? Why would I be haunted by such everyday people and ordinary menace? Would the details of a dream not be odder and yet less coherent? Their accents are real to me but their faces are elusive. Did I ever really see or dream their faces?

I hope that they were real.

SEVEN

ON THE FOLLOWING AFTERNOON, I telephoned a friend of mine in Belfast. We had shared a flat for most of the two years that I had spent as a Northern Ireland correspondent. He was an expert journalist with an encyclopaedic knowledge of the Republican underworld. We made small talk; because of some obscure sense of embarrassment, I didn't want him to know the real reason for my call. He asked about Laura. Although she had remained in Dublin while I commuted, she had often visited Belfast. There was no one about whom I could ask. His homosexual world was entirely private. He had never brought anyone to the flat. I had sometimes, mawkishly, thought of him as being even lonelier than I was, although he always seemed to be in reasonably good humour.

'Is there a publication called *The Voice of Tone?*' I asked him with that assumed casualness with which we can unintentionally betray our most important thoughts.

'Yes,' he said, 'of course there is. That's Doyle's broadsheet. Why are you asking?'

I felt elated at this confirmation of the accuracy of a detail that I could not have dreamed.

'I wanted to use the name in a story I'm writing but obviously not if it's a real publication. Is it fairly recent?'

'No,' he said with some evident exasperation. 'I don't know how you could have forgotten it. The Provos fund it and it's sold in some pubs on Saturday nights. Doyle was bringing it out in your time here. He used to send both of us a copy.'

'I'm beginning to remember,' I said with disappointment, picturing a logo of a sharp-faced man in profile beneath an Irish harp. An underground press flourished in Belfast, producing pamphlets and broadsheets on old-style printing machines that smudged the ink and left phantom indentations on the paper.

'Rough stuff,' my friend said. 'Lots of quotations from Tone. Fairly murderous actually. Doyle writes virtually the entire thing himself. He's something of a blast from the past.'

'You're right,' I said, 'I remember him now,' picturing a man with a severe limp who approached one awkwardly at the bar of the Europa Hotel. I had often accepted a copy of his publication and I suppose that I may occasionally have read it. I remembered that I had once invited him to have a drink and that he had refused abruptly. He was one of the old style: sober, learned, ascetic and bloodthirsty.

'Yes, it all comes back to me,' I said. 'He had a pronounced limp.'

'Nothing changes! I read a copy last week. Terrible stuff! I hope that you're working on another book.'

'I've some ideas,' I said defensively, the standard answer. I was disappointed by the call, frustrated that another possible point of confirmation had been taken away from me. I knew that I had to speak to Cromer and would like my story to have been fortified by something that looked like an independent source or, at least, by something other than alcohol.

It was a grey and showery day. My fractured conversation seemed to make each hour drag past with intolerable slowness. I attempted to think about Ingrid but there was little consolation there. I assumed that she would feel contempt for me. I wandered from room to room like some ancient retainer, acting out, uselessly, the routines of the past, and I obviously was getting on Laura's nerves.

'Why don't you go for a walk?'

I trudged along the road without any pleasure. The rain got worse, then, like a clichéd theatrical effect, the sun broke through the clouds and a rainbow looped southwards towards one of the American writers and his crock of gold. I passed Barbara's house, a long, low bungalow with wide windows looking down on a narrow but deep valley. Her car was outside but the curtains were still across on most of the windows. Her lawn needed cutting – we both availed of the services of a somewhat unreliable local man, Tim Byrne – but her flowerbeds were vivid in the damp sunlight. The road stretched ahead, curving towards the mountains, passing the ruined and ivy-covered walls of what had once been the local demesne. The house had been burned down during the War of Independence, then demolished several decades later but the woods always merited some exploration. There was a summer house, an elaborate folly designed to look like a miniature Hindu temple. Names and messages of sexual candour were scrawled on the walls inside but if one looked carefully one could still distinguish the traces of older and more thoughtful graffiti, pencilled in angular writing. 13/4/08 Tea with Florence. Discussed Terence. Due home next year. Please. 21/8/11 Picnic with the children. Toys from the big red box strewn everywhere. Recognised my own horse and cart.

I had often looked at these faded notes from the dead and wondered about the compulsion that lay behind their composition. Was there the basis of a novel there, contemplating lives passed amongst trees and behind walls that had not yet crumbled and before the first shots fired at a groom or a gardener or an elderly relative had signalled the beginning of the end?

I walked to where the outlines of the foundations of the house were still visible. A basement had crumbled inwards. Grass and gorse bushes flourished. It would be possible to pass ten yards from this outline of the past without noticing that it was there. I always experienced a strange, dull feeling when I stood within the large rectangle that I guessed had once been the drawing room. The windows would have looked out not only towards Barbara's valley but towards a small but energetic waterfall that poured across dark rocks into a fast-moving stream. I would sometimes feel that this place had played some part in my life, yet I had discovered it only three or four years before. The feeling was one of an awareness of intensely concentrated lives; all the births and deaths that must have taken place in these invisible rooms, all the acts of lovemaking and humble servitude that had stained the atmosphere with some indelible refusal to pass away completely. Once, I had convinced myself that I had heard voices, someone complaining about a task not performed, someone apologizing. I had brought both Laura and Rachael there and they thought that my feelings were nonsense.

'Why don't you feel it in our own house?' Rachael had challenged me. 'It's old enough. Dozens of people have lived there before us.'

'It must depend on the people,' I had said weakly. 'Perhaps you need to want to be a ghost really badly before you get to be one. The people in our house must have lived passive, contented lives. And aren't we lucky that they did?'

The grass was wet; the trees dark and dripping. Brambles pulled against my coat as I made my way back to the road. Startled birds flapped awkwardly from the undergrowth and something larger and more determined moved across the path ahead. I concluded, without any real evidence, that it was probably a rabbit, but it may have been a rat.

I kept on thinking about the woman and her children, playing with some toys that had once been her own. Had Terence returned from some improbable part of the Empire, after years of discomfort and petty frustration? What had he defended or achieved under an inhospitable sun, surrounded by natives who probably despised him, when he could have been here with his wife and children, looking out at the waterfall? It was the presence of the woman, a cool stillness, and the voices of her children, squabbling because tea had not yet been served which seemed to move with me along the rough path. She was at least as real to me as the men at the back door of Cromer's house. I attempted, yet again, to isolate some detail of that confrontation that might validate it, but nothing came to mind. When I came to the road, many of the clouds had dissolved and the scene sparkled in oblique sunlight. I made up my mind that I would go and talk to Cromer the following morning.

Ingrid opened the door.

'Oh,' she said, 'I wasn't expecting you, was I?'

She was wearing a loose U2 tee-shirt and a tight pair of worn denim jeans and I thought that I had never seen a more desirable or less accessible woman. I stared at her like a schoolboy on a first date that is going wrong, gauche and unable to anticipate what is likely to happen next. She stared back at me, not unfriendly, merely curious.

'No,' I said. 'I was hoping to have a word with Bill. If it isn't convenient I'll call again.'

'He's not here,' she said. 'Didn't he tell you? He heard on Friday that a friend of his from the old days, a novelist from the same town, is dying in Liverpool. He went over yesterday to see him.'

'I'm sorry,' I said mechanically. 'I didn't know that or I wouldn't have called.'

'Come in,' she said, holding the door open. 'It's not too early for a drink, is it?'

'No indeed.'

I followed her into the living room. There was no trace of the party; everything was back in its proper place.

'I know that Laura has posted you a thank-you note.'

'She shouldn't have bothered. Would a gin and tonic be nice?'

'It would be lovely. The Ritchies have gone?'

'Yes. They're touring somewhere in the south of the country. Kerry, I think. I don't think that I could have coped with them for much longer.'

As she poured the drinks, I was acutely aware of the shape of her body, the swell of her buttocks, her long lean thighs. She turned suddenly as if to catch me looking at her, then handed me the drink.

'Did you want to talk to Bill about anything special or was it only for a chat?'

'I was just passing,' I said ineptly. 'I wondered if he'd like to go for a walk.'

She must have known that this was untrue. There was no conviction in my voice, no acceptance in her reaction to it.

'Were they close friends?'

'I think they were at one time. He encouraged Bill. Alan Maxwell. Do you know his work?'

'Not really. I've read a few of his short stories. They tend to turn up in anthologies.'

'Won't you sit down?' she said. 'You seem very stressed. Is something wrong?'

'Well, I suppose I'm at least a little embarrassed,' I said, relieved that we could talk about something real. 'I didn't behave very well at the party, did I?'

'We all had taken too much to drink. What else are parties for?'

We sat opposite each other, on two armchairs, like strangers in the lobby of some hotel. The atmosphere was filled with an equivalent anonymity.

'Yes, but I was probably the only one to express my feelings. Or maybe Ritchie did as well. In a different way. Let me be clear about it. They were sincere feelings but I accept that it was neither the place nor the time.'

'You did take a risk, didn't you,' she said, 'and you came very close to being caught.'

I noticed that she appeared to be more speculative than angry, yet she still seemed totally distant.

I decided to press on, however awkwardly.

'It puzzles me slightly that I feel the way I do. I'm confused by it.

I'm guilty but I'm pleased as well. I think about you all the time.'

This confession seemed to lie between us like an example of extreme bad taste.

She drank from her glass and I waited, rather hopelessly, for her to say something. I didn't think that I could cope with the prospect of not seeing her again. Her feet were bare and vulnerable, the toenails painted a startling and inappropriate red. The tightness of her jeans emphasized the angularity of her hips and the softness of her calves. The tee-shirt revealed wide, firm shoulders but disguised her breasts. She ran the fingers of her left hand through her hair in a gesture that may have indicated either embarrassment or irritation.

'You're very direct,' she said. 'I don't believe that anyone has ever been so direct with me before. I've tried to be annoyed but I'm not annoyed. I've tried not to be flattered but I'm a little flattered. I've got to say this to you. I don't know whether I'm attracted by you or by your directness. If you hadn't spoken as you did, I don't believe that I would ever have thought of us as lovers. Friends yes, but not lovers. You say you're confused but I'm confused as well. I'm confused about my own feelings, so how can I hope to understand yours?'

It was like a reprieve; the condemned man listening to the governor reading out the message that had arrived at the very last minute.

'You seem to understand that I had to tell you,' I said. 'That mattered hugely to me.'

'I suppose it means something,' she said, 'but I asked myself yesterday and last night and this morning, why do it? I'm happy. And everybody will get hurt. Everybody always does.'

'Why can't it just be our private thing?' I asked dishonestly, delighted to hear that I had occupied her thoughts. She shifted her weight on the chair and I longed to touch her.

'Do you think that it ever could be?'

'Why not?'

'It never is,' she said. 'And we live so close. Wouldn't you always be afraid that Laura would find out? Or your daughter? What would you do if your daughter found out?'

I didn't want to think about this; it interrupted the fantasy; it was the reality from which I wished to turn aside.

'No one need know,' I said. 'Come on. We can make each other happy. I want to be with you more than anything in the world.'

She finished her drink, took my glass and went to a table with bottles on a tray. She must have known that I was watching her and wanting her and perhaps she enjoyed that provocation for every movement that she made as she poured out our drinks seemed to be slow and deliberate. I ached for the sight of her naked body but failed totally to imagine it in any detail. When she handed me my glass I noticed that her scar, although still very faint, appeared to be more faded blue than white.

'How did you get that scar?' I asked her, as if we had reached a point of intimacy that made intrusive questioning acceptable. She touched it with a finger; she might have been tracing the shape of the old wound.

'Two men fought a duel over me,' she said, 'many years ago and I flung myself between them to prevent the certain death of the one I cared about.'

She stared into her glass as if capturing some images of the past in the clear liquid. Because she was German, I wanted to believe that answer and attribute to her such an interesting past but she laughed.

'When I was five or six,' she said, 'I was playing with some of my friends in the garden of a neighbour's house. They had a summerhouse, a house of glass, and our ball hit into it and broke one of the pieces. The door was locked, so I reached in through the broken part to get the ball. I fell against the edge and cut my cheek and then I panicked and screamed and pulled back my head and did the real harm. I had a white dress and it went totally red with the blood. You couldn't imagine the blood! I remember that some of the other children cried and some of them laughed. It was as if the world was coming to an end. I can't remember how many stitches I had to have. For years I believed that my face was hideous.'

'That's difficult to believe.'

'You can believe it all right. Even today, when I look in a mirror I sometimes fear that I'm going to see my face the way it was then.'

'You're very beautiful.'

'You're good to say so, but it isn't true. I have good features, good eyes, a good mouth and I make the most of them but I've certainly never thought of myself as beautiful.'

'I can't describe the effect you had on me the first day that we met.'

'That day with Bill? In the pub? What can have been special about that?'

'Everything. I was so jealous when you kissed him!'

'How could you have been?'

'I love you,' I said.

'No you don't. You love some invented version of me that you want to go to bed with. That's a completely different thing.'

'Then let me get to know you properly.'

'It's too much pressure,' she said.

'I'm sorry.'

'Half of me likes it. More than half of me maybe. Oh why not?'

Her sudden agreement caught me by surprise. I stared at her, attempting to think of something appropriate to say, feeling inadequate.

She stood up and I followed her out to the hallway as if I were going to get my coat. She went up the stairs towards the bright, abstract-stained glass window and the unknown rooms.

'We'll use one of the guest rooms,' she said, pointing towards a door at the end of the landing. 'I'll be with you in a minute.'

I went into the room. It was small and almost gloomy, darkened by the branches of a beech tree that pressed against the window.

I could look down at the road and saw, incongruously, the local parish priest trudging past with a small dog on a lead.

The double bed had a dark, old-fashioned mahogany headboard and a red quilt that looked as if it had come from some part of South America. There were three framed architectural drawings on the wall, exploded views of elaborately shaped buildings, and a pile of paperback books on the bedside table. I wondered if the Ritchies had slept here, finding the idea a little distasteful. There was a smell of apples and of old wood.

I took off my sweater and left it on a chair. I heard a lavatory being flushed, an oddly intimate sound, and some pipes gurgling. When I took off my shirt I felt overweight and unattractive. Since giving up cigarettes I had developed a series of mild skin allergies that came and went in unpredictable sequences. I had grown accustomed to the hand-sized patch of redness on my chest but felt nervous about her looking at it and then looking away, wishing that she were somewhere else. I put my shirt back on as she came into the room. She was wearing a large tartan dressing gown that probably belonged to Cromer.

'Why aren't you in bed?'

'I'm embarrassed. I've got this skin allergy. It's utterly harmless but it looks fairly hideous.'

'Let me see.'

I pulled open my shirt and waited for the verdict.

'It's nothing,' she said, touching my chest with cool fingers.

I put my arms around her, excited by her proximity. Her hips appeared to be boneless yet I was conscious of their force. As I kissed her neck, she leaned her head backwards, her hands moving to the buckle of my belt. When my jeans fell to the floor I opened her dressing gown and saw her breasts, blue-veined and heavy.

'Yes, you are beautiful,' I said. 'I've never wanted anyone so much.'

I kissed her breasts, tasting a faint saltiness, wondering at the smoothness of her skin and the gentleness with which she held me.

'Let's get into bed,' she said.

She was naked. I was wearing shoes and socks and my jeans and underpants were draped around my ankles. I could think of no graceful way of completing undressing and was aware, with some surprise, of my own inhibitions pressing in like some sense of doubt. Her dressing gown had fallen to the floor where it lay provocatively like a symbol of satiation, retaining some of the heat that it had absorbed from her naked body. Her nakedness dominated the room, demanding one's full attention. The curve of her stomach had a tonal richness, like some rare and exotic fruit. Her pubic hair was sparse and dark in colour. She stood, watching, apparently amused, as I pushed off my shoes and stooped to take off my socks and jeans. There was nothing in the least provocative about the sight of my clothes on the floor; they made an untidy, slightly ragged-looking bundle and I felt ashamed of them and uneasy about my own nakedness. She held out her hands and we took the few steps to the bed. I realized that she had assumed an air of authority and I found that exciting. She pulled aside the quilt and lay on the bed, pushing herself up towards the pillows with her heels.

'I didn't bring condoms,' I said.

'I take the pill.'

'Thank you,' I said meaninglessly, lying beside her. She looked along my body as if appraising it for usefulness, a detached examination that I found a little disconcerting. Then she kissed my cheek gently, her breath warm against my ear.

'My ears are an erogenous zone,' she said, 'and the back of my neck and all the usual places. How about you?'

'Almost everywhere.'

I was running my fingers along her body, accustoming them to the texture of her skin.

'I get ticklish very easily,' I said, 'if I'm touched where I'm touching you.'

'Do you!' she said, moving her hands repeatedly along the inside of my thighs. 'Do you? Do you?'

I squirmed and wriggled like a child.

'Please!' I gasped, 'Please!', managing to hold her wrists, using physical strength to reverse our roles. She loomed above me, then fell on me as I released her wrists, her body moving against mine with a sudden urgency. We made love quickly and without speaking. Afterwards we both reassured each other that it had been good.

'Would you like some wine?' she said.

I kissed her. Her body was damp and exciting.

'I'll get it,' I said. 'Don't you move.'

'Will you know where to look? It's in the fridge.'

I got out of bed and put on her dressing gown. On my way to the stairs I passed the open door of their bedroom and was pained with jealousy at this glimpse of their life together. The large bed was unmade and there was a breakfast tray on the bedside table. A small colour television set was showing a game show but the sound was turned down. Perhaps she had been in bed when I had knocked at the door or had just got dressed in preparation for a totally different day. Cromer's jackets were visible through an open wardrobe door and his presence haunted the room with objects and pieces of furniture that seemed too masculine to have been her choice.

I went downstairs to the kitchen and found a bottle of Rhein-gau in the fridge. I opened the porch door and looked around in the hope of seeing something that would validate my memory but nothing helped. In the dining room, I found glasses and a cork-screw. I hadn't noticed, before, how loudly the floorboards creaked, a pronounced staccato sound from door to window. I opened the door of what I guessed must be Cromer's study. It was a small room with a basic office desk and chair. Tea chests filled with books were lined up against one wall. Over the mantelpiece there was a small but striking Lowry; children playing with a bright red ball, unaware of the poignancy of a poorly attended funeral in the next street.

I brought the wine, the glasses and the corkscrew upstairs. She had covered herself with the duvet and appeared to be asleep, one naked shoulder visible and a tangle of hair. I kissed her shoulder, relishing its warmth and she turned and smiled at me. I opened the wine.

'What part of Germany do you come from?'

'From near Schloss Vollrads. Like the wine.'

'It's an erotic combination! A woman and her local wine!'

She looked at me speculatively as I poured the wine. Its colour resembled her skin. I sat on the side of the bed and we toasted each other. There were some minutes of awkwardness as if neither of us was confident enough to know what to say. Then I got into bed and caressed her and we made love again, more slowly and adventurously, tasting each other.

Afterwards, as we lay together in our small and intense world, she asked me about my parents and my childhood and she told me about hers. This was interesting, yet I knew that we were really avoiding talking about each other's partner. She told me about her childhood with a vividness that made it possible for me to picture a tall, long-legged girl in green cords, a tee-shirt and a baseball cap who had grown into the woman whom I held.

I think that we may have slept for some time. I realized that Laura would be on her way home from work. I kissed her and said, evasively, 'I suppose I'd better go.' 'Stay another hour,' she said. 'This is nice. What's the hurry?'

'It's just that I'm afraid someone will see the car.'

'Why would that matter?'

'Only if Laura came this way,' I said reluctantly.

'Oh,' she said, 'Laura!' taking her hand away from my penis. 'Of course!'

'It's not that I don't want to stay. I want it more than anything in the world.'

'If you wanted it that much, you'd stay.'

'Please be fair,' I said. 'If you were expecting Bill, you'd feel the same urgency!'

'Would I?'

'Let's not argue and spoil everything.'

'All right!' she said. 'Off you go!'

I reached out to touch her shoulder but she shrugged my hand away.

'I'm sorry,' I said, hearing an unattractive, placatory tone in my voice.

'I liked having you here,' she said. 'I'm just sorry to see you go.'

We clung to each other as if participating in some long-delayed ritual of reconciliation. The warmth of her body was intensely exciting; she emanated a force that I absorbed like a feeling of strength.

'All right,' she said. 'Go now. Don't risk getting caught.'

I felt awkward as I dressed, aware of her watching me, wondering what negative feelings she might experience as she appraised my naked body with a new objectivity.

'Will you invite me again?'

'I'll think about it.'

'I know that I'll think about little else.'

'When you're gone,' she said, as if she hadn't heard me, 'I'm going to take a big, squishy bath.'

I wondered if this remark had some emblematic significance, a cleansing ritual after an experience already regretted. Then the telephone rang in another room. She acted as if she hadn't heard it.

'Hadn't you better answer it?'

'Why?'

'It could be important.'

'I doubt it.'

The ringing went on and I was unnerved by its persistence and the thought of someone waiting for it to be answered.

'Stop worrying,' she said. 'Nobody knows you're here.'

The sudden silence was almost as intrusive as the sound had been. I found that I was waiting for other sounds; a sudden knocking on the door, a voice accusing me of disloyalty.

'Thank you for everything,' I said. 'May I phone you in the morning?'

'If you want to.'

There was no way of leaving that would not seem like a betrayal. I stood at the door, hesitating. She looked at me as if I were an intruder.

'All right?' I said.

'All right.'

I went down the stairs. The front door closed behind me with a decisive clunk. The evening was warm and fragrant and two magpies hopped inelegantly across the grass beneath Cromer's trees. I heard a car coming up the road but knew, from the sound of the engine, that it was not Laura's Renault. Barbara's car came around the corner and she waved at me expansively, perhaps even a little drunkenly.

I drove home. Laura was there. She was sitting at the kitchen table, reading an evening newspaper. She looked tired and her eyes were strained and faded.

'Did you go for a drive?'

'Just down to the pub,' I said.

I looked away from her, nervous that guilt was evident in my expression. She had been working all day while I had been trying to put her out of my mind.

'Had you a busy day?'

She nodded, distracted by what she was reading. I looked and saw that it was a hostile article about the British royal family.

'There can't be anything new to learn about them?'

'I feel sorry for that girl,' she said.

'Would you like to go out somewhere?'

'I want to get Rachael's room looking nice.'

I had forgotten that the school holiday began the following day.

'I'll help you.'

'Don't worry. I just want to get some bits and pieces done.'

I was so obviously dispensable that I wished I were back with Ingrid.

'We'll have some supper later,' Laura said.

I was touched by her vulnerability. The back of her neck looked narrow and insubstantial. She was slumped on the chair, her elbows on the table, her suit looking a little like a uniform. From the doorway, she could easily be confused with Rachael who often sat in the same position reading music magazines. I thought of Ingrid in her bath, her skin growing pink in the heat, suds moving across the curves of her body and swirling between her legs. I wished that I could see her, touch her, be with her, escape from dullness.

I went into my study and jotted down the notes that have formed the basis of this part of my journal.

EIGHT

LAURA SAID that she would collect Rachael on her way home from work.

'It could be eight o'clock before you see us.'

'Don't worry,' I said, elated at the thought of the long day stretching ahead. 'I'll put a nice supper together.'

As soon as she had gone, I dialled Cromer's number, letting it ring for three or four minutes. There was no reply. I could imagine the exact sound that the phone was making and became convinced that Ingrid was there ignoring it. I hung up, then dialled again almost immediately, impatient to make contact, angry at being ignored. There was no reply. I tried again, knowing that it was pointless. I was surprised to notice that my hands were trembling. I took a bath, shaved, listened to a radio programme and felt more calm and in control. I dialled the number and listened to it ring. I know you're there, I thought, why are you doing this to me? Answer it now.

I drove to the house. There was no car parked outside but I couldn't remember having seen one the previous day. I knocked on the front door, using a big, old-fashioned black knocker shaped as the head of a lion. The sound seemed to echo back as if there was nothing whatsoever behind the door. I knocked again, impatiently, like a policeman in a bad drama, but there was no response.

I went around to the back door and found myself standing where I believed the men had stood on the night of the party. I knocked and tried the latch but the door was bolted. I returned to the front of the house and looked up at the windows. No curtain stirred, no figure moved back from the light. I was attempting to see between a gap in the curtains of the dining-room windows when I heard a car stopping outside the gate. I turned around guiltily, hoping to see Ingrid. Barbara got out of her car and leaned on the gate.

'Have I caught you in the act of robbing the place?'

'I was just looking for Bill.'

'But you must know he's away,' she said.

'Is he?'

'Didn't I see you here yesterday?'

'I thought that Ingrid said something about his getting back this morning.'

'I doubt that. She told me that he'd be gone for at least a week.'

'How is Aidan?' I asked, hoping to disconcert her. I resented her tone of voice and conspiratorial smile.

'He's no more,' she said with no evident regret. 'Celibacy beckons.'

'That seems a little grim.'

'So are the alternatives, darling.'

I was standing beside her at the gate, wishing that she'd go away.

'Any news?' she asked. 'I'm out of touch.'

'Nothing much. Rachael gets her summer holidays today.'

'Lovely. I'll invite her over for a chat. Will you be in the pub later?'

'I'm sure I will.'

'I'll see you later then.'

She got into her car and looked at me quizzically, as if expecting some revelation.

'Yes,' I said. 'Yes. I'll see you then.'

I watched as she drove away, the sound of the car's engine

fading, some glimpses through the thick hedges of its roof, diminishing in the distance. I went back to the door and knocked without hope or conviction. I was about to leave a note but decided against it. I felt very much alone.

I went home, made some coffee, then dialled the number again. There was no reply. I felt guilty about Rachael. Her return from school would usually be a major event but it now seemed like a complication in the progress of my infidelity. I went up to her room. Laura had left flowers in a vase on the bedside table and a 'Welcome Home' card on the pillow beside a bear that had been worn almost one-dimensional with love. It was a happy room and I felt miserable.

The telephone rang. I rushed into our bedroom to answer it.

'Hello. Are you free to talk?' she asked.

'Yes, of course I am. Of course. How are you? I've been thinking about you and telephoning you all morning.'

'I went into the city early this morning to go to Kennedy's of Harcourt Street. For art supplies. Bits and pieces.'

'Of course. It's great to hear from you.'

'I was curious to know if you'd rung.'

'I was longing to talk to you.'

'Were you really?'

'Of course I was!'

'I bought lots of mussels. Would you like to share them with me?'

'There's nothing I'd like better!'

'Give me half an hour, then join me here.'

'I look forward to that!'

She hung up without replying. I felt absurdly happy that she had contacted me and wanted to see me. I had a good bottle of Sauvignon Muscadet that had survived our last dinner party. I put it into a carrier bag and looked at my watch. It was less than five minutes since she had called. I walked around the house as if attempting to imprint the shape and character of each room on my memory. I was touched by the sight of the flowers in Rachael's room and guilty at how anxious I was to shut the front door behind me, discarding precious memories. I was excited at the thought of Ingrid undressing, the sway of her lovely breasts, the tattoo vivid against the smoothness of her skin.

It was even better than on the previous day. We were more relaxed, more at ease with the reality of each other, less surprised at what was happening. Afterwards I helped her to cook a meal, chopping shallots and parsley as she scrubbed the mussels in the sink. We ate at the kitchen table, giggling like conspirators at something silly that had happened to her in the city, reaching out to touch each other and leaning close to kiss. She had cut brown bread into very thin slices. My wine, although not properly chilled, was good.

'I wish I had known that you were driving into Dublin,' I said. 'I'd have gone with you. It would have been fun.'

'I just got what I wanted and came straight back home.'

'We could have had a drink or something.'

'Where do you like to go to drink?'

'There's a small pub close to Leeson Street Bridge called O'Brien's. I was a regular there for years.'

'You must take me there some time.'

'Of course I will.'

It was exciting to be plotting a future, days shared, appointments arranged, new places to fill with our feelings. She was wearing black denim jeans and a loose white blouse, her hair held back from her face by a childish piece of red ribbon. I stood to fill her wine glass, kissed the top of her head, stroked the back of her neck.

'That feels good.'

'I was in despair,' I said, 'when I couldn't get through to you. I thought that you couldn't be bothered answering.'

'Silly!'

'I wanted to see you so I'd know that I wasn't imagining yesterday.'

'You'd need to have a very good imagination!'

This tempted me to tell her about the men at the back porch but I feared that it would spoil everything. I had more or less decided to tell Cromer as soon as he returned from England but I wanted this day to be perfect. I wanted to hear her saying that she loved me.

We finished the meal and I took the plates and cutlery to the dishwasher.

'Good wine,' she said.

'I'm glad you liked it. What kind of art supplies did you need?'

'I want to do some sketching here. I'm out of practice but once I was quite good. I illustrated two books in Germany.'

'Do you have copies of them here?' I asked, hungry for any fragment that might help me to know her better. To see something through her eyes would be a new kind of intimacy.

'They're in London. I'll show them to you some day.'

'I'd like that.'

'I want to read one of your books. Will you give one to me?'

'Of course.'

'Are they very sexy?'

'Not at all!'

'No?'

'No. The characters brood about motive and religion. The sex takes place quickly in the dark.'

'I know you're joking.'

'I'll bring you one the next time we meet.'

'I think Bill is a good writer,' she said unexpectedly, 'but he doesn't write very well about women. His women are the way that men like Bill would like them to be. I've tried to explain this to him but he doesn't pay any attention.'

'On second thoughts,' I said, 'I probably won't bring you a book.'

She laughed, came over and put her arms around me. Her proximity was a new sensation each time. We went back upstairs to the same spare room. The untidiness of the bed was provocative. She put a tape into a cassette player.

'Do you like Leonard Cohen?' she asked.

'Actually I do. Very much.'

'Good.'

She switched on the tape. Cohen was singing 'Chelsea Hotel', the account of his affair with Janis Joplin, and I wondered if she had chosen it deliberately, knowing that it ended with the affectionate indifference that can so often follow passion. She undressed quickly and neatly, leaving me going through my awkward routine with clothes left on the floor like shabby plumage. We made love. I felt that she trusted me and the pleasure was intense. Afterwards we lay holding each other.

'Bill's coming back tomorrow,' she said. 'He's bringing Jack, his son.'

'Rachael's coming back this evening.'

'That's that then,' she said, pulling away from me.

'What do you mean?'

'We won't have a house that's private.'

'Nonsense. We'll find a way. There'll be plenty of opportunities.'

'Not if we're always afraid of being caught.'

'I'll work out something,' I said, as if comforting a child.

'You're kind,' she said without any conviction.

'Do you think you could love me?'

'Maybe.'

'You could love Bill as well.'

'Oh I don't think I've ever really loved Bill,' she said. 'And he doesn't really love me. We like each other in special ways. We met when we were both lonely.'

'And it's been like that for all these years?'

'They've been good years and we like each other a lot. And the sex has always been good. Bill isn't a very emotional man. His childhood was cold. His mother was a very ambitious woman. He told me that he had no memory of any physical affection between them.'

'Would you be very upset if he got involved with someone else?'

'Of course I would. You don't have to love someone madly to need them or depend on them.'

'Do you think he feels the same?'

'I'm sure he does. I've had some affairs but they were never of any importance.'

I was chilled by this answer and by the calm manner in which she dissected her feelings for Cromer.

'Is this just another unimportant affair?'

We lay separate and constrained in the untidy bed.

'No, this might be different,' she said. 'I don't know but it might be different.'

I reached out and touched her shoulder, sleek beneath my fingers, delighted at the interest that she had expressed yet noticing that she had closed her eyes as if to mask her feelings.

'What about you?' she asked. 'What about you and Laura?'

I knew that she would not believe me if I attempted to explain how successfully I had avoided the implications of that question.

'I never knew,' I said, 'that it was possible to be in love with two people at the same time.'

The words sounded glib to me. Her closed eyes were like a rebuke.

'I never loved anyone except Laura before I met you. I had some relationships but they were superficial. As soon as I met you, I knew that my feelings were just as strong.'

'It's all so complicated.'

'We can unravel it.'

'Don't talk nonsense,' she said, opening her eyes and staring at me with what appeared to be dislike. 'There's no way of making any of this simple.'

I was hurt by her rebuke and uncertain how to respond. We seemed to have moved a long way from our sexual closeness.

'I need to be close to you,' I said honestly. 'Despite all that may be right in my life and despite all the complications, I need you in a way that I wouldn't have thought possible.'

'I like you for saying what you feel. I need someone I can be honest with.'

We moved close together again and embraced but there was a definite awkwardness after the first articulation of the price to be paid and the risks that would have to be taken. Laura had been forced into our consideration and my disloyalty to her and to our life together came like the chill of a bad memory. Cromer was more difficult to comprehend; he was merely a part of an uncertain future. If her need for him could not be defined as love, there would still be a considerable reservoir of shared feeling.

'What's Jack like?' I asked, in an effort to relax and dispel my guilt.

'He's all right,' she said without enthusiasm. 'He's fine.'

'It doesn't sound as if you like him.'

'I don't like some of the things that he's done to Bill.'

'But he's only a boy, isn't he?'

'He's seventeen.'

'So what can he have done?'

'I'm sure that divorce is very difficult for children,' she said, 'but he found advantages for himself in the situation. Bill can be very vulnerable. Jack knows how to make the most of that.'

'Is he at university?'

'He's just finished school. He went to somewhere famous. I'll think of the name. Listen, you'll know what I mean when you meet him.'

'I'm sure you're right,' I said. 'I had rather hoped he'd be company for Rachael. Ever since we moved from the city she's felt a little isolated during the holidays.'

'Maybe Rachael will think that he's nice.'

'Anyway,' I said, uncomfortable at the thought of Rachael's possible feelings, 'there's something that I want to talk to Bill about. I'll probably call tomorrow. Will you mind?'

'I mind that you have to go now.'

This was like a declaration of love and I welcomed it into the awkwardness of our conversation. When she yawned, her tongue arced against her bottom teeth which were small and very white. I was preoccupied with all her movements, loving the way that she frowned when she looked to see the time. Leonard Cohen's voice had already become a part of our world. 'Like a worm on a hook, like a knight in some old-fashioned book, I have saved all my ribbons for thee.' The voice had a hypnotic charm. I found myself staring at the cassette player as if there were a message to be decoded there. Something prompted me to ask her if she were superstitious.

'Not really. I used to go to fortune-tellers when I was a teen-ager but all my friends did. There was a woman living near us who read Tarot cards.'

'Was she good?'

'Too good. She scared me.'

The telephone rang and I felt like an intruder. She reached over and switched off the tape then got out of bed and walked, naked, from the room. She answered the call in their bedroom and I noticed that she made no attempt to speak quietly.

'Hi! Where are you? Oh really? That's nice. With Jack? How is he?'

I felt sad and jealous that a telephone call could alter every-thing so radically. All the intimacy had been transferred to the other room; they would interpret the pauses in speech as precisely as the words they used.

'Yes, me too,' she said. 'Yes, of course I do. I can't wait. There's been nothing much here. I hope that Jack likes the house. He hasn't been to Ireland before, has he? He may find it very quiet here. Do you think so? Okay, I'll see you then.'

She came back into the room wearing a long, black silk dress-ing gown with a sash tied at the waist.

'That was Bill,' she said. 'They'll be here in a few hours. Earlier than I thought.'

'I'd better go then.'

She sat on the edge of the bed and kissed me.

'You're like a child,' she said, 'all worried. Don't you remember that you said we'd find a way?'

'And we will,' I said. 'I know we will. It's just that I feel we're being invaded by everybody. Even Barbara. She was so full of curiosity yesterday when she saw me knocking on your door.'

'Isn't Barbara always curious?'

'Why doesn't everyone just fuck off and let us have some time for ourselves!'

She smiled and switched on the music. Cohen's voice evoked what we had experienced earlier, a conspiratorial closeness. She untied the sash of her dressing gown and slipped it off by moving her shoulders. This chameleon process was deeply exciting. When she lay beside me, it was as if we were close for the very first time and our lovemaking reflected an additional sense of discovery. I needed the reassurance of her desire. Her nails scraped painfully across my back as if she resented the presence of my body looming above hers but I accepted this like a caress.

Afterwards, there seemed to be little enough to say. I could sense that she shared the paradox of sudden constraint. Perhaps both of us were thinking about the summer that stretched ahead or the partners whom we had betrayed.

She watched me as I dressed. The cassette came to an end; the machine hissed, then subsided into silence.

'So I'll call round to see Bill tomorrow.'

'Why not?'

I thought that she suddenly looked young, vulnerable and uncertain.

'What would be the best time?'

'Why not telephone first?'

She turned away from me.

'What's wrong?' I asked.

'What a stupid question!' she said without looking at me. 'I don't want to be involved with you. Go home to your wife. What are you doing here anyway?'

I was disturbed by the hostility in her voice and when I said 'Can we not just see what happens?' I hated the mendicant sound of my own. When I thought of my first impression of her, so openly sexual with Cromer, I was ashamed that our relationship had brought about such furtive sadness. It was even difficult to recall that just minutes before we had made love with unsuppressed excitement.

'I suppose that we can.'

'It's only because Jack and Rachael are coming on the scene,' I said without conviction. 'But we'll get around that.'

'Will you pass me the dressing gown?'

She put it on while sitting up in the bed without either the exuberance or grace with which it had been discarded.

'I must change the sheets,' she said, as if speaking to herself.

'Can I help?'

'No, it's all right. Don't worry,' she said, attempting a small, crooked smile, 'I'll cheer up.'

'I hate leaving.'

'You've got to go.'

'I don't even know how to end this conversation. I don't know how to walk from the room. Can I phone you when I get home? That might make it easier.'

'If you like.'

I kissed her on the lips and, somewhat to my surprise, she responded. I went down the stairs without saying another silly or self-pitying word. I telephoned from my study and knew before I had dialled the last two digits that her telephone would be engaged. I felt some relief; saying goodbye again might have made things even worse. A search for reassurance could become ritualistic and hostile, yet I longed to hear her voice. I telephoned again and again over the next few hours. The number was engaged each time.

Later, I remembered that I had promised to make a supper to celebrate Rachael's return. I had neglected to get anything at the shops so I made a spaghetti Bolognaise from ingredients that I found in the pantry and refrigerator. I knew that it would be good but I was sorry that it wasn't more special. I decided to try Ingrid's number one last time and got a ringing tone, then heard Cromer's voice. I was so shocked that I just stared at the receiver as he said 'Hello. Hello. Hello?' He hung up before I did. I poured myself a drink, knowing that she would guess that I had been the caller. The sadness of it seemed to suggest the world towards which we were moving; furtive assignations and phones clicking off, photographs hidden between the pages of books. I wondered if he would be suspicious about the call and if she would be angry with me. Despite the intimacy that we had experienced it would be easy for us to be distanced by misunderstanding. I moped around the house, feeling old and joyless until I heard the sound of Laura's car in the drive.

'Welcome home!' I said to my daughter, standing on the front steps. 'Now I know that it's summer.'

Rachael looked happy and awkward in her school uniform. She had outgrown it in a matter of months and reminded me of a schoolgirl in a Ronald Searle cartoon.

'I can't believe how much you've grown,' I said, feeling a little uneasy as I hugged her, as if my faithlessness to her mother would be in some way evident.

'It's brilliant to be home!' she said. 'I'm the second-tallest girl in my year. Only Alison Farrell is taller.'

Laura was smiling at her in a way that suggested some surprise. Then she turned to me.

'Had you a good day?'

'Not bad,' I said. 'I didn't do anything in particular.'

'Mum said that you were making supper,' Rachael said.

'Spaghetti. And garlic bread.'

'That sounds great. The food this term was even worse than before.'

She ran up the stairs with a mixture of noise and grace that was totally endearing. Laura was looking at me speculatively as if expecting me to say something of importance.

'I bumped into Ingrid,' I said, compelled to speak her name. 'Bill Cromer and his son are expected back today. I hope the boy might be some company for Rachael.'

'Do we know anything about him?'

We went into the kitchen and I was comforted by the smell of garlic and Italian herbs. I had opened a bottle of Valpolicella.

'Well, we know who his parents are.'

'You know what I mean. We don't need anyone too alarming.'

'All I know is that he's been to some good boarding school. Ingrid couldn't remember the name but she said it was famous.'

'I suppose that Bill could afford that easily enough.'

'We can look him over in any case,' I said.

Rachael came into the kitchen and hugged Laura.

'Thanks a million for the card,' she said.

'There's a good weather forecast,' I said. This information appeared both irrelevant and foolish. 'In case you want to play tennis. Apparently it's going to be sunny for the next day or two.'

'I want to do nothing for a while except lounge around the place. I love being here. I love having nothing to do.'

'Of course. I just mentioned it in case you were afraid you'd be bored.'

In this faintly uneasy atmosphere, we sat down for our family meal.

NINE

CROMER TELEPHONED early the following morning. I was both embarrassed and uneasy, wondering how much he knew.

'I was sorry to hear about your friend.'

'Big C,' he said in that solemn tone reserved for death and unpalatable medical prognosis. 'The poor bastard could go any day now. His youngest kid is only nine. A little girl.'

'That's terrible.'

'Intimations of mortality,' he said vaguely and then, in a conjunction of ideas that I found a little disturbing, 'Have you been keeping well yourself?'

'Very well indeed,' I said, over-emphatically, wondering if he were in their bedroom or alone in his study. Could he see her from wherever he was? Did he want her as much as I did? I was deeply jealous at the thought of the lovemaking that they would have enjoyed since his return home.

'Good,' he said. 'How are you fixed at lunchtime?'

'There's nothing happening.'

'Ingrid tells me that your daughter's home from school.'

'She came home yesterday.'

'And my boy Jack is here. Why don't the four of us meet in the pub at half twelve? We can have a chat and the kids can get to know each other.'

'That's a good idea,' I said without enthusiasm, remembering Ingrid's unfavourable opinion and Laura's hesitations. 'I'll just make certain that Rachael's free but if I don't phone you back you can take it that we'll be there.'

'I look forward to that.'

Laura was getting ready to go to a medical conference in a hotel outside Dublin. Her hair, still wet from the shower, was plastered against her skull and her cheeks were flushed to the colour of the pink bathrobe she was wearing.

I kissed her, but she was in a hurry, moving away impatiently.

'I can't be late. I'm introducing one of the speakers.'

I told her about Cromer's invitation. She paused, a hair dryer held above her head as if she had been frozen into some act of masochism. I wished that we were about to get into bed but knew, with a sharp feeling of self-dislike, that I was aroused as much by the thought of Ingrid as by the sight of my almost-naked wife.

'Well I'm sure that Rachael will like that,' she said finally. 'Let's hope that he's not too alarmingly sophisticated. It's probably being over-protective of me to have any worries about it. It's just that his mother is kind of extravagant, isn't she?'

'Yes. If press reports are to be believed, she seems to have acted her way through life. She probably doesn't know who she is any more. But the boy might be a rock of sense.'

'I doubt it!'

'I wish you were coming,' I said, wishing that Ingrid would be there.

'I'm really interested in this conference,' Laura said as if she had not heard me. 'I think it's going to be very important.'

Her enthusiasm made me feel guilty about the triviality of my life. When I wasn't working, I was doing very little except wasting time. I sometimes surmised that the sense of unreality that I occasionally experienced might emanate from the lack of commitment in my days. I was a man with few beliefs and even fewer causes.

'I'll let you know what happens,' I said.

When I told Rachael about the arrangement, she was obviously disconcerted.

'You could have given me more notice.'

'How could I? He only suggested it a few minutes ago.'

'Jack,' she said. 'It's quite a nice name, isn't it? It's like something out of a nursery rhyme. I never actually met someone called Jack before. What age is he?'

'Seventeen I think.'

'I've seen his mother in two movies. I wonder if he looks like her. I'm going to be so nervous.'

'You don't have to come if you don't want to. I can easily make an excuse.'

'Of course I want to come! Don't be silly! It's just that I've hardly had time to think about it. I don't know what I'm going to wear. I'll think about it in the shower.'

It was warm and bright in my study. I looked at some books that I had been sent for review: a Celtic blockbuster by one of the American writers who lived ten or twelve miles away and a paperback thriller with a lurid cover, set in Northern Ireland, by an English journalist whom I had known and liked when I worked there. Both looked tedious. The Celts spoke in an irritating singsong manner, and the thriller, which read as if written by Peter Cheyney, claimed to be 'the first authoritative investigation of the real forces at work in Northern Ireland'. It would be difficult to feel any enthusiasm for them, yet they made me wish that I had completed a sustained piece of writing. Every day that passed increased, by some immeasurable fraction, my sense of failure. I longed to capture the reality of my life, to explore the relationships that mattered to me but the manner of doing so, the creation of a device that would pull the pieces together, had become obscure. It appeared that I could no longer enter into the personality of a narrator. My attempts never provided me with the reality of a voice. There is a temptation, in fiction, to devise the additional fiction and make oneself look good, to end a chapter before the truth dawns or the recriminations begin. I had no difficulty in identifying this fault in the work of other writers but in draft after draft of works partially in progress I would find myself sympathizing with a heroic point of view. The falsity of that writing was offensive.

Rachael came into the study. She was dressed in a black top and a black mini-skirt; the effect was totally surprising. The gangling teenager had transformed into a young woman whose sexual allure was strikingly evident. I was touched and a little shocked.

'You look wonderful,' I said. 'I don't think I've ever seen you so dressed up before.'

'What do you mean?'

'So grown up. So sophisticated.'

'Dad! You don't think it's too much, do you?'

'Not at all,' I said, afraid that she would detect some doubt in my expression or in my tone of voice. She was unselfconscious about her looks and that was too precious a quality to jeopardize. 'I'm so proud of you.'

'You don't think it's too much for the pub? I can change back into jeans.'

'Don't be silly. You look absolutely great!'

'Good,' she said. 'I just didn't know what you'd think. Mum got me this outfit in case I was going to a party but I wanted to try it out.'

She chatted animatedly as we drove to the pub. It was as if she were practising an almost adult line of brittle conversation. I felt slightly uncomfortable.

'Is everything all right?' she asked as we pulled into the carpark. The anxiety of her expression, her evident need for reassurance, robbed her of whatever sophistication she had attempted.

'Are you certain that I look okay?'

I switched off the engine and took her right hand in mine.

'Absolutely,' I said. 'You're a beautiful young woman and I'm very proud of you. I think young Cromer is very lucky to be meeting you.'

'I didn't dress up for him,' she said quickly.

'I know that, but I still think he's really lucky.'

She kissed me on the cheek.

'You're good to me,' she said.

We went into the pub. Cromer was standing at the counter talking to Mr Moore.

'We've just arrived,' he said a little drunkenly. 'I was telling mine host about some recent trends in the English licensed trade.'

Mr Moore's expression was impassive. He glanced briefly at Rachael and nodded to me.

'And this must be your daughter,' Cromer said. 'I was expecting someone totally different. Tram tracks on the teeth and a healthy enthusiasm for ponies. Nothing could have prepared me for this beautiful creature.'

He took Rachael's hand and kissed it. I noticed with some surprise that she did not appear to be disconcerted. She smiled and said 'I was sorry to hear about your friend.'

When he asked what drink she'd like, she looked at me briefly then said a Coke. I wondered if she'd have ordered differently if I hadn't been there. This thought made me feel elderly and plodding, an enemy of youth. I asked for a gin and tonic.

'I'll bring them to your table,' Mr Moore said in a tone of voice that suggested an enormous favour was being done.

'My son's over there,' Cromer said, nodding towards the farthest corner. 'He's getting stuck in to his very first pint of Guinness.'

We went across the room.

'This is Jack,' Cromer said.

The boy looked at Rachael and stood up, still holding an almost-full pint glass. He was tall, with narrow shoulders and a lean face. His dark hair reached down to his shoulders. He had prominent upper front teeth which pressed against his lips and parted them slightly. He wore a black shirt and black denims and I noticed that despite his expensive education he spoke with a North of England working-class accent that made him sound like a character from one of his father's books. The confidence of his manner made Rachael appear doubtful, as if she were a fan meeting someone whom she had long admired. I saw that she blushed when they shook hands and then folded her arms in a gesture of recoil. I must admit that I regarded him with an instant, largely irrational dislike. I knew, instinctively, that he would think of me as an old fool who would have to be tolerated because of the desirable presence of an attractive daughter.

'Jack's never been in Ireland before,' Cromer said. 'He assumed that I'd be living in a cottage in a bog.'

'Not exactly in a bog,' Jack said, 'but nowhere in particular. At the end of a lane or something. You didn't describe it all that well in your letters.'

He sat down beside Rachael, stretching out his legs in exaggerated ease. There was something proprietorial and faintly patronizing in the way he spoke to her.

'You like living here?'

'Well, yes,' she said, 'although I'm away at school a lot of the time. I think I might get bored otherwise.'

'It's not exactly a place for teenagers,' Cromer conceded. 'Although it's easy enough to get to Dublin.'

Mr Moore brought us our drinks.

'Will ye be staying for lunch?' he asked without much interest.

'We will,' Cromer said.

'I'll send the young one over with a menu so.'

'Why does he bother?' I asked when he had gone back to the bar. 'The menu hasn't changed for years. Soup of the Day. Egg Mayonnaise. Lasagne. Steak and Kidney Pie, in which, incidentally, no piece of kidney has ever been found. Fish of the Day. Ham Salad. Tea or Coffee.'

'Oh for some Coquilles St Jacques au Vin Blanc,' Cromer said, 'or perhaps a simple Omelette aux Truffes.'

'A selection of freshly cut sandwiches,' I said, 'is available throughout the day.'

111

Mr Moore's niece, Lily, even a little more glum than usual, wrote our orders into her notebook. Jack was talking to Rachael in a confiding manner, not quite loud enough for me to hear. She was listening to him with apparent interest.

'You wanted to talk to me about something?' Cromer said to me. He was leaning back in his chair preparing to go through the ritual of lighting a pipe. It occurred to me, like a moment of inspiration, that it was an ideal opportunity to get in touch with Ingrid.

'Just excuse me for a few minutes,' I said.

The telephone was in an alcove between the doors to the toilets. I dialled anxiously, fearing an engaged tone, but she answered almost immediately.

'But you're supposed to be with Bill and Jack, aren't you?'

'I am. I wish that I were with you.'

There was a long pause. I could hear a radio in the background. A weather forecast predicting sunshine with occasional showers.

'I wish you were too,' she said.

'Do you really? Thank you for saying that. I'm so pleased. It's one of the nicest things ever said to me. Why did you leave the phone off the hook yesterday?'

'I'm sorry,' she said. 'I was sad. This is absurd. Can they not see that you're on the phone?'

'No. When am I going to see you?'

'You know the problem,' she said, 'with Bill and Jack here. It would have to be somewhere else.'

'Okay,' I said. 'I'll work on it. I love you.'

'Are you not taking a risk now? What if somebody hears you?'

'They'll assume that I'm talking to Laura.'

'I'd like to see you.'

I was pleased by this but disappointed that she made no declaration of love.

'I'll keep in touch,' I said.

'Do that.'

'I suppose I'd better go back to the others.'

'Have a good lunch.'

'Are you glad that I phoned?'

'Of course I am.'

'All right,' I said. 'I'll be in touch with you soon.'

When I got back to the table, our lunch had been served. Rachael and Jack were speaking intently to each other. Cromer gestured towards them with his pipe and raised his eyebrows.

'I've been totally ignored,' he said, with comic intonation. 'I might as well not have been here.'

'The thing I wanted to talk to you about,' I said, 'is a little embarrassing. I don't know if you remember but I got fairly drunk that evening in your house.'

'Did you?' he said. 'Didn't we all? I have absolutely no memory whatsoever of getting to bed.'

'At some point near the end of the evening I was in your kitchen. You had been there earlier but you had gone somewhere. I'm vague about the details.'

'I think I remember talking to you in the kitchen,' he said. 'I had gone there to enjoy a cigar. Ingrid has banned it in most rooms.'

'Exactly,' I said emphatically, as if I had stumbled on some important evidence. 'Exactly.'

'Exactly what?'

'I think that I may have nodded off,' I said. 'I'm not sure. Maybe I did, for a few minutes or even for a few seconds. I think that Laura may have woken me. Anyway, that's what has caused the confusion.'

Cromer was picking, without enthusiasm, at his steak and kidney pie.

'You've lost me,' he said with understandable impatience. 'What confusion?'

'This is important, Bill,' I said. 'I wouldn't be putting myself through this embarrassment if it weren't.'

Rachael and Jack laughed at something that he had said and I envied them their freedom.

'Sorry,' Cromer said. 'I didn't mean to snap.'

'The point is that late on the night of your party, two men, who may or may not be members of the Republican movement, came to your back door. Or I think they did. They mistook me for you and suggested it would make good sense and be good politics for you to make a substantial contribution to the movement.'

There was something almost comic about his reaction. He had put down his knife and fork and was looking a little bored as if waiting for me to admit to some misdemeanour. Now he looked as if I had hit him; there was shock and surprise and pain in his expression.

'What the fuck are you talking about?' he said.

'I'm sorry that I can't explain it more clearly.'

'But are you saying that this really happened or that you dreamed about it? You must know the difference.'

'I don't. I'm almost certain that it happened and I've checked out some details that match up but I can't say that I'm absolutely certain. I was drunk and I nodded off and that complicates things.'

'Bloody hell!' he said, 'I just don't believe what I'm hearing. And I know who's behind it, what's more. That ghastly old bastard we met by the river. I had really bad vibes from him.'

'I don't accept that,' I said. 'O'Dalaigh belongs to a totally different era. He's a dinosaur. They'd have nothing in common with him. One of the men was definitely from Belfast. They'd have no interest in someone like him.'

He shook his head to express some dimension of disbelief. Then I told him all the details I could remember. 'I checked out the magazine,' I said, 'with a friend in Belfast. I was obviously hoping that it didn't exist which would have shown that it was a dream. But it does. In fact, he reminded me that I even knew the editor.'

'Bloody hell!' Cromer said again. Rachael and Jack were still intent in conversation. 'Look,' he said quietly, 'I don't want Ingrid or Jack to know about this until I've decided what to do. What should I do? Should you not have gone to the police?'

'I didn't want to do anything before talking to you. And it's all so vague. Anyway, technically speaking, I'm not sure that any wrong has been done. All they did was solicit a subscription to a magazine.'

'Yes but you know and I know...'

'Of course we do but that's a different matter entirely.'

'It's a fucking disgrace!' he said bitterly. Rachael and Jack stopped speaking to each other and looked at us.

'John was just telling me about some people in Dublin,' Cromer said. 'You wouldn't know them.'

'Let me get some drinks,' I said.

I went to the counter, ordered our round and carried it back to the table. I was glad of the diversion; the force of Cromer's worry had left me with a fresh awareness of my incompetence. I had sought no identification from the men, no token of their authenticity. The reason that I had not gone to the guards was almost certainly a fear that Ingrid would become inaccessible because of their surveillance. I had behaved with a marked degree of selfishness.

Rachael and Jack had resumed their conversation and were at ease with each other in a manner that I resented. I attempted to ignore them and concentrated on Cromer, who had lit his pipe and was leaning towards me.

'You know the score,' he said. 'Do you think I'm in danger?'

'I have no direct experience of anything like this, although I've heard rumours in the past about other English writers who've been put under pressure. If I wasn't dreaming, and I'm sorry that I have to go on making that qualification, then I'd have to say they looked as if they'd be fairly bad enemies. The guy from Belfast was a type I got to know there, a type who means business.'

'Let's face it then,' Cromer said; 'there are only two things that I can do. Go to the police or try to settle with them.'

I resented being drawn into the labyrinth of his plans almost as much as I resented his closeness to Ingrid. Sitting there, opposite him, I felt, irrationally, that I was the one who had been betrayed.

'We don't know that it isn't just a racket,' I said. 'You could call their bluff and perhaps nothing at all will happen.'

'That's an awfully big perhaps,' he said in a tone of voice which made it clear that he had detected my callousness. 'You could lose your life over a perhaps like that.'

'Let's keep it in some context,' I said, attempting to sound more compassionate. 'There are a lot of English people living in this country. Even in this county. I've never heard of hard evidence of a threat being implemented.'

'There's always a first time.'

'You can say that about almost anything.'

'It's just that I keep on remembering that malevolent old cunt.'

'Forget about him. He's a spectre from the past.'

'I'm not convinced. There was something very personal in his dislike of me.'

He spoke with such conviction that I found myself wondering if he could be right. I dismissed the possibility. The IRA of that generation, with their memories of Padraic Pearse and the General Post Office and of ambushes at lonely crossroads, were an altogether different phenomenon. They were a collection of old men, rapidly diminishing in number, who turned up at funerals or local memorial services, wearing felt hats and greasy overcoats on to which they had pinned the medals that commemorated their military records. They were almost entirely without influence; they were sad; they were relics from another time.

'Why would they pick on you?' I asked with exasperation, as if it were his fault or as if he could provide me with an answer. 'Why hasn't this happened to Barbara and all the other English writers here?'

'How do you know that it hasn't happened? How do you know that they didn't just pay up? This could be going on for years for all you know. If I pay up, it's not the kind of thing I'll go around talking about. It would make me vulnerable to the next demand.'

'Do you believe for even a moment that if anything like this happened to Barbara that she wouldn't talk about it?'

'Why not?'

'It just isn't the way she is.'

'What kind of money do you think they're talking about?'

'Substantial was what they said. Fifteen thousand?'

'Jesus! That's a lot of money!'

'There is one thing you could do if you're determined to get to the bottom of this. You could go to Belfast and talk to the editor of the magazine. He must know something about what's going on.'

'Did you say you know him?'

'I've met him,' I said reluctantly.

'Will you come to Belfast with me? You know your way around.'

'You haven't seriously considered whether or not it's a good idea.'

'It's the only idea,' he said. 'What else is there to consider?'

Looking out of the window I saw that Barbara was parking her car. I knew that if she settled into conversation with us, she would eventually say something about my having been to his house.

'If you want me to of course I will.'

'I'd really appreciate that,' he said.

'I've got to go now but we can keep in touch and decide on a suitable day.'

'Do we have to leave now?' Rachael asked.

'I'm afraid so.'

'We shouldn't let too much time pass,' Cromer said.

'We'll have to set up an appointment.'

'Can you arrange that?'

'I suppose so,' I said.

Barbara arrived at the table preceded by a perfume of a faintly unpleasant sweetness.

'Darling,' she said, kissing Cromer on both cheeks. 'Home is the hero. How is your poor friend?'

'Poor,' Cromer said, 'as I expected him to be.'

'And this must be the next generation! No need to contemplate mortality when confronted by such youth and beauty!'

Rachael and Jack looked uncomfortable and smiled awkwardly. Barbara was wearing a purple jumpsuit that emphasized the amplitude of her attractions. I realized that I was studying her body with an involved curiosity. What would Rachael think if she noticed?

'I'm going to buy all you nice people a drink.'

'Unfortunately,' I said, 'Rachael and I are just about to go.'

'What a pity! I have so much catching up to do.'

'We'll meet soon.'

'So will we!' Jack said to Rachael as she stood up to join me.

'Sure,' she said. 'It was nice meeting you, Mr Cromer.'

'Entirely my pleasure,' Cromer said. 'I just wish that my unmannerly son hadn't insisted on keeping you entirely to himself.'

I muttered something to Jack, kissed Barbara and followed Rachael to the carpark.

'What did you think of Jack?' I asked her, attempting to sound disinterested.

'He's all right,' she said; 'he seemed dead-on.'

'You seemed to find lots to talk about.'

'He's interested in stuff,' she said vaguely. 'We agree about a lot of things. His Dad seems nice.'

'Did he talk about his mother?'

'Not really. He's got an older brother called Adam. He's in Germany on a holiday job.'

'Germany?' I said, thinking about Ingrid. 'That sounds interesting.'

'He's a photography student in London.'

'What does Jack want to do?'

'He wants to be a gardener.'

'A gardener?'

'Yes,' she said in a tone of rebuke. 'A gardener. Have you got a problem with that?'

'Not at all. It's just that he doesn't look the type.'

'What are gardeners supposed to look like?'

'He looks indelibly urban, that's all.'

'I don't think the divisions are as clear cut as that any more. Our generation is going to be much more fluid than yours.'

I turned out of the carpark and drove towards home. I felt that she had already been distanced from me by the encounter; my resentment was like a bitter feeling of rejection.

'Anyway,' I said with patent insincerity, 'I'm glad you got on so well.'

'I didn't say that. I said that he was dead-on.'

'Why are you in such a bad mood?'

'Did we have to leave so soon? I was enjoying the conversation. Now we're going home to an empty house.'

'I'm sorry,' I said. 'When you put it like that, I admit that it seems a little bleak. It's just that I saw Barbara in the carpark and didn't feel up to a conversation with her.'

'I thought you liked Barbara?'

'I do. But not anytime, anywhere.'

'I don't mean to be in bad humour,' she said. 'I had a brilliant time. It was great to have someone of my own age to talk to.'

'He obviously liked you.'

'Do you think so?'

'Well of course I do. He hadn't a word for anyone else.'

'He's interesting,' she said in a tone of voice that she would once have used to describe a kitten as lovely, and I ached with the contradictory needs to reassure her of her own value while undermining Jack. I resented his potential influence, his intrusion into our lives, a bored youth in search of sexual opportunity.

'Do you like his Dad?'

'I don't know him all that well but, yes, I suppose I do. I respect what he's written and I've enjoyed talking to him. Mum and I had a nice dinner in his house some time ago.'

'What's the house like?'

'They've done a very good job.'

'What's she like?'

'Ingrid? She's German. She's a theatrical designer. She seems charming.'

'Jack doesn't like her much.'

'Does he not?' I said, feeling oddly hurt. 'Why not?'

I felt protective towards her, wanted to shield her from the opinions of two observers who probably valued youth above any other quality.

'He didn't say why. He just said that she's not a very nice person.'

'I suppose,' I said, suppressing an urge to say bitter things about him, 'that he feels obliged to be loyal to his mother. But they must have broken up years before Bill met Ingrid.'

'Maybe that's it,' she said without conviction.

I turned into our drive, calmed by the sight of the house, its solid, dependable lines etched against the afternoon light.

'I often picture here when I'm at school,' Rachael said. 'It was comforting to imagine both of you here.'

'I'm glad you feel secure about it.'

'The parents of two of my friends have separated in the past few months. Jack says it's awful when it happens. Everyone wants you to take sides and put pressure on you to have opinions. I'd hate to be in that position.'

We went into the house.

'You never worried,' I said unhappily, 'that Mum and I would separate?'

'No, but Stephanie, my friend, told me she hadn't a clue until it happened. She never even heard her parents have an argument. She said it was weird. They just called to the school one day and told her about it. Both of them had other relationships. She said her Dad was upset but her Mum seemed quite cool about it.'

'I'm glad that you feel secure,' I said ineptly.

She smiled and went upstairs. I telephoned Ingrid, assuming that she would still be alone in the house. Jack answered. In the background, I could hear Barbara laughing loudly. I hung up. It then occurred to me that Cromer, if he heard about it, would almost certainly assume that the call had something to do with the visit from the men, that it was a hostile intervention designed to unnerve him, a message from the IRA. I was assailed by the complexity, real or imaginary, of other people's lives. Or was I creating these complexities? As I sat there, I felt like a puppet-master capable of jerking people into action by a telephone call, condemning them to some kind of stasis if I failed to dial their number. It was an unpleasant feeling, followed by a more familiar feeling of unreality that permitted me to become more detached. Even Rachael, whom I could hear moving around upstairs, was distanced by this process. It dispelled my feelings of over-protec-tiveness. I telephoned my friend in Belfast with little hope that he would be there on a Saturday afternoon but he answered almost immediately as if he had been waiting for the call. I asked him if he could arrange the appointment for me. He replied, a little hesi-tantly, that he probably could.

'Do you want to tell me what this is all about?'

'I will when I see you.'

'He's an awkward kind of a man. You know that yourself. What will I tell him if he wants to know?'

'Would it be enough to tell him that William Cromer, the English novelist, wants to talk to him about a personal matter?'

'Cromer?' he said, sounding a little impressed. 'I have two or three of his books upstairs. Did I read that he was living in Wicklow?'

'We're more or less next-door neighbours.'

'I suppose that might intrigue him. When do you want to meet?'

'How about Tuesday?'

'I'll see what I can do.'

'I really appreciate it,' I said.

I hung up; almost immediately, the telephone rang. I longed for it to be Ingrid. It was Laura. The conference had gone very well. She wondered if Rachael and I would join her for a meal.

'I thought it would be fun. I'll treat you both,' she said.

'It's a lovely idea.'

We arranged to meet in the Unicorn Minor.

'Rachael will be pleased,' I said. 'I think she finds it something of an anticlimax here. She got on alarmingly well with Jack Cromer.'

'What's he like?'

'He seems okay,' I lied. 'It's not a particularly attractive age for a boy.'

Rachael was pleased that we were driving to Dublin. She had put on jeans and a tee-shirt, had tied back her hair, and looked like the younger sister of the girl who had sat beside Jack Cromer at lunchtime.

There was surprisingly little traffic along the way and we arrived in Stephen's Green a quarter of an hour earlier than planned. I found a parking place opposite the Shelbourne Hotel and we went into the Horseshoe Bar. It was crowded with American tourists and a boisterous collection of locals just back from a race meeting, still wearing their stand badges, crumpled race cards protruding from suit pockets. A well-known politician and a sports commentator were conspiring in the farthest corner. I bought us drinks and Rachael told me about the summer plans of some of her friends. Unnervingly, she referred to a number of broken marriages and sad children bewildered by the behaviour of their parents.

'It's additionally awful,' I said, 'in a society that denies its citizens the fundamental human right of divorce.'

'Do you believe in divorce?' she asked, sounding surprised.

'I believe that people who want it should have it.'

'If it's too easy to get, does it not mean that people will stop working at their marriages?'

'Most people who want it will have come painfully to the decision. People can fall out of love with each other. That's a sad fact. I'm sorry about your friends, but forcing their parents to stay together wouldn't make them any happier.'

'I suppose not.'

I felt corrupt and self-interested in this argument; her acceptance of it was like a rebuke.

'Have you given much thought to what you'd like to do after school?' I asked her in a deliberate but, I hoped, not obvious attempt to change both the subject and the mood.

'Kind of,' she said, her face unfolding from the worry that had tightened it. 'I've been thinking about law. I think I might like to be a barrister.'

'Really? I can introduce you to some people I know.'

'Some time,' she said. 'I haven't made up my mind, it's just something that I'm thinking about. I'll have to find out more about it soon.'

'I suppose we'd better go,' I said, finishing my gin and tonic. 'I don't want to keep Mum waiting. She'll be tired after the conference.'

The politician was drunk. This became obvious when he attempted to stand and the act required a sudden, visible intensity of concentration. He swayed, used his hand to balance against the wall, then fell back into his chair.

'She's not in very good form, is she?' Rachael said.

'Why do you say that?'

'She looks tired all the time. She hasn't been herself since I came home.'

'She's been working very hard,' I said as we left the hotel.

I was reluctant to consider what she was saying. It seemed to be charged with an implied criticism. We walked along Merrion Row, past the Huguenot Cemetery and the new block that, years before, in a more innocent city, had been the site of the Swiss Chalet. I could never pass there without recalling the girls with whom I had danced when I was young and hopeful. I could remember not only their names but the quality of their nervous kisses and our conversations and the music that seemed so modern to us then but was about to become impossibly dated. These girls were fixed in my memory, always young, like specimens in a case. They were only a few years older than Rachael was now, with their sixties' hair-styles, dresses and mannerisms. On the other side of the street was the building that had once been the Unicorn Restaurant where waitresses who seemed to have stepped out of a Victorian twilight served good Italian food in an atmosphere that was redolent of a private club. In the days of our courtship and early marriage Laura and I had been regulars on Friday evenings, with a proprietorial preference for a certain table. Its successor, the Unicorn Minor, was in a laneway around the corner. We went in and Mrs Dom greeted us with characteristic enthusiasm.

'How nice to see you! And your lovely daughter! Your wife just got here before you.'

We joined Laura at her table and I found myself looking for signs of tiredness. She smiled and I was suffused with guilt. In some confused way I attributed her feelings to contemplation of my betrayal.

She told us about the conference. It had been a success.

'Was it all very tiring?' I asked her.

'Rachael has just asked me that,' she said. 'What's going on? Do I seem very tired? I'm going to get paranoid!'

'I said to Dad that I thought that you looked a bit tired,' Rachael said. 'That's all. I'm sure you've been working too hard.'

'Yes, I suppose I have,' Laura said, mollified. 'Everybody in the hospital is busy. The health cuts have made a real difference. It really is a scandal.'

'By the way,' I said, after we had ordered. 'I told Bill Cromer that I'd show him something of Belfast soon.'

'Just for the day?'

'That's right. He's curious about it. I think he feels a little embarrassed that he's never been there.'

'Will Jack be going with you?' Rachael asked.

I resisted the temptation to tease her, pleased at how success-fully I had turned a portentous visit into a casual trip.

'No, it's not a social occasion,' I said vaguely. 'He just wants to be filled in on some of the facts.'

'Maybe he'll write about it,' Rachael said.

'Who knows?'

'It's fairly quiet there recently, isn't it,' Laura said. 'I mean, most of the violence seems to be in rural areas like Fermanagh.'

'More or less.'

'You might bump into some old colleagues.'

'I'll arrange for us to meet someone for lunch. I wouldn't mind having an update myself.'

We chatted easily and, after the meal, thanked Mrs Dom and strolled to Pembroke Street where Laura had parked her car. It was a warm evening and people were having drinks at tables outside the Pembroke Bar. A yeasty smell came from the open doorway like some exotic suggestion of pleasure. There was a festive feeling, a sense of something exultant about to happen, yet I could not relax. I pretended to be interested in the contents of the window of a print shop so that Laura and Rachael could walk ahead, then I followed them, noticing that they were exactly the same height and held their shoulders in a similar lopsided way. I wondered what they really thought of me. It is easy to assume that the feelings of others will remain constant and that there will be no surprise confrontations, no suitcases in the hall, no tears. I had been unnerved by Rachael's conversation about broken marriages. Did she know something?

She turned and said, 'Do you mind if I travel back with Mum? I've been telling her about Jack and things.'

'Of course,' I said, with some kind of indefinable relief. 'I'll see you both later on.'

I watched as they drove towards Leeson Street. A middle-aged prostitute, tall and stout, was standing at the corner of Fitzwilliam Square, brought out early by the sun, a somewhat unlikely heliotrope in her tight red skirt. A car passed me and pulled up beside her and the driver rolled down the front passenger window so that he could lean across and discuss prices. I walked back towards the Green, feeling the onset of self-pity like a physical symptom. I wished that I were with Ingrid, drawing comfort from her body, discovering something new about her. I crossed the street to the Shelbourne and, almost without thought or plan, walked through the foyer to the telephones. I gave a girl Cromer's number and she directed me towards a box. I heard the phone ringing. Ingrid answered. Her voice, sounding a little bewildered, increased in volume as she repeated 'Hello? Hello?'

'It's me,' I said.

'Yes?'

'Is it difficult for you to talk?'

'A little.'

'I'm sorry. I know that it's indulgent and intrusive of me to ring but I had to hear your voice.'

'Where are you?'

'The Shelbourne.'

'The Shelbourne Hotel? What are you doing there?'

I found that I did not want to mention Laura. It was as if the centre of my loyalties had shifted and that having a wife was a slightly disreputable secret.

'I was restless,' I said, 'so I came into town. It's a lovely evening. I wish you were here with me.'

'Barbara is with us. Did you telephone earlier and hang up when Jack answered?'

I was about to deny it, then realized how pointless that would be.

'Yes, I did. I'm sorry. From now on I won't phone unless we've got a prior arrangement.'

'Bill got really upset when Jack told him. I don't know why it mattered so much to him.'

'I'm sorry,' I said again. I wanted her to feel positive towards me but this conversation was teetering towards something totally different. 'Would you like to be here?' I asked her, ashamed at my need for easy reassurance.

'I suppose so. Bill says that you're going to Belfast together.'

'Yes. He's curious to see it.'

'Is it safe?'

'Perfectly.'

'Look, I'll have to go now.'

'Please say something nice.'

A silence echoed along the line between us, cold and reproachful.

'Yes,' she said quietly. 'Of course I'd like to be there.'

This small concession was all that I had been looking for.

'Thank you. I'll get in touch properly. Good night.'

I paid for the call, went into the Horseshoe Bar and ordered a coffee. The tourists had gone somewhere else and had been replaced by more of the regulars; businessmen, journalists, an opposition politician and the actress with whom he was having an affair. I joined some journalist acquaintances and caught up on current gossip.

'When did he stop trying to hide her?' I asked, nodding towards the politician who had his hand on the actress's thigh.

'It's more a case of when did he start showing her off. He wants everyone to know. That's why nobody is interested. His wife told a friend of mine that she couldn't give a fuck in every possible interpretation of that phrase.'

This was the familiar atmosphere of the world I had occupied for so many years, a cynical insight on the weaknesses of the newsworthy. It could often be small-minded and envious and not always free from a desire to hurt, but I could miss it in moments of loneliness and imagine that there was a supportive camaraderie on which I had turned my back.

I drove home slowly, through the suburb in which we had once lived, and then along the almost-empty country roads. I avoided going past Cromer's house.

Laura and Rachael were in the kitchen having coffee. They stopped talking when they saw me; their complicity excluded me and I guessed that they had been talking about Jack and men in general and, indirectly, about me.

I went into my study. The telephone rang. It was my friend in Belfast.

'He was intrigued all right,' he said. 'And bloody suspicious. To be honest, I don't think he'd have wanted to have anything to do with the pair of you if I hadn't been the intermediary.'

'I have no doubt that's true,' I said. 'I really owe you one.'

'He doesn't want you going to his office. You'd probably be followed anyway. He'll see you on Tuesday, at two o'clock, here in my place.'

I said that we looked forward to seeing him, then I telephoned Cromer. I notice that telephones are assuming a central role in this narrative; their ringing punctuates the pages, a lonely sound as I reach out for contact with someone.

Cromer answered. He sounded drunk as I told him about our appointment in Belfast.

'In Belfast, did you say?'

'You can't have forgotten already,' I said, losing patience.

'There's no need to shout at me! Of course I haven't forgotten. I'm just surprised at how quickly you've arranged it. I mean, we only talked about it today.'

'There's no point in losing time.'

'I couldn't agree more.'

'Do you know what you'll say when you meet him?'

There was a long pause.

'Between one thing and the other,' he said, 'I haven't had much of a chance to think about it. Have you any feelings?'

'Not really.'

'We can discuss it on the way there.'

'Of course.'

I felt impatient with him. I was too involved with his wife to feel any tolerance.

'All right,' I said. 'I'll talk to you about it then.'

TEN

ON THE JOURNEY between Dublin and Dundalk, Cromer was emphatic about the stance he intended to take. Demanding money with menace was a particularly serious crime and there was absolutely no way whatsoever that he was going to be bullied or threatened into cooperating with the perpetrators of such an abysmal act. An Englishman's home, regardless of where it stood, was his castle. It could not be violated. And he certainly wasn't going to contribute as much as a penny to a cause that had brutally murdered so many young, working-class British soldiers. How could he live with himself, how could he face family and friends if he were to depart from this fundamental principle? They were terrorists, pure and simple. He intended to make that clear and they were not going to bully him into changing his mind.

When we passed through Dundalk I mentioned that we were only a few miles from the border. His mood changed.

'Don't you think I'm right?'

'I've been trying to think how I might react in the circumstances. On the one hand, they haven't really taken any action in the Republic. On the other hand, is it worth taking the risk? But if you feel as definite as you're saying, why are we going to Belfast? Should you not just have reported the whole thing to the guards?'

'Wouldn't that have put you in an odd position?'

'I suppose so.'

'Anyway,' he said, with a certain satisfaction, 'just how efficient and professional can these people be if they don't even know what I look like? If they mix me up with someone who's been living in the neighbourhood for years?'

'You don't need to be excessively professional to toss a petrol bomb through the window of a house.'

'I don't know what your argument is,' he said, with understandable exasperation. 'Are you saying that I should or shouldn't pay the bastards?'

'I'm not going to pretend that I see the matter in black and white. I don't. I wouldn't like a threat hanging over the safety of my own family, so I'm not going to give you superficial reassurances. Remember that the whole point of making this journey is to authenticate the incident. After that, you can decide what you want to do about it.'

'This is bleak countryside, isn't it?' he said, staring morosely out of the window at the small farms and ugly bungalows. The traffic was getting heavier. I drove past an articulated truck, enjoying the sudden surge of acceleration, then slowed as we approached the border. We were waved past the Irish Customs.

'Is that all there is to it?' Cromer said.

'Now we'll have your lot up the road.'

We joined a long line of slow-moving cars as we approached the Northern Ireland checkpoint. There was an intimidating technological presence. I assumed that soldiers in the raised observation posts could listen in to what was being said in any of the cars. A section of the road was covered with horizontal spikes that would spring upward if any unchecked car attempted to drive through. We drove slowly towards two armed soldiers.

'It brings it home to you, doesn't it?' Cromer said. 'To see them so heavily armed. Take a look at them! They're only kids, for fuck's sake. They don't look much older than Jack!'

One of the soldiers noted the car's registration number, then spoke into his radio. He had a thin, pale face, redolent of urban poverty, with a faint suggestion of a moustache. His camouflage jacket looked like something that he might wriggle out of, snake-like, to emerge as an ordinary streetwise youngster hanging around outside a pool hall. He continued to look at our registration as he spoke into the radio.

'Why is he checking us out?' Cromer said. 'He didn't do that to the two cars in front of us.'

'I suppose it's because we've got a southern registration.'

The soldier put the radio away and walked over to us. He looked in the passenger window. His cheeks were pitted with acne and he was nervous.

'How long do you intend spending in Northern Ireland?' he asked.

'Just for today,' I said.

'Just for today,' Cromer repeated.

'You got any identification?'

I had kept up my membership of the NUJ and was able to show him a card.

'That's okay then,' he said, as if some contentious matter had been resolved. He walked away and we drove into Northern Ireland.

'That wasn't too demanding,' Cromer said. 'I think I expected something much heavier.'

'Yes and no. I've never been asked for identification before.'

'I still can't get over how young he was.'

'Talking about youth,' I said. 'Jack made quite an impression on Rachael.'

'He made an impression? What about the impression that she made? He kept on bringing up her name and asking Barbara questions about her. I can't say that I blame him. She's a delightful girl.'

There was a long pause in our conversation as I pretended to concentrate on my driving. I knew that he had expected me to say something favourable about Jack but I could not bring myself to do so. Outside Newry, an armoured car came crawling towards us, like some enlarged and menacing insect. We continued to be silent, even tense, until it had driven past.

'So you think I should make some kind of deal with them?' he said suddenly, as if we were in the middle of a conversation.

'Let's take it one step at a time.'

'Why did they have to pick on me? Do you think that I was right not to tell Ingrid?'

'Would she be nervous?' I asked, delighted with this opportunity to talk about her.

'She might be. She wasn't very enthusiastic about coming to Ireland in the first place, you know. I don't want her spending more and more time in London. I need her here with me.'

'I'm sure that's true for her as well.'

'Don't be too sure of it,' he said. 'She's a very independent woman. I think that I'm beginning to settle in well but she seems really restless. Add some new tension and she mightn't want to live here any more.'

I was surprised at how dispassionate he sounded. He made the prospect of losing her sound like little more than an inconvenience, yet a minute before he had declared his need for her. I would have liked to pursue his thinking and learn more about their relationship but he changed the conversation to questions about Belfast which lasted until we were driving through the suburbs. It was a bright, sun-filled afternoon and the hills around the city were a light and luminous blue. I turned off Donegall Road and drove along Botanic Avenue towards the house in which I had once lived and worked.

'This is very nice,' Cromer said. I sensed that he was a little disappointed at the middle-class imperturbability of the scene. He had probably expected a war zone, vehicles burning at deserted corners, the whine of sniper fire from distant roofs.

'Life has continued more or less as usual in large areas of the city.'

'Remarkable. And this is where you lived?' he said as I pulled up before a detached red-brick house with a neat lawn and ornate, black railings.

'Yes. I shared it with the owner. It's he who's set up everything for us today.'

Charles was effusive in his welcome.

'So something has finally happened to entice you back to us!' he said. 'I was afraid you had shaken the dust of Belfast off your shoes for ever.'

He looked a good deal older than I remembered; dark red veins were blotched against his cheeks and he had developed a pronounced stoop, yet his manner was noticeably more flamboyant than in the past. I introduced him to Cromer.

'You seem really well,' I said as we sat in the living room with the large glasses of gin and tonic that Charles had carried in from the kitchen.

'I am. I'm much more in tune with myself. I've relaxed. I feel that I'd let far too many years pass by without really discovering who I was. I know myself much better now and it's invigorating.'

He appeared to be quite sincere as he spoke this jargon, like someone who has experienced a religious conversion and believes that life will never be the same again. I looked around the familiar room for some signs of a new way of life, but very little had changed.

'It's good of you,' Cromer said, 'to set up the meeting. It can't have been easy.'

Charles looked at his watch.

'He'll be here in about twenty minutes,' he said, 'but only because he knows John and myself and has heard of you. Are you going to tell me what this is all about?'

We had agreed not to emphasize any doubts that I had about the reality of the incident. Charles was a good journalist and would not have been impressed by such vagueness. It was sufficient to say, when recounting the details, that we had some reason to doubt the authenticity of the messengers. Charles saw through that immediately.

'If they weren't authentic how could they benefit from eliciting a donation to the magazine?'

'Unless it's a plot between the editor and the two who called to my house,' Cromer said. 'A freelance job that hasn't been authorized by anyone else.'

'Absolutely not! There's no way in the world that Doyle would have anything to do with that sort of thing. You must know that,' Charles said, turning to me. 'He's one of the old school, a pious, practising Catholic and a fanatical follower of Republican orthodoxy. There are literally hundreds of fiddles and frauds and protection rackets of every kind going on here but Doyle would have nothing to do with that.'

The doorbell rang.

'Could that be him now?' I asked.

Charles looked at his watch again.

'If it is, he's a little early.'

He went out to the hall. Cromer and I sat in silence as if feeling guilty about something. I could hear them talking, the tone of their conversation without any varying emphasis, the words spoken too quietly to be overheard.

'I'm bloody nervous!' Cromer said. 'I don't know what to expect.'

Charles followed Doyle into the room. As soon as I saw him I recalled late-night drinking in the bar of the Europa Hotel, the exchange of gossip, the sense of more-or-less friendly rivalry. He would come into the bar wearing the same, inappropriate charcoal-grey overcoat that he was wearing now, to distribute copies of his murderous little magazine. I had forgotten how unnaturally pale he was. Once I had asked him if the title of the magazine, *The Voice of Tone*, was a deliberate play on words and he had just stared at me with evident dislike before moving on to someone else.

'You know John and this is William Cromer,' Charles said. 'Let me take your coat.'

'No, no, there's no need for that,' Doyle said as if offended by the idea.

He sat, suspiciously, on a corner of the sofa, his feet placed neatly together, his long, pale hands resting on his knees. He reminded me of a man about to listen, respectfully, to a sermon.

'You haven't been here this long time,' he said to me in a faintly accusing tone of voice.

'I was just thinking that myself,' I said. 'Time has passed very quickly.'

Doyle made me feel uneasy; his cold, grey formality was something that he could hide behind as effectively as a disguise.

'I know there's no point in offering you a drink,' Charles said. 'Can I get you a coffee?'

'I'll have a mineral, thank you.'

Charles took our glasses to the kitchen. I made some uneasy small talk with Doyle, asking him about other journalists. I was relieved when Charles returned. Cromer remained silent, as if detached from the scene. Charles gave us fresh, strong gins and tonics and handed Doyle a tall glass of red lemonade which he held balanced on one knee.

'I have a number of other appointments,' he said, ' so could we get down to why you wanted to see me?'

He looked from Charles to Cromer. They both looked at me. I resented Cromer's passivity. Upstairs, in the front room that we had shared as a study, the telephone rang and Charles went to answer it.

'Do you want me to start?' I said to Doyle.

'Please.'

I outlined the details of the incident. Doyle stared at me as I spoke. It was possible to believe that he wasn't even blinking. His face remained totally without perceivable expression until I explained that the money was to be paid to his magazine. He reacted to that by a slow scratching of his chin.

'So that's about it,' I said, feeling that I had related the story badly. 'I don't know who they were. They didn't authenticate themselves in any way, so naturally we thought that we should ask you.'

'Ask me what?'

'Ask what you know about it.'

'Why should I know anything about it?'

'You must know something,' I said helplessly.

'Not so fast. Are you accusing me of being a part of some plot against your friend here?'

'Not at all,' I said. 'No, not at all. I was just hoping that you could tell us whether or not, in your opinion, these men were members of the Republican movement.'

'How in God's name could I do that? You come here with a daft story and try to involve me in it!'

'Well, you'd be the beneficiary if someone gave you money for your magazine.'

'I wouldn't be the beneficiary. The cause that the magazine serves would benefit.'

Charles came back into the room in time to hear this. Something humorous that he had been about to say had animated his expression; it was replaced by immediate concern.

'What's the matter?' he asked, looking at me.

Doyle drank some of his lemonade, then left the glass on the floor.

'Did you know why they wanted to see me?'

'I got filled in on the details just before you arrived.'

'Do you think it was worth my while to come all the way across to here to listen to such rubbish?'

'We'd gladly have gone to you,' Charles said. He was visibly disconcerted. I guessed that he feared a loss of credibility amongst sources close to Doyle. 'I'm sorry that you feel inconvenienced.'

'That's not the point,' Doyle said. 'The point is the slur that's been made against me.'

Charles looked at me accusingly.

'That certainly wasn't the intention,' he said in a placatory tone of voice.

'Nor was it what happened,' I said. 'The only object of the exercise was to find out if the two men had the authority to speak for the IRA.'

'How could I know that?'

I was irritated by Cromer, who continued to sit there like someone who has stumbled into an argument and is embarrassed by the intimate details he is hearing.

'You're an apologist for the movement and they mentioned your magazine,' I said. 'Surely it was reasonable to assume that you might know.'

Despite a tremble of annoyance in his voice, he retained his menacing immobility.

'I have always supported the armed struggle for the liberation of all this island,' he said. 'That's my historical right. I take my mandate for that position from the generations who shed their blood for this cause. That's a very different thing from being a part of a protection racket or whatever it is you're talking about.'

Charles, who was standing where he could not be seen by Doyle, was staring at me and making small, pacific gestures.

'I was simply looking for some information,' I said weakly. 'I didn't intend to accuse you of anything.'

I wished that one of the others would say something. It was as if I had made a fool of myself and they were too embarrassed to be identified with me.

'Can I get someone another drink?' Charles asked, bustling into action as if it were a normal social occasion. To my surprise, Doyle held out his glass.

'I'll have another mineral,' he said, 'before I go.'

I drank some of my gin and tonic. Its potency was cheering and in that surge of feeling I thought of Ingrid and wanted her, wanted to be with her, resented time spent away from her. I thought of her voice on the telephone, the unusual way that she accented some vowels. I wondered if she had made love with Cromer the previous night and the thought embittered me. I wanted to hurt him.

'You've been very quiet, Bill,' I said and he looked at me, startled, as if I had betrayed him to the enemy. 'What do you feel about the situation now?'

'I feel disadvantaged by being the only Englishman present. It hardly seems appropriate for me to comment on many of the things that have been said.'

I was tempted to remind him that he had expressed very definite opinions earlier but, even in my mood of treachery, I could recognize that to do so would be excessively disloyal.

'I obviously accept everything that Mr Doyle has said, so that leads me to the conclusion that we can now treat the event as if it had never happened.'

I took it that this was intended as a coded message to me but could not agree with the conclusion.

'The fact that Mr Doyle doesn't know anything about it,' I said, 'doesn't, in itself, prove anything. We still don't know who called to the house.'

'I'm sorry that you've been inconvenienced,' Cromer said, as if I had not spoken, and Doyle nodded noncommittally.

Charles gave him a glass of lemonade which he accepted without comment.

'If you thought it appropriate, I'd like to take out a subscription to your publication,' Cromer said.

The three of us stared at him with surprise.

'We're always glad to have another reader,' Doyle said. 'In our own small way we believe that we're not without influence.'

Cromer produced a chequebook and pen. After his long silence, his actions appeared to be elaborately dramatic.

'I want to find out more about the conflict,' Cromer said. 'Who should I make out the cheque to?'

'The magazine, as such, doesn't have a separate account,' Doyle said, 'so you should make it out to me. Seamus Doyle.'

Cromer wrote the cheque, wrote something on the back of it and handed it to Doyle.

'I've put my address on the back.'

Doyle didn't look at it. He folded it and put it into the inside pocket of his coat.

'I'll be on my way,' he said ponderously, 'as there's no more business to be done.'

We shook hands in a constrained atmosphere as if we were all meeting for the first time. Doyle's handshake was cold and limp. Charles followed him out to the hall. I turned to Cromer, who was looking pleased with himself.

'Was that wise?'

'You can talk!' he said, 'after the way you antagonized him. If you want my frank opinion I think you got the thing off to a very bad start.'

'You were struck dumb as soon as he came into the room!'

'I wanted to be measured in my speech. I've got to say that I regret you didn't follow a similar course.'

'You amaze me,' I said. 'As far as I'm concerned, you left me to do all your dirty work.'

We heard the hall door closing. Charles came into the room looking flustered and unhappy.

'That was a real cock-up,' he said. 'I could have done without it. Doyle may be one of the old brigade but he's not without influence.'

'He was quick enough to take a bribe,' Cromer said.

'Don't be silly. He won't keep a penny of your subscription for himself.'

'How much was the cheque for?' I asked, alerted by his use of the word bribe.

'Four thousand pounds.'

'What the hell did you do that for?' Charles said.

'With the greatest respect,' Cromer said, 'I don't see how that's any of your business. I take it that there's no law here prohibiting the writing of cheques.'

'I don't think you acted wisely,' I said. 'If the demand was genuine, you show some strength in refusing to pay anything. By making what looks like a part payment, you seem to at least partially accept their right to demand payment from you in the first place.'

'That's right,' Charles said. 'Genuine or not, you've now marked yourself out as someone who'll hand over money after very little pressure.'

Cromer looked crestfallen, then angry.

'I assumed,' he said, 'that I was taking out insurance. And doing it in a clever, indirect way.'

'You should have talked to us,' Charles said. 'You should have considered the implications.'

'Oh bugger it anyway! I hardly know why I wrote it. It seemed like a good idea, a way out of this mess.'

I felt sorry for him and regretted my earlier words. I had turned him into a victim. Our relationship appeared to be based on nothing but a series of betrayals. He sat there, ready to listen to an analysis of his action, like a schoolboy who has done something wrong and is ready to accept the consequences. Charles collected the glasses and returned with yet more large gins and tonics.

'I'll be driving,' I protested without much conviction. 'Enough is enough.'

'You'll be eating before then.'

'I could always cancel the cheque,' Cromer said.

Charles shook his head.

'That's about the only thing you could do to make things even worse.'

'Doyle's an odd fish, isn't he?' Charles said to me. 'He's still got some influence but I've never met anyone who actually likes him. Perhaps that's the definition of a local patriot.'

'I'll never get the hang of you Irish,' Cromer said.

He was subdued on the journey back to Wicklow. He had seen very little of Belfast but did not complain. Charles had produced plates of sandwiches and cheese and fruit to counter the effects of his liberally poured drinks. We were waved across the border by bored soldiers. A customs man took a perfunctory look in the car and nodded. We listened to the news and to a quiz programme, hardly speaking. As we drove past Dublin Airport I asked Cromer if he'd like to stop off somewhere for a drink but he refused curtly, then apologized. There was a traffic jam in Drumcondra and roadworks in Gardiner Street. I would have liked to call into the Shelbourne but drove past.

'I was beginning to think of here as home,' Cromer said suddenly.

'There's no reason why that should change.'

'Every day will be full of suspense now. Could you write under those conditions?'

'I can't write under any condition.'

'I'm sorry,' he said. 'That was insensitive of me. And you're right, of course. Everything could be fine in the future.'

'That's the spirit!'

'I was never a quitter.'

Our clichés hung uneasily between us, a barrier to anything like sympathy. We listened to music on the car radio until I pulled up outside his house. I left the engine running to indicate that I did not expect to be invited inside. He sat as if reluctant to leave, pressing forward against his safety belt.

'What a day!' he said. 'Who can ever know the way that things are going to turn out?'

Ingrid opened the gate. I longed to be alone with her. She was wearing a short black dress and looked even more desirable than in my memories of her naked.

'Had you a nice time?' she asked Cromer, then looked at me as if assuming that I would be the one to answer.

'What a day!' Cromer said vaguely. 'It's a most interesting city.'

'I'm afraid I've got bad news,' she said. 'He died at ten past eleven this morning. They say that he died very peacefully.'

'Balls!' Cromer said bitterly. 'Why do people say stupid things like that? I'd guess that it was a horrible death, all blood and shit and tears.'

'I've written down details of the funeral. I didn't know he was a Roman Catholic.'

'I suppose he was,' Cromer said, 'for all the good it ever did him.'

He got out of the car and she placed her left hand on his shoulder. He leaned his cheek against it and they stood there, in a tableau of intimacy that I hated. I felt my exclusion like a chill current of disapproval. I waved at them vaguely and drove home. Rachael met me in the hall. She was vivid with excitement.

'You must have got good news!' I said.

'No,' she said, 'why do you think that?'

'Your impersonation of the cat that got the cream is rather impressive.'

She pouted and went upstairs. Laura was in the kitchen. She had poured me a glass of red wine. A Bolognaise sauce was bubbling in a copper pan. Her kiss was dry-lipped and assertive. It was all so welcoming that I felt additional guilt about my longing to be somewhere else. I tried not to think about Cromer being comforted by Ingrid.

'Rachael's in very good form,' I said.

'That boy telephoned. Bill Cromer's son. He's invited her to go for a drive and a meal tomorrow.'

'A drive and a meal,' I repeated, as if this codified some particular insight. 'I should have guessed.'

'I suppose that it's all right? At least we know who he is, more or less.'

'I suppose so,' I said without conviction. 'Did you hear about Bill's friend?'

'No?'

I told her and she looked concerned. The pan bubbled noisily; the kitchen was filled with the aroma of tomato sauce.

'God rest him,' she said vaguely 'We should be grateful for all that we've got.'

ELEVEN

JACK'S POLITENESS did nothing to dispel my antipathy towards him. He stood in the doorway, looking around the room, more shy and more shambling than he had been in the pub and wearing the same clothes. Rachael was obviously pleased to see him. She radiated an energy that disconcerted me and made me feel elderly. I offered him a drink but he declined, explaining that he was driving. I walked with them to the front door. Cromer's car was parked in the driveway. Yes, he said to me when I asked, they had driven to the airport earlier and his dad had been more upset than might have been expected. Ingrid had offered to accompany him to the funeral but he had insisted on going alone. Perhaps this was the piece of information that I had been seeking. I waved to them as they drove away, then dialled her number.

'Can I come round?'

'All right,' she said without enthusiasm.

'Just give me a few minutes.'

'Okay.'

'I love you.'

'Thank you.'

I had a quick shower, dressed in a blue shirt and cords and drove to her house. It was a warm afternoon; the hedges were bright with blossoms. As I went around a corner, a fox stood, lean and tense by the side of the road, looking towards me. I slowed and it went in a leisurely, loping way across the road. I attempted to invent a meaning for such a welcome happening, to invest it with the mysterious properties of a sign of good luck.

When I knocked, the house appeared to have the empty feeling with which I had become familiar but, after only a few seconds, she opened the door.

'Come in.'

I attempted to embrace her but she turned and walked towards the stairs. I closed the door and followed her. We went upstairs. She was wearing a blue tracksuit and trainers. When we got to the door of the guest room she turned and we kissed, then went into the room and, without even fully undressing, made love quickly and urgently. I remember a slight feeling of unreality, some part of me speculative and detached. Afterwards we lay together, comforted.

'Let's get into bed,' she said eventually.

We undressed. She had an enviable assurance when naked as if the wearing of clothes was the cause of some kind of reticence. I was touched by the innocence of her tattoo and a little embarrassed by the marks made by my fingers on her hips. She switched on the Leonard Cohen tape and got into bed.

'Do you never get tired of him?'

'Not really.'

'Do you believe that there ain't no cure for love?'

'How would I know?'

I held her closely, breathing in the faint dampness of her skin. When she began to cry, I felt guilty and helpless. Her body seemed to convulse with the force of her grief; her wet face, pressed against the pillow, was red from the exertion.

'Please talk to me about it,' I said, worrying that our closeness was illusory.

'There's nothing to talk about,' she said. 'I'm lonely. That's all.'

'For Bill?'

'For Bill, for you, for someone else. Maybe for a child.'

She got out of bed and left the room. I felt foolish and inadequate. I could hear her in the bathroom, opening and closing cupboards as if she had lost something. Then I heard a car stopping outside. I got out of bed and looked, cautiously, out of the window. Cromer's car was parked beside the Discovery. I heard the familiar sound of Rachael's laughter.

I remember thinking that this had been waiting to happen for years and years, that the shadow of this predestined moment had fallen across much of my life, spoiling moments that should have been more precious. I went to the door and called to Ingrid.

'Jack and Rachael are outside!'

'Oh no!' She remained in the bathroom. I dressed as quickly as I could, attempting to think of a lie that would vindicate me. As I gathered up Ingrid's clothes I expected to hear the sound of a key turning in the front door but when I looked out they were still sitting in the car. Jack had his arm around Rachael's shoulders. I felt like an intruder and I suppose some jealousy of his youth rose up from the pelagic caves of male competitiveness. I went out to the landing.

Ingrid had put on jeans and a shirt and was making-up in the bathroom.

'Do I look as if I've been crying?'

'No,' I said, without really looking. The atmosphere between us was hostile. 'I'll go downstairs so they'll assume that we've been there all the time.'

'I'll follow you.'

I went downstairs, poured a vodka and a whiskey and left them on tables beside two armchairs. I heard Rachael laugh as the front door was opened.

'Hi Dad,' she said as she came into the room. 'We saw your car outside.'

'I just dropped in to have a drink with Ingrid.'

'That was thoughtful of you,' Jack said in a tone so even that it was impossible to decide if any irony was intended.

'I thought you two were going for a drive.'

'The trouble is,' Jack said, 'because I haven't been here before I haven't a clue where to drive to. And Rachael hadn't many ideas. Then I remembered that I had seen an Ordnance Survey map in the study. I'll check that it's there.'

'I heard you laughing,' I said to Rachael. 'I'm so glad that you've got some decent company.'

She was sitting on the arm of a chair, legs crossed, her arms folded.

'Yes, he is lovely, isn't he?' she said with an assumed archness.

She appeared to have no difficulty in accepting my explanation for being there.

I wondered what Jack thought. I could hear Ingrid talking to him. When she came into the room, she was relaxed, even cheerful. She kissed Rachael, as if they were old friends and went, unprompted, to the chair beside which I had left her drink. We were sitting well away from each other, sociable neighbours enjoying an afternoon drink.

'I was sorry to hear about Mr Cromer's friend,' Rachael said.

'I've just been talking to your father about that. Bill was very sad and upset. They were close friends many years ago.'

Jack came into the room, holding an unfolded map.

'Now at least I'll know where we're going,' he said. 'To put it mildly, Rachael lacks skill as a navigator.'

I wanted, absurdly, to defend her from this affectionate criticism.

'The roads in this country!' Ingrid said. 'There are so many small roads leading to nowhere in particular. I drove along one last week and ended up in a field. And if you try to explore, there are always black and white dogs that bark at you and cross old men who look as if they're going to expose themselves.'

'We'll be on our way then,' Jack said. Rachael stood beside him in the doorway as they said goodbye. We sat in silence until we heard the sound of the car engine starting.

'I feel like shit,' Ingrid said after they had gone. She pushed hair away from her forehead. 'In front of your daughter and his son. How have I got myself into such a shit situation?'

I knew what she meant and would not have been able to put any conviction into disagreeing with her. The open enthusiasm of Rachael and Jack made us look furtive and corrupt, our plotting a travesty of love.

'It is a shit situation,' I said defensively. 'I wouldn't have wished it on either of us. But I still think it's worth it.'

The inadequacy of the words was evident to me. I was ashamed of the superficiality of my insights. She shrugged impatiently.

'All I know is that I'm going to get hurt. I'm hurt already. Why don't you just go?'

'Rachael and Laura will be going to England soon,' I said. 'They'll be there for a month or so.'

'Is that the only problem that you can see? A shortage of beds to fuck in?'

'I think that the lack of privacy makes things very difficult for us.'

'That's pathetic!' she said.

I went across to where she was sitting and knelt beside her chair. She would not let me touch her.

'Please!' she said. 'What are you trying to do? Please!'

'It's not my fault that I'm married to someone I love and in love with you as well.'

She did not answer. She stared past me towards the empty fireplace.

'This is the best it'll ever be,' she said. 'What's the good of that?'

'No, it will be much, much better. I promise you. When we have time to relax and talk and be with each other. We're under too much pressure now.'

'I don't believe that.'

She began to cry. When I attempted to hold her, I found that her shoulders were as rigid as a protective armour against me, like some primitive accomplishment suddenly recalled. Large tears rolled across her cheeks, trembled at the corner of her lips and then appeared to vanish. I touched her cheek. She pulled away.

'Please,' I said, uncertain of what I was requesting. 'Let me help.'

'You know I'll want to see you,' she said unexpectedly.

'Thank you.'

She reached for her glass. I watched as she drank, aroused by the movement of her throat and the slight flattening of her lower lip and her half-closed eyes. I know that I often seem to write about her as an accumulation of intimate physical details. I also know that some of her unhappiness came from a belief that my feelings did not transcend this sexual longing, yet whenever I attempted to define a greater need or talk about needs and love, she would move on brusquely to something else. I began to feel silly kneeling there, like a bumpkin in a ballad.

'Who could have guessed,' I said, 'that they'd come back?'

'It's not their coming back,' she said. 'It's that we have the kind of relationship that makes their coming back so important.'

I went to my chair, feeling rebuked. I wanted to think of something hurtful to say in reply but, looking at her, I feared that she would simply tell me to go. She sat there, looking mysterious, like a woman in a painting, oddly posed, her left hand on her knee, the long fingers spread as if clutching something. Light from the window accentuated her cheekbone in a manner that an artist might have favoured. I hated being so remote from her.

'It isn't what I'd have chosen,' I said, and, almost immediately, wished that I had not spoken for the sentiment emerged as yet another cliché, dull and mundane. She smiled in a way that I could not interpret, then looked around the room as if it were somewhere new.

'We need to think it out,' she said. 'Seeing Jack and Rachael so happy just wasn't a help. What would they think about us if they knew? They'd think we were pathetic.'

'Can we not make the most of what we have?'

'And settle for second best? Why should I do that again? I've probably done it with Bill. He's spent his entire life avoiding commitment.'

We talked in a desultory way after that for as long as it took us to finish our drinks. Then I stood up to go.

'Can I get in touch with you?' I asked, not knowing what the answer might be.

'Of course.'

'I'm sorry that you've been so upset.'

'It wasn't your fault.'

I kissed her lightly on the lips. It was difficult to believe that we had made love so recently. I drove home, suffused with self-pity. I stopped on a straight stretch of the road beside a gateway where I could see fields rolling towards a river that looked metallic in the sunlight. A boy was fishing inexpertly, casting into a part of the river that was too unshaded to be attractive to fish. I sat there and thought about leaving Laura.

Like other men, I am capable of self-deception and emotional immaturity. I have made no attempt to disguise these facts in this narrative and I am prepared to accuse myself directly at this point. The women I have known, including both Laura and Ingrid, have not demonstrated these characteristics. The outlines of their lives contain a greater grasp of reality. They have the strength to confront the truth. I had also noticed, during my years of reporting from Northern Ireland, that the mothers of murder victims had, invariably, greater strength than other members of their families. They accepted their grief while the men in their families spoke wildly and fantasized plots of revenge that would never happen. This is something of a diversion. I suppose I am attempting to examine the fact that my own inability to face up to the truth is a common male failing. I sat there, looking down towards the river and attempted to deceive myself into believing that there were simple solutions to the problems that I had made for myself.

I could leave Laura. I could tell her, some long evening, as we sat apart from each other in the quiet room, that, although I still loved her, I had met another woman, yes, someone whom she knew, Ingrid actually, and my feelings for her were so overpowering that I was prepared to destroy everything that I had previously treasured. On the other hand, I could stop seeing Ingrid. It isn't as if we had shared a long and enduring relationship, filled with mutual dependencies and private agreements and things that didn't need to be said. I could explain to her that I had changed my mind or come to my senses, that it had been great but that we both had other commitments.

I knew that I could not do either of these things. The outcome of such confrontation was unimaginable. Why did I have to make a choice? Why couldn't we go on as we were?

Later, while I was talking to Laura, my sentences infused with a self-important guilt, Rachael came noisily into the room, her energy like a rebuke for all the small tediums I had unleashed. She could not hide her happiness; it was there in the way that she walked, in the way that she flung herself onto the sofa.

'Good day?' Laura asked, smiling at her.

'We went for a drive and a walk near Roundwood. Did you hear that we bumped into Dad?'

'No. Where was that?'

'In Jack's house. We had to go back there for a map.'

'Yes, I was passing,' I said quickly. 'I just looked in to see if Ingrid was all right.'

'All right?' Laura said. 'Why wouldn't she be all right?'

'I knew that Bill had been very upset, so I thought that she might be as well.'

She looked at me as if she knew I was lying.

'Would anyone care for a coffee?' Rachael asked.

Neither of us answered. She went into the kitchen. Laura was flicking through the pages of a magazine. She put it down and I could see that she was thinking carefully about what she was about to say.

'You don't think people would get the wrong idea if you were seen calling on Ingrid while Bill is away?'

'Who would even think about it?'

'Barbara for one.'

That disconcerted me. I had yet to discover Barbara's reaction to having seen me leaving Cromer's house.

'Do we really care what Barbara thinks?' I said defensively. 'We usen't to.'

'And other people. You know yourself that there's nothing people around here like so much as a juicy piece of gossip.'

'I'm sorry if you think I've provided them with that.'

'I'm probably overreacting. Do you like Ingrid?'

'I find her interesting.'

'*Very* interesting?'

'Not as interesting as you.'

'I don't feel interesting,' she said. 'I feel like a drudge. The job seems to have taken over everything.'

'I'm sorry that you have to work so hard. I know that I must seem incredibly indolent. Does it make you bitter?'

'I know it's not your choice. And you'll write again. But at that party I felt I wasn't really a part of things, that my life was happening somewhere else.'

'Remember me at any of your medical dinners? I always felt like an intruder.'

'Really?'

'Absolutely. I must have mentioned it. When you all get together you seem to be speaking in a different language.'

'You don't find me boring?'

'How could you even begin to think that? You lead a much more interesting life than I do.'

'That's not what I mean,' she said, looking away from me. 'I'm not glamorous like Ingrid.'

'Of course you are! Why is Ingrid suddenly so important?'

'It's only natural. She's suddenly in our lives. She comes from another world. I don't know who she is.'

She came across the room and sat beside me. I wondered if she would detect my inner panic, hear it like a heartbeat. I put my arm around her, immediately conscious of how much more narrow her shoulders were than Ingrid's.

'I love you,' I said, remembering myself using the same words so recently to another woman.

'I love you.'

I attempted to think of ways to reassure her but was afraid that my tone of voice would betray my duplicity. As I held her, I was disconcerted by the unfamiliarity of her body. I was even surprised by the texture of her hair and when I kissed the back of her neck, her skin had an unpredictable sweetness. After all the years, one would have assumed that our bodies would deliver instinctive physical recall but I might have been holding a stranger. She kissed me, her tongue moving lazily across mine. I should have been aroused but the time with Ingrid, although brief, had been sufficiently intense to leave me unresponsive. Laura detected this, looked at me quizzically, kissed me again, moving her body against mine as if in an act of seduction. I pretended a degree of enthusiasm, much greater than I was just beginning to experience, while thinking that to tell lies with one's body was a sadness more usually associated with the female experience.

'Let's go up,' Laura whispered.

'What about Rachael?'

'She's too pleased with herself to notice!'

Loud music was coming from the kitchen as we went up the stairs. The bedroom had the look of early morning; clothes on the bed, make-up scattered on the dressing table. The curtains had not been pulled. It had a disreputable, rather exciting air. We undressed. Laura's mood was passionate but her caresses were different and lighter than Ingrid's and my mind seemed to lock into measuring these differences rather than allowing my body to react.

'I'm sorry,' I said. 'I don't know what's wrong. I love you and want you.'

'Don't worry,' she said. 'Give yourself a chance.' Her lovely, suddenly familiar breasts were close to my face and I kissed them.

I felt challenged by her understanding. There might have been a more immediate solution in a quarrel. I closed my eyes and in an act of betrayal that filled me with shame pretended that it was Ingrid's body I was caressing, her fingers that were stroking me as I grew hard in her grasp. Then, for moments of disturbing unreality I hardly knew who I was in bed with or whom I was entering.

Afterwards, we lay quietly and I waited for Laura to say something. We would usually comment on our feelings, express opinions.

'That was good,' she said.

'It was lovely. You're lovely.'

'I suppose Rachael will be making love soon.'

'What put that into your head?'

'I don't know. Well, we've talked about it.'

'What kind of talk?'

'Woman's talk. The part that sex plays in a relationship. All her magazines write about it as if it is the relationship. I've attempted to give her a perspective. And I've emphasized the importance of contraception.'

'You don't think that she's too young?'

'She's certainly not too young for contraceptives. Do you mind about Jack?'

I had been wondering that myself as I had listened to her. Perhaps my dislike of him was formed from an awareness that he was sexually attracted to my daughter.

'A little bit, I suppose. You forget that I'm a Catholic. Not a good one, but it stays with you. Whatever happened to guilt and mortal sin?'

'Aren't you glad that she doesn't think like that? You've often said that it was a huge burden in your childhood.'

'I suppose so.'

'You only suppose so?'

'No. I'm glad. It's just that she seems very young and he seems old beyond his years. It's not the happiest of combinations, is it?'

'I don't think that covers everything.'

'You think that I'm some kind of Victorian throwback? Barrett of Wimpole Street?'

'No, but I think you might find it difficult not being the only man in her life.'

'That makes me sound rather pathetic.'

She moved against me so that our naked bodies seemed to adhere. I didn't want to go through the pretence again and disliked myself for being so dishonest with somebody offering love. She kissed me lightly then lay back sleepily and I realized that I had misinterpreted her movements.

'I love you,' I said.

'I love you.'

'You haven't gone off me?'

'It doesn't look like it, does it?'

It was the kind of reassurance that we had exchanged so often in the past that it was like hearing something I had written being read back to me. One accepts the truth of these reassurances as an act of faith; the fantasies of the loved one remain like a land-scape out of sight. I felt the distance between us keenly as we lay there, knowing that she had bared her trust and her concern and her body to someone who had betrayed all three. I touched her stomach, enjoying the warmth of her body and thought, almost against my will, about Ingrid, wondering what she was doing. Laura stirred beneath my fingers but she was asleep, dreaming of whatever it was that was forcing itself up from her subconscious mind to masquerade as the present. What would she think if she knew? This night's conversation and false reassurance and dishon-est lovemaking would be seen as the greatest betrayal of all. I felt oppressed by the stillness in the room, by a perception of old air, trapped heat, the energy of sex. It was then that I noticed that I could no longer hear music from the kitchen. I made an effort to concentrate on listening but there was nothing to hear except Laura's breathing. I got out of bed, put on a dressing gown and went quietly out to the landing. I heard Rachael's voice and realized that she was speaking on the phone. 'It's not that I don't like you,' she was saying. 'I do like you but it's been a very short time. I don't want anything to spoil it.' I resisted the temptation to go on listening and went to the bathroom for a shower. I wondered again what Ingrid was doing, imagining her standing beside me, the water cascading from her naked body.

When I went back to the bedroom, Laura was awake. She had put on a dressing gown and was sitting at the end of the bed, watching the news on television. There had been another murder in Belfast, a Protestant van driver shot twice through the head as he waited at a traffic lights. The images were, as usual, small and pathetic; the van, with bloodstains on its open door, a shoe left mysteriously on the pavement, the young widow and her two frightened children sitting in the kitchen of a neighbour's house. There was someone to express outrage and someone to express regret. A bishop expressed the simplistic and improbable hope that the people who had perpetrated this outrage would finally come to their senses and recognize that nothing was achieved by violence. He seemed like a foolish figure saying easy things. I wondered if Cromer were watching the news and what he would think now about the contribution that he had made towards the cause. I longed to speak to Ingrid.

TWELVE

WHEN CROMER RETURNED from England, he telephoned me and asked me over to his house for a drink. It was early in the afternoon and I was alone, so I was glad of the invitation. He sounded subdued and perhaps a little hostile, although I knew that I could be imagining this. I also thought that his regional accent had become more pronounced, as if the funeral had in some way drawn him back to his roots.

'Ingrid's in town,' he said when he opened the door. 'And Jack's out somewhere with your daughter. I was feeling lonely.'

We went into his study and he poured me a Powers Gold Label. When he went to the kitchen to get water I glanced at the correspondence on his desk. A woman in St Louis, Missouri, was preparing a critical account of his work for a series being issued by a university press. 'I hope that the enclosed chapter meets with your approval. I have endeavoured to show how the English anti-hero was almost totally different from his counterparts elsewhere. The references to Sillitoe and Amis may be of some interest to you.'

'Was it a terrible ordeal?' I asked him when he came back carrying a jug of water.

'It was sobering,' he said. 'The poor bugger had testicular cancer.

It doesn't bear thinking about. Biggest bloody womaniser I ever knew in the old days. He got all wizened up like some East European politician.'

'I've seen a few of my generation go,' I said lugubriously, as if I were seeking sympathy. 'It makes you think.'

'It's a bloody disgrace that they haven't cracked cancer yet with all the thousands of millions that they claim to have spent on research.'

'But the treatment seems to be improving.'

'For a while, then the inevitable takes over. And what about AIDS? Do you worry about AIDS?'

Although I had never been sufficiently promiscuous to regard myself as being under real threat, I was surprised that neither Ingrid nor I had ever discussed this new area of risk. I had avoided the subject because there was already enough danger in our relationship. I had no idea what she thought about it.

'I worried, like we all did, at the beginning, but the opportunities are limited enough here.'

'They're the very circumstances that would lead to being infected,' Cromer said enigmatically. 'Settle for anything, wouldn't you, after a while?'

I assumed and hoped that this was a hypothetical question rather than the preface to some accusation.

'I saw girls at the funeral,' Cromer said, 'whom I used to think that I loved. They looked like their grandmothers used to look. Little old ladies. For Christ's sake, I'm getting old. I kept on looking into any reflecting surface that I passed, hoping that I looked better than they did.'

I was disconcerted by the conversation, increasingly certain that he was talking in some circuitous way about Ingrid and me. Perhaps Jack had dropped some hint, some sly allusion that had bothered Cromer sufficiently for him to play this game with me, waiting for me to fail some unspecified test.

'I think that it happens in every generation,' I said. 'The same feeling of anticlimax. Remember Dickens and Mrs Whatshername? Total disillusion.'

'It unnerved me,' he said, 'on top of our trip to Belfast. And now there's something else.'

'What?' I asked, unable to hide impatience in my voice. 'What else?'

'I've had three telephone calls this morning. Someone has been phoning recently and hanging up but these were proper calls from the same guy. The first time I answered he said "Are you comfortable where you're living, Mr Cromer?" I asked him who I was talking to and he just laughed. Then he said "A spokesman for the people whose land your house is built on." Then he hung up. That shook me a fair bit. It would shake anyone, wouldn't it? The second call was even worse.'

I'm ashamed to confess that all I wanted to do was to stand up and walk away from his predicament. I had lived in the area for years without even hearing of anything like this. Now he was insisting that I share in an uneasy world and I was already tired of it.

'I don't know how you've managed to attract all this attention.'

'That's not a very sympathetic response! I thought that you, of all people, would know what I was feeling.'

'But if you hadn't paid money in the first place ...' I said.

'I don't care what you say. I still think that malevolent old fucker is behind it.'

'That's nonsense. I've told you. He's a dinosaur. Tell me about the second call.'

'That came about twenty minutes later. The same fellow. There was a silence at first, so I knew who it was. I said, "What exactly do you want from me?" He said, "Brits out!" Then he hung up.'

'What kind of accent did he have?'

'He didn't sound as if he were reading history at Balliol.'

'Northern or southern?'

'Southern. He sounded exactly like any of the people in the shops around here.'

'What about the third call?'

'That was about an hour ago. He said "You should listen to what I'm saying, Mr Cromer. I amn't playing a game." I didn't say anything and he hung up. That's why I didn't tell you as soon as you got here. I kept on waiting for the phone to ring.'

'What are you going to do?'

'I thought I'd ask you for some advice. I have no one else to talk to about it.'

'Why don't you go to the local gardaí? They'll probably know immediately who's making these calls.'

'Suppose they find out about the cheque?'

'It was a perfectly legal donation.'

'Yes, but they're going to think I'm a total fool.'

'That's something you could learn to live with.'

'If Ingrid finds out, that'll be it. She's already far from happy as it is.'

'You haven't told her about any of it?'

'No.'

The telephone rang.

'I knew it,' he said. 'Here we go again. It's just going to get worse and worse.'

'You'd better answer it,' I said, aware that I had heard these exact words spoken in a number of mediocre films.

'You do. Then you'll be able to judge the accent.'

I picked up the receiver.

'Who's that?' Ingrid asked, a note of exasperation in her voice.

This was more startling than any expected threat from an anonymous caller.

'It's me,' I said. 'John. Bill had just gone out of the room but he's here now.'

Cromer was miming extravagant bewilderment.

'It's Ingrid,' I said.

He laughed as he took the receiver. I walked over to the window as if offering privacy but I was, of course, listening, hungry for anything that I could add to an unfavourable interpretation of their relationship.

'Just asked him around for a drink,' Cromer said. 'Were you able to get everything you wanted?'

There was a long pause. I wished that I could hear her voice, the sing-song quality of her spoken English.

'Well, that's pretty good then,' Cromer said. 'You can get everything else back in England, can't you?'

A cat strolled past the window, a small tabby with its tail erect. It paused and stared at me with large, expressionless eyes. I attempted to outstare it but failed; its mindless curiosity was too strong to be easily deflected.

'If you happen to see that Coogan book on the IRA,' Cromer said. 'If you happen to be near Hodges Figgis. But don't go specially.'

I had recommended that book to him. I wished that I were talking to her about it.

'That's great,' he said. 'I'll see you when I see you.'

He replaced the receiver and laughed. I experienced a wave of dislike for him as if he had suddenly revealed some particularly unpleasant aspect of his personality. I resented his easy access to Ingrid and his casual declaration of love.

'That was something of an anticlimax,' he said. 'Just Ingrid ringing from town. I had almost forgotten that there were such things as friendly telephone calls.'

'She seemed to be quite surprised when I answered?'

'Did she?'

'You mentioned that she wasn't happy.'

'It's the countryside,' he said. 'Not just here. Any bloody countryside. She doesn't like fields and she doesn't like mountains or old people on bicycles or cows. Funny thing is, she comes from the countryside herself. Or maybe that's the reason for it? Anyway, you know what Krauts are like. Once they've made up their minds, they never change their opinions.'

'I'm sorry,' I said. 'I assumed that she liked it here. So it's not really working out then?'

'Not really. On top of the calls and that business in Belfast I'm beginning to think that the only sensible thing I can do is pack up and get out.'

'That's fairly drastic, isn't it?'

'Do you think so? Everything seems to be slipping out of control. The next time the telephone rings, the entire situation could get worse. That's no way to live one's life. I came here for peace. It's ironic, isn't it?'

'I'm absolutely certain that if you go to the guards they'll be sympathetic.'

'But they're not going to agree to my saying nothing to Ingrid, are they?'

'Probably not.'

'Maybe you're forgetting that I'm in a foreign country? All your suppositions are meaningless to me. There are times when I feel that I don't even understand the language. I had hoped that I'd be well into a book by now but I haven't written a thing. It's all a complete mess.'

He finished his drink and brought the bottle to the table.

'What would you do if you were in my shoes?' he asked as he poured out large measures for both of us.

'I'd wait to see if the telephone calls were crank or serious. If they were serious I'd go to the guards.'

He looked pleased at this weak decision. I suspect that he welcomed the lack of commitment to any action that it contained. I left as soon as I had finished my drink, ashamed of the way I was abusing his trust. I was displaying weaknesses that I had never suspected existed but which must have been there, dormant, waiting for the right emotional temperature to emerge. I was acting in such a self-interested way that I didn't even know what I felt about Cromer. Did I like him? Did I seek his friendship? I had no answers. I regarded him as some kind of obstacle placed between myself and Ingrid. I was probably beginning to treat Laura in exactly the same way.

Later, when I returned from a walk, I was a surprised to see that his car was parked in the driveway before our house. I stood and looked into it as if seeking some kind of evidence. There was a copy of the previous Sunday's *Observer* in the back seat and a walking stick, roughly fashioned from ash. I went into the house. Rachael called to me from the kitchen.

'We're in here, Dad. Would you like a cup of tea?'

'I've just been talking to your father,' I said to Jack.

He nodded.

'We went for a walk,' Rachael said.

She poured me a cup of tea and I sat with them at the table. I was uneasy. I retained the impression that, to Jack, I was some kind of comic figure, old-fashioned and dismissible.

'Where did you go?' I asked.

'We parked at the crossroads and went over to the river. It was really beautiful there. There was a man and two children in a boat.'

'It's very good countryside,' Jack said. 'I thought it was going to be like the Lake District but it's not like anywhere else.'

I noticed that Rachael listened to him as if everything he said was imbued with some special interest.

'Jack really likes it here,' she said in a slightly proprietorial way.

'Quite a change from London,' he said.

'That's another thing,' Rachael said. 'Great luck. When Mum and I go to England next week, Jack will be going home to his own house. We'll get to see each other.'

'That's nice,' I said.

'Isn't it?'

Rachael made no effort to hide her enthusiasm at the prospect. I wanted to warn her he would be more impressed if she didn't appear so eager but that advice seemed to come from a world more mean than the one that she occupied. I wanted to reach out and hug her; she appeared frail in her attempts to be adult. She must have noticed that I was staring at her. She smiled, hesitantly, as if afraid that I was about to say something embarrassing. Her smile was similar to Laura's, spreading slowly but widely to reveal her teeth. Jack sat slightly sprawled on his chair, looking superior and fashionably unkempt.

'Rachael tells me that you want to be a gardener,' I said, investing the word with a certain degree of disapproval.

'I've been thinking along those lines,' he said. 'It more or less appeals to me. I like Kew Gardens. I like plants. I think that I understand them.'

I wanted to challenge him on this statement but was aware that my motivation would be far too obvious. I suppose that the source of my caution was the fear that Rachael would be ashamed of me.

'That's interesting,' I said. 'So you'd go to some kind of horticultural college?'

'I've been looking into that.'

'Have you done a lot of gardening at home?'

'Not really. It's only a back garden. You know the kind of thing. It's not the scale that I want to work on. I want something more natural where plants can have their own integrity. I hate to see them regimented into beds and borders.'

Rachael was very impressed. She nodded in agreement at this evident nonsense. She turned from staring at him and looked at me as if to share her enthusiasm. I don't think I succeeded in forcing a positive expression on to my face.

'Fascinating,' I said. 'Does your brother have similar views?'

'All he wants to do is make money.'

'That's hardly totally discreditable.'

'Doesn't that depend on the methods that someone chooses?'

'You don't approve of his methods?'

'Not at all. I hate them.'

'He's an investment banker,' Rachael said with a distaste that she must have learned from Jack. 'He has dealings with countries in the Third World and apparently they do nothing but rip them off.'

'Being ripped off is the destiny of Third World countries,' I said, 'but it's usually their leaders who are doing the ripping.'

Rachael looked at me with disappointment, her eyes seeming to darken. I cared so much about her good opinion that I was surprised that I was not more adroit in hiding my antipathy to Jack. I did not want to see disappointment turn to disillusion as she detected the real nature of my flaws.

'I'm sorry for being flippant,' I said. 'It's an important subject and it deserves to be treated seriously.'

We talked about the nature of capitalism. Jack's intelligence, although sometimes weighed down by fashionable principles that he had accepted too readily, was sharper than I had expected. I became aware of his liking for his father and his pride in a working-class inheritance. He was conscious of the rigidity of the British class system and had experienced kaleidoscopic variations of it at his school. He knew a number of Labour Party MPs and was scathing about the tepidity of their socialism. I had to admit to myself, after a while, that he bore little resemblance to the parody figure I had imagined. My dislike for him, my inability to see him as anything other than a predator on my family were tempered by a certain respect. I made a number of attempts to include Rachael in our conversation but she remained on the sidelines like a neutral observer, smiling awkwardly, frowning occasionally. She was just a year or so too young to have political convictions.

We made more tea and, as the conversation slowed, I realized that I was in the way. I felt a kind of absurd loneliness as I went into my study and looked for something to read. I took down some novels by my contemporaries but in each case I was deterred from reading past the first page by the self-satisfaction of the style. I had reviewed one of the books only a year before and had admired it. Now I wondered why I had not seen that the elaboration of the prose was a screen hiding any true feeling. I put the books away and wondered what I should do with the rest of the day.

In the afternoon, I drove down to the pub. Barbara's car was parked outside. I had an instinct that she would be there with a new boyfriend and this was almost enough to make me go somewhere else. When I went inside she was sitting by herself and there was only one glass on the table. She looked up from the book she was reading and gave me a casual wave.

I went to the counter. Mr Moore's niece, Lily, asked, 'Are you all right?'

I particularly dislike this expression and wanted to ask 'Would I be standing at the counter of your grossly inadequate hostelry if I were all right and not in need of a drink?' Instead, I asked for a Gold Label and watched as she looked and then looked again at the small line of bottles beside the till.

'A Gold Label?' she said as if my order were unusual.

'It's the second bottle.'

'Oh, a Gold Label,' she said, without any embarrassment. 'Would you like ice?'

'Just water.'

This exchange irritated me so much that I feared that I would have an argument with Barbara. I was glad she was alone. If she had something to say about my visit to Ingrid, I could at least deal with it in private. I carried my drink over to her table.

'Do you mind if I join you?'

'I'd mind if you didn't.'

She was reading *The Great Hunger*, Cecil Woodham-Smith's account of the Irish Famine.

'All of a sudden,' I said, 'everyone is interested in the history of our beleaguered nation.'

'This is research.'

'I can't imagine that there's much romantic potential in the Famine.'

'Don't be naughty!' she said. 'My heroine leaves Connemara in 1846 to go to the New World.'

'One has to admire her prescience!'

165

'Where have you been hiding anyway? I've been here for several lunchtimes but I'm told that you're never around.'

'It's probably because Rachael's on holidays.'

'I've seen her a number of times being escorted by a handsome young man.'

'Jack Cromer,' I said.

'That's right.'

'I've just been talking to him. He's really quite an interesting lad.'

'And totally smitten?'

'I'm sure it's just a holiday romance.'

'I don't know about that,' she said with an emphasis that left me wondering about the contexts in which she may have encountered them.

'It's good for Rachael to have company,' I said.

'I have no doubt that it is!'

There was no reassurance in that reply but I was determined not to be seen to be looking for information. Barbara would derive far too much satisfaction from that small act of abasement. I wanted to fill the space with some irony but nothing came to mind. It was a day in which everything contrived to undermine. Barbara was smiling at me encouragingly as if waiting for me to answer some question she had asked. A breeze from an open window blew some of her cigarette smoke back towards her face and, as she squinted, her face seemed to implode into old age, lines turning into wrinkles.

'Any gossip?' I asked her.

'If there is, I suppose it's about me.'

'Surely you're leading a blameless existence?'

'That's exactly it,' she said. 'Very sad. I'll soon have to go scouting.'

'Have you ever heard of any political pressure being put on any writers around here?'

'Political pressure? You mean visits from the local TDs or whatever they're called.'

'No. Did anyone ever threaten you, for example, because you're English?'

'After one of the shootings in Northern Ireland, when the army shot someone or other, a man shouted "Brits out!" at me when I was leaving the pub. I assumed that he was drunk.'

'Doubtless he was.'

'Why are you asking me this?'

'There's a rumour going around that one of the American writers near Ashford has been asked to pay protection.'

'Protection from what?'

'I don't know really. From having a petrol bomb lobbed through his window.'

'Good God! Why pick on an American?'

'Why not?'

'Do you believe it happened?'

'It's not impossible. I'd like a little more evidence.'

'Should I be worried?'

'I've really got to remind you, Barbara, that I'm talking about the most vague of rumours.'

'Where did you hear it?'

'I think it was Rachael who mentioned it to me. Or somebody in the village. Somebody in one of the shops.'

'Why do I feel that you're not being completely frank?' Barbara asked. 'You'd certainly remember where you heard something like that.'

She was lighting a cigarette. Two local sheep farmers, gloomy men who seldom conversed, even with each other, came quietly into the bar and sat on stools by the counter.

'I'm sure that it must have been Rachael.'

'Was it you who got the call?'

'Oh for God's sake, Barbara!' I said, irritated at how enmeshed I had become in my own lie. 'It's that tall, bald American who writes science fiction. The fellow with the irritating laugh. Bob somebody. And anyway, it may not even be true. I'm sorry that I ever mentioned it!'

Mr Moore had pulled pints of Guinness for the farmers. He placed the glasses carefully before them and all three stared as if they had been presented with some unusual objects that they had been challenged to identify. Then one of the farmers, a small, fat man who was rumoured to have had incestuous relationships with two of his daughters, took a glass and raised it slowly to his lips.

'You know what they say about him?' Barbara said.

'I was just thinking about that myself.'

'One of his daughters committed suicide.'

'Yes, she drowned in the lake.'

'The inquest said that she was pregnant.'

'That's right.'

'How can we bear to be in the same room as him?'

'We don't know if it's true.'

'Of course we know it's true! We just don't want to confront the implications. Do you know anything about his wife?'

'I know her to see. So do you. A tall woman on a bicycle. She always wears a brown coat and a headscarf.'

'Good God! Of course I know her. We've often said hello to each other on the road. What can she be thinking of to let that despicable little monster abuse her children?'

She was speaking quite loudly. Both the men turned their heads and looked across at us.

'Do you think they heard me?' Barbara said quietly.

'They seem to have heard something.'

'Have I put my foot in it this time?'

'I wouldn't think so,' I said, without any real concern.

'So you don't really think they heard me?'

I looked across at the farmers. Both were slumped forward, their elbows on the counter, their broad backs straining against old sweaters.

'They seem quite agitated,' I said.

'Do they really?'

She looked across at them.

'They seem pissed to me!'

'Let me get you a drink,' I said. 'Then I'll have to go.'

I liked to invent small urgencies for myself to make the time pass. I strolled across to the counter and went through the boring business of ordering drinks. Both farmers stared at me and made no effort to look away when I stared back.

'Nice day,' I said.

'Oh it is, it is,' the fat one said. 'It's a nice one sure enough. A very nice day, thank God. You're right there.'

I guessed from his almost excessive friendliness that he hadn't heard what Barbara had said.

'It's nicer than yesterday,' he said as if this were of some importance.

'Would you like ice in the whiskey?' Mr Moore asked.

'Just water.'

When I went back to the table, Barbara was eager for information.

'I saw him talking to you.'

'Yes. We had quite a conversation.'

'What was he saying?'

'He expressed the opinion that today was a nicer day than yesterday.'

'Is that all?'

'Were you expecting something less controversial?'

'I was expecting some kind of complaint.'

'Even if they heard you, they wouldn't say anything.'

She considered this for a moment.

'How are you getting on with Bill Cromer?' she asked.

I sensed that the conversation was about to become more hazardous and that Ingrid's name would soon appear, unobtrusively at first and then in some challenging way. Barbara's smile invited confidence; some lipstick had smudged across her teeth, making her vulnerable. She looked down at her glass of gin and tonic as if it were a crystal ball.

'What a strange question!' I said, aware that I sounded defensive. 'We're getting on fine. I enjoy his company. I think that he enjoys mine.'

'That's nice,' Barbara said, 'I've often noticed your car outside his place. Even when he's away.'

That could not be ignored.

'Yes, I've called to see Ingrid once or twice. She's rekindling my interest in theatre.'

'Rekindling it?' Barbara said, making the word sound lewd and provocative. 'That's nice!'

'Don't be heavy-handed, Barbara,' I said. 'I haven't stepped out of one of your books.'

'That's very hurtful.'

I felt, in some obscure way, that the worst danger had passed. Any suspicions she may have could not be confirmed without additional information. I was fully aware of her malice but felt that it was tempered by the fact that we got on well. We enjoyed these adversarial encounters.

'I insist on buying you a drink,' she said.

'I shouldn't. I intended to go home early. Anyway, I haven't even finished this one yet.'

'Yes, but the second you do, you'll be gone unless there's one waiting. I suppose it's too much to expect that girl to even glance in this direction. Why isn't Mr Moore here? At least he moves occasionally. That girl just sits on her fat arse and stares into space.'

'An Irish contemplative,' I said. 'A not altogether unfamiliar sort.'

'Hello!' Barbara called very loudly. Lily and both the farmers looked in our direction.

'I'm so very contrite to disturb you,' Barbara said, 'but would a new round of drinks be out of the question?'

Lily came across and stared at us sullenly.

'A gin and tonic and a Powers Gold Label.'

'Would you like ice with the Powers?'

'No.'

'Do you suspect that there's much inbreeding in this district?' Barbara said when Lily had gone back to the bar.

'Only amongst the newcomers.'

'Is that a confession?'

'Would I be so indiscreet?'

'I don't know,' she said. 'You seem to be spreading your wings. You're much more ... outgoing than you were.'

'Am I?'

'Oh much more. Are you working?'

'Not yet.'

'You've got to. It's silly to let time pass by.'

'I know,' I said defensively, 'but I just don't have the confidence yet.'

Lily came back with our drinks. She had fat arms and substantial hips. I suddenly felt sorry for her. She was only a few years older than Rachael but already she must have felt that the future was closing in, the fund of hopes dwindling.

'Where did you bump into Rachael?' I asked Barbara.

'What's that?'

'You said that you bumped into her. With Jack.'

'No, I said that I saw them around the place. Walking. Holding hands. Love's young dream and that kind of thing.'

'I hope that she won't end up out of her depth.'

'That's most unlikely. Young girls nowadays are wiser than their years. Do you ever see their magazines?'

'I've seen some of them. I'm not certain they're reassuring. I don't want to be over-involved and Laura is really very good about it but, still, she seems very young.'

I noticed, with alarm, that there were tears in Barbara's eyes. She took a handkerchief from her bag and a tear rolled down her face, tracking its way through her make-up.

'Barbara,' I said, 'I'm really sorry. Did I say something?'

I knew that when she got drunk she could be maudlin and filled with old regrets but I had never seen her get so upset so quickly. I felt awkward and intrusive.

'You didn't say anything. I'm getting old. I cry easily when I think about it. I hardly know where my life has gone. So much of it is no better than a bad dream.'

'Don't forget all you've achieved. Your books are read everywhere.'

'We both know they're not any good. They'll die with me.'

I didn't know what to say. It seemed that I was doomed to be the recipient other people's worries, other people's sense of defeat, yet I was the greatest failure of them all. The emptiness of my days was like a wound. I seemed to live a life of mere acquiescence. I wished that I had the generosity to tell her all this but I did not. Looking at her crumpled face I felt nothing but a kind of irritated pity. She had not grown accustomed to being alone. Perhaps there was something heroic in her relentless search for companionship.

'Would you like to come round to supper this evening?' I asked her, hoping that she wouldn't want to do so.

'I'm actually going into town,' she said. 'To the Gate. But it's nice of you to ask. Don't worry. I'm feeling much better already.'

We both left shortly after that, subdued, as if we had had an argument and too easy a reconciliation.

I telephoned Cromer. He answered almost immediately.

'That was fast,' I said.

'I'm still jumpy when it rings.'

'You haven't had any more calls?'

'No.'

'In all probability you won't have.'

'But you don't know that, do you?'

'It's just a feeling.'

He was childishly anxious to accept reassurance. His gratitude came down the line like an additional burden.

'You're good to be thinking about it,' he said.

'Ingrid and you must come round to supper soon.'

'We'd love that. She actually decided, on the spur of the moment, to go to London this afternoon.'

'Really?'

I hoped that dismay wasn't evident in my voice.

'Yes, she's making these masks and she couldn't get everything that she needed in Dublin. And anyway, as I think I mentioned to you, she misses her friends. A few days in London will do her nothing but good.'

'Exactly. She'll be back in a few days?'

'Yes,' Cromer said, as if a little surprised by the question.

'It's just that Laura will be going soon to visit her parents, so we may have to postpone that supper for a while.'

'It'll be something to look forward to. Jack actually mentioned Laura's holiday to me. He hopes to see something of Rachael over there.'

'I heard that.'

'Do you feel all right about it? I mean, if I had a daughter of that age I know that I'd be on tenterhooks all the time.'

'I'm delighted she has the company. There are very few people of her age around here.'

'That's all right then,' he said.

We both hesitated, as if reluctant to be the one to end the call. I wished that there were some way of looking for Ingrid's telephone number. I wanted to hear her voice, needed to know that she would want to see me in the weeks ahead when I would invite her into my home. The thought of her being there, standing beside familiar objects, intensifying them with her beauty, filled me with excitement.

It is some weeks since I have broken into this narrative to comment on its progress. I kept up a steady output of words through the shortening, melancholy days of autumn. It is now just three weeks before

Christmas and a grey, translucent mist hangs heavily over the landscape, obliterating many of the features I have already described.

Two things happened this week, one interesting, one terrible, and have prompted this intervention. In the pub a few days ago I learned that Cromer's house had been sold. Outside these pages it will take on a new identity and the character of its rooms will change. It was sold privately and, according to rumour, cheaply, so that the identity of the new owner is prompting a certain amount of speculation. I discovered that, in some odd way, I had proprietorial feelings about the house or, at the least, about its future. I resented not knowing the details. Mr Moore told me that it had been bought by a film star, who intended converting it into a holiday home. Someone else heard that an ageing pop star, now largely forgotten, would live there with his alarmingly young fourth wife. Time will tell. New characters will come into this district too late to play a part in these pages and others, like Cromer and Ingrid, will walk out of the end of a chapter, not to be seen again.

The terrible thing that happened was Barbara's death. She killed herself the day before yesterday. She planned it with a precision and implemented it with a determination that showed it was never intended to be a cry for help. She wanted to die and her body, having been subjected to whatever indignities the pathologist found necessary, is waiting to be flown back to England. She requested that there should be no religious ceremony of any kind, so there is no obvious way of paying one's respect to her remains. Poor Barbara; she will live on in these pages for a little longer, unaware that she is about to plan her own death. Or perhaps she did know and put a brave face on it and derived some courage from the fact that she would be in control of those final moments. So now there are several Barbaras; the dead body waiting to be flown to a crematorium; the woman whom I remember with her enthusiasms and her small malices and her boyfriends, signalled by closed curtains; and the Barbara of these pages, uprooted from time and strange like the moments of unreality I have attempted to explain.

She hanged herself. An oak beam, decorative but sturdy, ran across the ceiling of her living room. Some previous owner of the house had driven a large copper hook into it. Barbara had once pointed it out to me and said 'Weird, don't you think?'

I saw her five days ago. We met in the village shop as we waited behind a crowd of schoolchildren, buying sweets. I had thought that she was in unusually good spirits.

'I've finished my new novel,' she said. 'The one about the girl who leaves mid-nineteenth-century Ireland. I think it's rather good.'

'Have you sent it to your publisher?'

'I posted it to them last week. They're happy.'

'Aren't you lucky?'

'Come on now! We've got to put you to work.'

She was served before I was. 'See you soon!' were the last words we spoke to each other. Some time the following morning she attached a strong electric cable to the hook and made a simple hangman's noose. She stood on a chair and the last thing she would have heard was some programme on the radio. Her small transistor radio was still playing when her body was found. She must have kicked the chair away with considerable determination. It was discovered, on its side, several feet away from where she was hanging. She had done her calculations accurately. When her body stopped falling and her head was jerked grotesquely by the cable, her feet were eight or nine inches away from the floor. I would like to think that she died quickly, in an uplifting spurt of intensive courage, but in all probability she choked slowly, her body jerking in a parody of dance. There was excrement on her legs. She was found later that morning by a young man called Basil. He had, apparently, had some kind of relationship with her which had ended three or four months before. It had broken up but, unlike so many of those who preceded him, he had hoped for a resumption. He drove to her house to talk to her. There was no response when he knocked on the door. He looked through the living-room window and saw her. She hadn't closed the curtains. There are those who would have got back into their cars and driven quickly away but, to his credit, he cared enough to break the glass of the window and enter the room in case that there was anything that could be done. Her back was to him; when he saw her face, which was grossly swollen and discoloured, he knew that the only action he could take was to call the guards. There was a letter addressed to her solicitor on a coffee table. In this, she expressed the wish that there should be no religious service, requested cremation in the town of her birth and confirmed the existence of a will, known to a firm of solicitors in London. That was all. I understand that these details were written in a businesslike tone, without any emotion or any explanation as to why she had decided to kill herself.

I must avoid being sentimental about her. They say that one should not speak ill of the dead but Barbara consistently spoke ill of the living and it would do no justice to her memory to reduce her into some kind of acceptable and anodyne caricature. When people whom we have known well die and turn into ghosts, they haunt our imagination and our memory with undetermined details of themselves. We remember them in the way that a novelist remembers a character into creation and in our insistence on their existence we make them real again.

THIRTEEN

I HEAR A TELEPHONE ringing and, as so often before, I wonder if it could be Ingrid. I answer it and when I hear her voice I am so startled that I can think of nothing to say.

'Is something wrong?' she said. 'Should I ring off? Hello?'

'No, please don't. I just can't believe it's you. When I heard a few days ago that you had gone to London I began to think that I'd never see you again. Where are you now? Can I see you?'

'I'm still in London.'

My surprise was replaced by disappointment.

'Will I ever see you again?'

'Why are you talking so strangely? I'm only here on a visit.'

'Don't you miss me?'

'All these questions! Of course I do. That's why I'm talking to you now.'

'I'm sorry,' I said. 'It's just that I've missed you so much.'

'It wasn't just that I needed materials, although I did. I also wanted time to think. I wanted to slow down for a while and find out what I thought.'

'Have you found out?'

'Yes, more or less.'

'Will you want to see me when you come back?'

'Yes.'

'Are you sure?.'

'Yes, I'm sure.'

She had never sounded so positive before. The words were like a revelation. It was as if I could see myself in an entirely different light: her lover.

'You sound very definite.'

'I know.'

'When are you coming home?'

'In a couple of days.'

'Laura and Rachael are going to England in a couple of days.'

'That will make it easier for us to have some time together.'

'Lots and lots of time.'

'Bill will be around, of course.'

'But you could be in Dublin or anywhere.'

She laughed and I realized that she sounded much more relaxed than on the last few occasions I had spoken to her. I felt so happy to be talking to her, to be the object of her attention, that I laughed as well.

'Oh God!' I said. 'I just can't wait to see you.'

'I'm glad you miss me. It's a nice feeling.'

'Miss is too mild a word. I long for you.'

'Aren't we absurd?'

'I don't care about that. I'm quite happy to be absurd.'

'I'd better go,' she said. 'I'll be home on Sunday or Monday. I'll phone you as soon as I get a chance.'

She hung up without saying goodbye; the suddenness of it was shocking. I stared at the receiver from which a soft, electronic moan was being emitted. Then I went into my study to consider the implications of the call. As the shock of the abrupt ending abated, the happiness returned. The very thought of her aroused me. I poured myself a vodka and tonic and wandered over to the window, then wandered back again, restless and disturbed by my desire. Laura was at work, Rachael had probably gone somewhere with Jack. I had often lived alone before getting married and usually enjoyed the sensation of an empty house, a feeling of unintruded-upon spaciousness, but now I found that the stillness added to my restlessness. I wished that there was someone to whom I could express my feelings without risking disapproval. I turned on the television and flicked from channel to channel to see if there was anything worth watching. There was not.

For five or six minutes I looked at an American chat show in which daughters of various ages, from young to middle-aged, spoke with alarming frankness about the dislike they had for their parents. Beside them, their parents sat complacently, listening to the lasting damage that they had inflicted on their children. I had always been surprised by the ability that some people possessed to express their deepest emotions to strangers. How could they expose their wounds in some brightly lit studio and admit to feelings of loss and betrayal? More mysteriously, how could the people who were alleged to have inflicted those wounds sit beside them with fixed smiles? Only one woman looked shocked at what she was hearing, turning to her daughter in an effort to protest that what she was saying wasn't true, that she had loved her, that her promiscuity had been her own business and that the strangers in the bedroom had been benign and friendly.

'It was terrible,' the girl said. 'I never knew who was going to be with her in that room.' She was crying, the tears welling from her very blue eyes with theatrical effect, as the programme cut to close-ups of members of the audience looking shocked or sympathetic.

I thought, guiltily, about Rachael. What would she have thought if she had encountered me in bed with Ingrid in Cromer's house? I couldn't imagine what she would have said or how she would have reacted.

The mother attempted to comfort her daughter, reaching out to stroke her shoulder but the gesture was angrily rejected. It was, all too evidently, too little too late. It was disconcerting that so much emotion could be unleashed for the purpose of entertainment, yet it had a fascination; one was catching a glimpse of two unusually sad lives. It was difficult to imagine what they would do when they left the studio. Would they travel in the same car, go for a drink, be, if only for a few moments, the most notorious mother and daughter in the United States? They would have to refine their hatreds and discover ways of being invulnerable to each other, like a couple who fall out of love and betray old memories with the least likely of partners. Although I longed to see Ingrid I knew that I would be guilty when I made love to her in this house, our house, not mine. Would I attempt to turn it into a ceremony of exorcism, banishing the spirits of so many other occasions?

'That's all my childhood was,' the daughter on television said. 'That's all my teenage years were, hanging out in the mall so that she could make it with some guy that she didn't even know.'

She had an effortless eloquence; her eyes were filling again with tears.

'That's not fair,' her mother said. 'When your father left me for that tramp, I couldn't just behave as if that was the end of my life. I wasn't going to let that jerk destroy me. Sure, I invited some guys home and a few of them were worthless but I always gave you love and attention.'

I switched off the television, chilled for a moment by the complexity entailed in any definition of family. I knew that I would retain a memory of their voices and of the mother's anger. I suppose she had little enough to look back on except those pretences of love with strangers, their overalls thrown on the floor, their trucks parked in some nearby lot, their names forgotten. They were adulterers, as I was. To represent these few tawdry memories as examples of parental neglect would be to define a life of unrelieved bleakness.

When Ingrid first comes to the house, I thought, I will entertain her formally to begin with, probably in this room. I will pour her a drink in one of our best glasses and draw her attention to some of the better paintings. I'm sure that she will admire the Collins with its mysteriously achieved rendering of land reflected in water, trees dissolving into their own images, light losing authority as shadows parody form. She should also like the Campbell of a wet day near a beach in Roundstone with its grey-blue light and turbulent sea and a scatter of birds taking off into flight. I attempted to imagine her standing there, looking at them, the promise of her nakedness filling me with excitement. There would be an awkwardness in the walk upstairs. I would avoid, as she had, the master bedroom and choose, instead, the room beside it. Laura's parents, on their visits to Ireland, have settled comfortably in there but the bed has no special secrets. We will undress quickly and I will be surprised yet again by her grace and by her beauty and notice her tattoo and the vulnerability of the hollows behind her knees. I was excited by this fantasy and disturbed at how easily I could imagine its enactment. It was as if it were a scene from the novel that I was unable to write. Was it all a fiction? That idea would certainly have offended her but, in some odd way, it appealed to me – as if in longing for her I was working.

Rachael came noisily into the room.

'I'm sorry,' she said. 'Were you asleep?'

'No, just thinking. I didn't hear a car.'

'Jack left me off at the gate.'

'You went for a walk?'

'Yes.'

She wandered around a little awkwardly, bumping against a chair, fiddling with an ornament.

'You like him?' I asked, half question, half statement.

'He's all right.'

I felt mean at the instant pleasure that I took in her apparent lack of enthusiasm.

'That's nice about London,' I said, trawling for information, shameless in my need to be important to her.

'We'll probably meet all right. But he has a girlfriend there.'

I didn't know if I should sympathize.

'Did he just mention her today?'

'No, he didn't mention her at all,' she said with adult bitterness. 'I found out.'

'But it isn't as if he had told you that he hadn't got a girlfriend, is it?'

'That isn't the point. I just don't think that he was upfront with me, that's all.'

'I'm sorry,' I said guiltily. 'I hope that you aren't hurt.'

'There's nothing to be sorry about. I didn't want to be his girlfriend anyway. I just wanted to be friends.'

She sat, slumped in an armchair, looking thin and dejected, a visual contradiction of the brave defiance of her words. I could remember her as a very small girl in our suburban house in Dublin, sitting on one of the steps of the stairs, refusing to cry despite some tragedy involving a kitten.

'How did you find out?'

'She telephoned him when we were in his kitchen today. He tried to talk in a kind of meaningless code but I knew right away. And although I couldn't hear what she was saying, I could hear her tone of voice. She was obviously so pleased to be talking to him and he had to say things like "I do. Of course I do" so I knew what was going on.'

'What a shit!' I said.

'Don't overreact, Dad.'

'I don't want you to get hurt.'

'It's no big deal.'

I thought that I could see the onset of tears in her eyes and wished that Laura were there to comfort her with intuitive understanding. She was determined to be brave and I felt crass and intrusive.

'We weren't going out together or anything,' she said, 'but I still feel that he should have told me. We had talked about things like that.'

'I understand,' I said without really understanding. 'I don't want to interfere. But I understand. I remember how deeply I felt about things when I was your age.'

'Really? I can't imagine you in this kind of situation. I only know what you were like from seeing the photographs of you. Tell me something about yourself. Something that happened to you.'

If you only knew what's happening to me now, I thought, and the layers of irony that it matters so much for me to hide from you.

She sat there, looking a little more cheerful and interested in what she was about to hear.

'Something awful?'

'Preferably.'

It was easy to decide on the incident.

'A million years ago, when I was young in Kells, the place that boys went to so that they could meet girls was a riverbank at the top of the town. Just a little bit out on a country road. You know the way that the river Blackwater curls around Kells so there are bridges on so many of the roads leading into it? Anyway, there was one part of the river where kids went to swim and there were relatively private places between trees where people conducted the fairly modest courtships that were common in those days. To a boy, girls were an exotic species who had to be approached with great caution. They travelled in packs and their special weapon was mockery. It could be absolutely devastating.'

Rachael laughed. Perhaps she had some sympathy with what I was describing or perhaps she was amused at the antiquity of that world. How could she possibly comprehend those long summer days when my friend Jim Muldoon and I would smoke Craven A cigarettes and wonder, with intense frustration, how we could contrive to bump into a particular girl and start a conversation that might lead to any kind of physical contact? Hours of intense and anxious planning seldom resulted in any success.

'So there was a girl,' I said, 'and her name was Alice Dunne, and I believe that she became a nurse. But I'm talking about when she was, say, fifteen, or perhaps sixteen, and I was more or less the same age. I was home on holidays from boarding school and I longed to get to know her properly and to kiss her. I'd guess that was about the pinnacle of my ambition. So there were agonizing weeks of hanging around, trying to encounter her as if by accident, while she was on her own, rather than with her two friends because while she was with them I'd never have the courage to talk to her. Then, one day, I was leaving a shop and there she was, about to come into it. I couldn't believe my luck. We said hello and then I asked her if she'd like to meet me by the river and she said, all right, she would, on the following afternoon, at three o'clock.'

As I recounted this to Rachael, the memory became more vivid. I could remember exact details of the town that summer, the people on the street, the warm, dusty stillness in the interior of Paddy Laracey's shop where I bought my comics, the old men who sat on the base of the market cross that had once been used as a gallows. The town was old and celebrated; tourists came there and stopped their cars and photographed each other against any of the crosses or St Columbcille's House or the Round Tower or the remains of the ancient fortifications. I had grown up in a world fashioned from old stones.

'Dad!' Rachael said. 'Do you realize how long it is since you've said anything? Are you dreaming?'

'Am I dreaming or remembering? Some memories are like dreams. Time loses its logic.'

'Before you get all morose,' she said, 'tell me about your date!'

'Well, the following day I was so excited I couldn't eat either breakfast or lunch. Isn't that ridiculous, but it's true. I told nobody that I was going to meet her. I didn't tell my best friend in case he turned up and spoiled it. I spent ages getting ready and set out in really good time. I actually had to walk past her house to get there. I walked past it quickly. Then I got to the bridge and went down along the bank of the river. There were some older boys swimming there. I knew them but they weren't friends of mine so they ignored me. After about an hour they dressed and went back to the town and I was there by myself. I think I waited until six o'clock. I really think that I can remember the Angelus ringing. She didn't turn up. I was almost sick with disappointment and the humiliation of knowing that all her friends would know that I had been left there.'

'Poor Dad!' Rachael said, half-sympathetic, half-mocking. I have no doubt that she saw me as a ridiculous figure in this doleful anecdote.

'That isn't the worst bit,' I said.

'There's more? What else could possibly happen?'

'Why am I turning myself into a figure of fun?'

'No, you're being good to tell me,' she said. Her own hurt or grievance had abated. She was involved in this anecdote; in some small way it was a part of her own past. She leaned forward expect-antly, looking young and pretty rejuvenated by my misfortune and for a few seconds I thought that she looked like my memories of Alice. How well did I remember her? Did she have sallow skin, a certain intensity of manner, curious eyes, a long, striding walk and a laugh that was adult in its expression?

'I walked back to town, wishing that I had brought my bike so that I could get past her house quickly. I went down Cannon Street and turned right to walk down past the cinema and there she was coming towards me with her two friends. I wanted to die. I really, really wanted to die. They seemed to be laughing. They always seemed to be laughing. I couldn't avoid them. I couldn't just walk past them. So I stopped and I said to her "I thought you were going to meet me?" "You must be mad," she said. "Why would I bother meeting *you*?"'

'Poor Dad!' Rachael said again but I wondered if she did not feel some retrospective shame at being the daughter of so pathetic a figure. As if to reassure me, she added, 'She sounds like a right little bitch!'

'Probably not,' I said, gratefully. 'It was a different era. There was very little openness. The games people played were entirely different.'

'So what did you say?'

'Nothing. I just stood there and they walked away.'

'You must have felt terrible?'

'Terrible.'

Despite all the years that had passed, I could still feel the shame as if it were something applied to my skin. Did that shame burn out some of my natural feelings and leave me a victim to predilections of disappointment?

'Did you ever see her again?'

'To be absolutely honest, and this is odd, I can't say whether I did or not. I'd love to be able to say that I met her years later and that she was fat and unattractive but I have no memories of her whatsoever after that afternoon. It was a small town and I must have seen her but the impressions are totally gone. I certainly never spoke to her again. Years later a cousin of hers I had gone to school with told me that she was a nurse somewhere or other.'

'It all seems like something from an old storybook.'

'It does even to me. I can imagine the illustrations! It was the end of summer for me. Not just of that summer but of all summers. It was never a season that I looked forward to again. I became an autumn person.'

'I'd like to have known you when you were young.'

'It was a different world,' I said.

'Jack's father was very poor when he was growing up. I mean seriously poor.'

'I know that,' I said. 'I've read the book that he wrote about his childhood. I'll loan it to you if you like. Would you like to read it?'

'Some time. Is it good?'

'I think it is. And I've got to assume it's honest.'

'I'm glad that we're not poor.'

'Did you ever worry about that?'

'Yes, I used to. Ever since I first heard about Cinderella. I used to worry that I'd wake up and everything would be gone.'

'I wonder where that insecurity came from?' I said, touched by the simple way in which she had expressed her feelings.

'Maybe it's just the reverse of people who are sad or poor dreaming about being happy.'

'That's a good point.'

'I used to fear that Mum and you would split up.'

'Never,' I said. 'It's great to have a beautiful and intelligent daughter.'

'I don't feel beautiful or intelligent.'

'You must. It's important. You should be enjoying both characteristics.'

'I feel a bit stupid with Jack.'

'Why?'

'He just seems to know so much more than I do. And he's done much more.'

'Well, he is older.'

'It's not just that. He takes an interest in all kinds of things.'

We heard the sound of Laura's car and our conversation ended in slight restraint.

'This is very cosy,' Laura said, when she came into the room. She spoke with a hint of irritation. I suppose that after a busy day she was affronted by our indolence. She gave me a tight-lipped kiss and agreed that she had earned a gin and tonic. The tension she brought into the room seemed to alter the space between objects. In some mysterious way, distances appeared to be greater.

'Did you have a bad day, Mum?' Rachael asked.

'Not particularly. Why do you ask?'

'You seem tired.'

'I've just done a day's work. It's hardly surprising if I'm tired. I work in a very stressful environment.'

'I'm not criticizing you. It was only an observation.'

'I sometimes feel that I'm on trial when I come through the door and get marked down for not being positive or cheerful enough.'

'Now you're just being silly,' Rachael said in the tone of a mother admonishing a naughty child. Laura turned to her in a conciliatory way.

'Am I being silly? I'm sorry. I'm so glad that we'll soon get away for a couple of weeks.'

'You work much too hard,' I said. 'I hope they appreciate you.'

'I certainly appreciate this,' she said, swirling the gin and tonic around so that the ice chimed cheerfully against the glass. 'What did you do today?'

'I was remembering things for Rachael. Coming of age in Kells. An attempt at anthropology.'

'The nineteenth-century childhood?' she said smiling.

'Something like that.'

'It was very interesting,' Rachael said. 'It's so different from the way things are now.'

'When I was growing up, it was a small town as well but obviously not as backward as Dad's.'

I found that I resented the word 'backward'.

'It wasn't Tobacco Road!'

'It's you who always describes it as a different world.'

'That doesn't mean that it was backward.'

'You're being over-sensitive!'

'You are, Dad,' Rachael said.

'Am I? Maybe I am. I think that talking about it today has made me feel protective towards it. I wish I had a better understanding of my childhood. Other people seem so certain about the implications of theirs. I'm sometimes lost in mine.'

'I think my childhood was very usual for the times,' Laura said. 'I'm not certain it has endless implications for analysis.'

'I love to know about you,' Rachael said. 'I think it was only a few years ago that I realized that both of you had once been young.'

'Born old,' I said. 'What a terrible prospect. Almost as bad as perpetual youth.'

'It just seems unfair that I know so little about you both when you know so much about me.'

I knew that she was attempting to make a serious point about roles but something about my involvement with Ingrid prompted me to avoid any discussion of family in case I betrayed the confusion I was feeling.

'I think I felt the same about my own parents,' I said.

'So did I,' Laura said as if to draw us all together in some treaty of accord.

'Jack told me that he hardly knows his own father. He's lived for most of his life with his mother. He says that he doesn't love her.'

'Did he say that?' Laura sounded shocked. 'Why would he say a thing like that?'

'Jack said that both his parents slept around a lot before they got divorced. He doesn't love his father either.'

'That's the world they lived in,' Laura said. 'I think that people in theatre are quite promiscuous.'

This proposition startled me. We could be within seconds of discovering what Jack felt about Ingrid.

'He said that both of them always slept with people much younger than themselves. I think that's disgusting, don't you?'

'I don't think I'd be quite so judgemental about it,' Laura said.

'What do you think, Dad?'

'I wouldn't like to generalize,' I said, remembering, suddenly, how, as a child, I used to blush when I was unable to give a direct answer to a question.

'Well I think it's disgusting.'

'You're fully entitled to that opinion,' I said, sounding defensive. 'But people can sometimes fall in love in ways that you might consider inappropriate.'

'It's creepy,' Rachael said.

'Anyway,' Laura said, 'Ingrid isn't that young.'

She went across the room to the drinks cabinet. Nobody spoke as she poured more gin and then tonic into her glass. The silence intensified; the tinkling of ice assumed a momentary menace.

'When Jack said young, he wasn't talking about Ingrid. He meant much younger,' Rachael said. 'He once found his mother in bed with one of his friends. Wouldn't that make you cringe?'

'And what happened?' I asked.

'Nothing. His mother didn't seem to care. He's not friendly with the guy any more.'

Laura had poured me a very large gin and tonic. The taste appeared to concentrate at the back of my throat and I coughed, an old and spluttering sound, like something heard in the smoking room of a club. They both stared at me with a kind of detachment, as if I were there to amuse them but was not succeeding. I remember how Rachael had almost discovered me with Ingrid and coughed again.

'Are you all right, Dad?'

'Your mother pours a lethal gin and tonic.'

'Will I get you more tonic?'

'No, don't bother. I'll just treat it with a little more respect. That's interesting about Jack. When did he tell you all this?'

'Over the past few days.'

'He obviously trusts you,' Laura said.

'Wouldn't you think so? Then I find out.'

'Find out what?'

'That he's got a girlfriend,' Rachael said in a dejected tone of voice, not looking at either of us.

'Oh darling!' Laura said. 'Do you mind? Do you feel really bad about it?'

'I'm going to leave you both to have a chat,' I said, bringing my glass into the study. I felt renewed by the stillness and by the sight of books on shelves. I went to the window and was surprised to see a man walking away down our drive. There had not been a knock on the door, so his presence was difficult to explain. Despite the mildness of the evening, he was wearing a raincoat and a tweed cap. As if he had sensed that he was being watched, he glanced back over his shoulder, then continued walking to the gate.

I left my drink on a table and went outside. I walked quickly down the drive, without a plan, without knowing what I would say to the man when I caught up with him. I hadn't seen the direction he had taken but since he wasn't on the long straight stretch of road to the right of the gate, I turned left where he might just have had time to go around the corner. Outside the gate, smoke curled from a cigarette butt that had been thrown into the middle of the road. I stopped and stared at it as if I could deduct some significant clue about the smoker. The evening was still and peaceful and I felt a little foolish about the logic of my pursuit. I walked quickly to the corner, not knowing what to expect. When I got there he would have to be in view because the road was straight until it reached the crossroads. I increased my pace, conscious of my breathing and the heavy, rather flat sound of my footsteps. Middle age, with all its attendant infirmities, was beginning to be the measure that defined me.

A car came accelerating towards me. After a few seconds I recognized the fat, red face of our local doctor. He waved at me and as he drove past I heard an incongruous snatch of loud pop music. I turned the corner and I saw the man well ahead of me, walking quickly but with a pronounced limp, towards a blue car. Instinctively, I increased my pace into a kind of trot or lope, like a participant in some minority interest athletics event. The man got into the passenger side of the car which, almost immediately, drove away towards the crossroads and the city. It was too far away for me to read the registration number. I was even doubtful about the make, although I thought it might have been a Volvo. I stood, panting, in the middle of the road, staring into the distance. The triumphant singing of a blackbird in a tree near to where I was standing was like an ironic contrast to the sense of failure that I experienced. Standing alone on the deserted road, I felt reluctant to commit myself to any course of action; anything that I did would be an acceptance of defeat. I attempted to remember the man's face from my brief glimpse of it. I remembered nothing, with the possible exception of a dark line of moustache. The blue car was no help, the raincoat and cap were anonymous and forgettable. The fact that he had got into the car ruled out any comforting possibility that he had been a passing walker who had come up the drive to get a better look at the house. In some way he had to connect to the series of odd happenings that emanated from Cromer. I felt threatened and concerned about the safety of Laura and Rachael. I pictured them back in the house, intent in conversation, the front door open, unaware that anything odd had happened. I walked back quickly. The cigarette butt had been flattened by the wheels of the doctor's car.

The house looked secure and peaceful, one window catching light in a shimmering reflection. I closed the hall door and listened at the kitchen door. They were talking quietly and, as I went into the study, I heard the welcome sound of Rachael's laughter.

FOURTEEN

THE DAYS BEFORE Laura and Rachael left for their holidays passed intolerably slowly. I seemed to be locked into a spirit of inaction, waiting for something to happen. I felt guilty not to be going with them and pretended that the time would be an ideal opportunity to begin work on a new book. Laura and I planned to spend two weeks in Amsterdam when Rachael went back to school.

I hoped that Ingrid would telephone again but she did not. One afternoon, I drove to the city suburbs with Rachael and we went to the cinema. The film had been widely praised and Rachael enjoyed it but I found it trite, although I was stirred by a sex scene. The naked body of the actress reminded me so vividly of Ingrid that I found myself looking for the tattoo. On another afternoon I spent some hours drinking with Barbara. She was in particularly good form, bawdily funny about the variety of her young lovers. I could imagine how deeply Rachael would have disapproved. One of her books had been bought for German television and she insisted on paying for each round. I remember wondering if I could use her as a character in something and what aspects I would change to prevent her from being recognized. It would be very difficult; her personality was very much a sum of its parts. She existed for me as a collection of traits, each interdependent on each other as in some cellular structure.

On the following morning I drove to Blessington and sat by the lake, considering the possibility of a book of short stories that would rediscover the world of my boyhood, the world that Rachael considered to be so inaccessibly remote but which was still sending out signals that came down through the years, powerful and persistent, to the present. I wasn't certain I could find the degree of objectivity that the project would require. Perhaps, I decided, it would be better to let it seep into something else that I was writing just as it continued to seep into my life.

I didn't contact Cromer. His house had become a shrine to Ingrid's absence. I didn't want to risk hearing another conversation between them that indicated their need for each other or the urgency of their desire. Driving past the house, I would look for some hint of her presence, some intangible suggestion that she was there. The days became aimless, time to be passed before she came home.

I drove Laura and Rachael to the airport just as, one year later, as I have described at the opening of this journal, we were to make an identical journey. I felt guilt and excitement. The thought of the two and a half weeks stretching ahead was like the prospect of a new way of life. In the city I bought flowers, champagne and three Leonard Cohen tapes. I had a drink in O'Brien's, the pub that I liked, in Sussex Terrace. An acquaintance of mine called to me from a shadowed corner where he was attempting to hide from his hangover and I joined him there, feeling so positive and optimistic that I lifted his low spirits up to a relatively good mood. He directed television commercials and was a reliable purveyor of gossip. I asked him if he had heard of any protection money being extorted from English people living in Dublin. He said that he had not and added that since he knew many in his own line of business he regarded it as improbable. However, he conceded, a television crew from the BBC making a documentary on women in Irish life had been put under pressure for refusing to hire, as security men, well-known members of a south city gang.

'I don't know why they picked on that shoot in particular,' he said. 'Someone told me that one of the sparks was a cousin of a member of the gang. But that may not be true.'

'What happened in the end?'

'Nothing much. They were given police protection for a while then the whole thing just fizzled out.'

Apart from two businessmen sitting at the counter and drinking pints of stout we were the only people in the bar. A barman came from a door behind the counter, looked around and enquired, without much interest, 'Everybody all right?' When nobody answered, he went back through the door.

'I've always liked it here,' I said, 'especially at times like now when it's not busy. Then it's caught in a time warp.'

On one wall hung a large oil painting by Harry Kernoff. It depicted two drinkers, one with a face of almost vulpine cunning, the other looking more convivial but stupid, squinting out with an air of baffled good humour that could turn sour very easily. The names of scores of Dublin pubs were painted in the background.

'I was here,' my acquaintance said, 'the day that Harry Kernoff came in to add the name of O'Brien's to that painting.'

'Really? Is that a kind of forgery or is it all right if it's added by the painter? I remember him well around town with his big black hat. He was hardly more than five feet tall.'

I had a second drink, then drove home, listening to one of the Leonard Cohen tapes, feeling almost happy. It was late afternoon and there was a good chance that Ingrid would have returned. She knew that this was the day I would start to have the house to myself. Because I was relaxed I expected I would hear from her, rather than assuming that she would have changed her mind. An envelope with my name written on it in large, angular, unfamiliar writing was lying on the hall floor. I took it into the study and my mood began to change to one of apprehension. The square, white envelope was made from fine paper. I opened it carefully with the seldom-used silver letter opener that I kept on my desk. Most of the letters that I received deserved no special treatment. I took out a single sheet of paper, folded in four. Her writing touched me by its childish precision. I had to remind myself that she was using a foreign language.

> *Dear You,*
>
>   *It is so long since we have been talking that it is strange to write to you now. The days I spent in London were good. I got the things I needed to make fine masks. I also discovered an alternative to gold leaf that is very nearly as good but costs much less so I can use it a lot.*
>
>   *I would like to see you. I will call around to your house at six o'clock today. If this is not all right telephone me. Let it ring three times and then hang up. That way I will know not to go.*
>
>   *Love, I.*

I read it twice; the first time for information, the second time for pleasure. The intimacy of the conspiracy appealed to me; we would be bound together by complex codes of behaviour. There was a commitment in 'I would like to see you' that delighted me. It seemed to promise that we had gone through the aphelion of our relationship and that we could expect warmth and intimacy.

It was twenty past four. In one hour and forty minutes I would hear her knock on the door. I would greet her. I would hardly know what to say.

At half past six I couldn't wait any longer. I telephoned her number. It was engaged. I had prepared the guest bedroom, arranged the flowers in a vase on the dressing table beside a bucket of ice. I couldn't help noticing that the room seemed a little vulgar; the appurtenances of a love nest made it look more like a photograph from a tabloid newspaper than a bright and welcoming room. I tried to understand why the room in which we had made love in Cromer's house had never assumed this characteristic but could not do so. Perhaps it had something to do with the guilt that I felt in using our home in this way; the closed door of Rachael's room across the landing was like a muted reproach.

I telephoned again; the instrument that conveyed so many faltering changes in our relationship had become malign once more. The number was engaged. The entire event was going out of focus and becoming unreal. If it were not for the letter, folded carefully and put back into its envelope on my desk, I would begin to wonder if I had got the details wrong. Simple details appeared to be complex; should I have rung her three times, where were we meeting, how could she be so late? I walked to the hall door and opened it, just as her car slowed outside the gate. I was tempted to shut the door quickly so that I could shake away my anxieties but she had seen me. She waved as she came up the drive, a small, sideways movement of her hand as if she were acknowledging applause. I waved back, then walked nervously down the steps to open the car door. She swung her legs out in a manner that was curiously athletic and attractive, a single, sprightly movement.

'I'm late,' she said, 'There was some difficulty about getting away. I'm sorry. Did you mind?'

'Not at all,' I lied. 'I guessed something must have happened. It's good to see you.'

She was dressed rather formally in a white silk shirt and a long black skirt. She looked like a member of an orchestra. She was beautiful.

I was disconcerted by the perfection of her appearance. My plans appeared tawdry and inappropriate. Did she think that we were going out to dinner? Perhaps I had read far too much into 'I would like to see you'. The phrase, on rapid reconsideration, seemed to hold very little promise. I couldn't understand how I had interpreted it so favourably. I followed her into the house. She looked at me questioningly for a moment as we stood in the hall.

'We're in to the right,' I said, pointing to the study door. She entered the room and sat down, unexpectedly, on the chair behind my desk.

'Gin and tonic?'

'Thank you.'

It disconcerted me to see her sitting there. I had imagined her on the sofa or on a chair near to the window. She looked like the receptionist in some upmarket business, cool and poised and not very welcoming to an unfamiliar face. As I poured the drinks I was aware of her watching me and this made me awkward. I spilled some tonic, put more ice into a glass than I had intended. I felt oafish in my sweater and cords, as if I had found myself attending the wrong event.

'You've been keeping well?' she said as I left her drink beside her letter on the desk. Her tone of voice conveyed this as information rather than as a question.

'Yes. And you?'

'Yes. I liked London. I always like London.'

'You say that you got everything you needed.'

'I did. And I saw some shows. And some friends.'

I immediately wondered how many of these friends were male and with how many of them she might have made love. Her eyes were frank and inquisitorial, inviting me to be candid with my comments. I sat on a chair near to the desk.

'When did you get back?'

'Yesterday evening. Laura left today?'

'This morning.'

She was wearing a diamond ring on her wedding finger. The large, single stone had an ice-blue, luminous intensity. I watched it, preparing to be hypnotized.

'Is that an engagement ring?'

'This? No, it's paste. It's only fun.'

'Did you get it in London?'

'No. I've had it for years. I actually got it in Stockholm. Why do you ask?'

'Just curious. I'd never seen you wearing it before. There are so many things,' I added, without caution, 'that I don't know about.'

'Ask me some of them.'

'Now?'

'Why not?'

She was smiling provocatively, daring me to meet some challenge. I couldn't remember any of the things that I really wanted to know.

'Have you brothers and sisters?'

'One brother. He's a lawyer in Düsseldorf.'

'Have you had many lovers?'

'Ah,' she said, 'this is something you really want to know, isn't it? Why do men always want to know? Women don't. Every lover I've ever had got around to asking that question.'

'What do you tell them?'

'I think of a number. Twenty-five? Thirty? Then I tell him he's the best because that's the question that's really being asked.'

'So you tell a lie and everybody's happy?'

'No. Not everybody. But the person the lie is told to is very happy.'

'I'm already sorry that I asked the question. Now I'll never know what you think of me.'

'I really like you,' she said.

The atmosphere changed and became more relaxed.

'You intimidated me,' I said, 'by being so dressed up.'

'I'm going into Dublin but not for two hours. I'm meeting a friend of mine for supper. She wants to talk to me. She's in some kind of trouble.'

My disappointment must have been evident.

'Come on!' she said. 'It gave me a good reason for going out. Bill thinks I'm on my way there already.'

'What if he sees the car?'

'He won't. He's settled in for the evening with two videos.'

'Or Barbara?'

'We can't just worry about everything. We can think of some excuse.'

'I'm sorry,' I said. 'I know that I'm making a complete mess of everything so far.'

'I like this room.'

'There's a nicer one upstairs.'

'Is there?' she said, standing up abruptly. 'Show me.'

As I followed her up the stairs, the movement of her skirt against the swell of her buttocks was intensely provocative. I could picture her skin and almost feel its warmth. She must have been aware of the effect that she had because, near to the top of the stairs, she glanced back over her shoulder and smiled.

'It's that door on the right.'

'Isn't this nice,' she said, although to me the room still looked tawdry. She turned and kissed me with a directness that reminded me of the first time I had met her with Cromer. Her tongue tasted of toothpaste. I couldn't bear to wait. We undressed each other quickly and made love with trust and excitement. Afterwards, drinking champagne and listening to Leonard Cohen, we talked quietly until I realized that I was attempting to postpone her departure.

'I wish you didn't have to go,' I said, wondering at the beauty of the tattoo against the paleness of her skin. She smiled at me, strands of hair falling across her forehead.

'We have what we have,' she said, an expression that sounded so idiomatic that she must have heard it from someone. 'I'm not going to waste any more time regretting what we haven't got.'

I kissed her and listened to the song, a bitter, brooding number from 'Death of a Ladies' Man'.

'Tell me about the friend you're meeting.'

She looked at her watch on the bedside table.

'I went to school with her,' she said. 'She married an Irish architect. He's a bastard. You would not believe the things that he says to her. She wants to leave him but because they got married in this country she can't get a divorce. And she has young children she worries about.'

I kissed her, moved by the real concern in her voice. She kissed me back abstractedly, her lips remaining puckered for seconds after we had moved apart. I reached out and held her tightly as if I could use strength to possess her. She frowned.

'I'm sorry,' I said. 'I didn't hurt you?'

'No, I was thinking about my friend. This isn't a very good country for women, is it?'

'It's getting better,' I said defensively, feeling that I had been accused of something.

'He beats her,' she said. 'He broke two of her fingers once.'

'She shouldn't stay with him.'

'She's pregnant.'

'Even so.'

'It isn't his baby.'

'Does he know that?'

'I don't think so.'

She looked at her watch again.

'Bugger!' she said. 'I've got to go. I don't even have time to have a shower.'

She got out of bed. Her perfume seemed to intensify as she dressed quickly and effortlessly.

'Up you get!' she said to me.

'Why?'

'Because you want to see me to my car.'

'I love you.'

'I love you.'

'Was it good?' I asked, wishing I didn't need the reassurance.

'It was lovely. Where's the bathroom?'

'Left and left.'

She took her bag and I missed her being there, felt a chill of loneliness enter the room. I got dressed. An odd silence settled on the house. I assumed that she was making-up and wished that I could witness this ritual. In the early years of our marriage I would watch Laura as she put on eyeliner or lipstick or brushed her hair, the narrow arc of her wrist blurring with the speed of the strokes.

The sensuality of these movements had always attracted me. One was witnessing a quest for some perfection.

When she came back into the room she looked as distant and as attractive as when she had arrived.

'You're beautiful,' I said.

'Thank you.'

'I wish I had seen you making-up.'

'You can the next time!'

'When will that be?'

'Soon. I'll call you.'

'I'll be really jealous thinking of you with Bill.'

'Don't be. The sex thing was big between us once but not really now.'

She kissed me lightly on the lips.

'I must rush.'

'Please call me as soon as you can.'

I could hear, with some disquiet, the pressure that I was putting on her as if contact was something that I had earned.

We went down the stairs. She stood for a moment in the hallway, looking around.

'I meant to show you some paintings,' I said. 'There's one or two that I think you'll like.'

'Show them to me the next time.'

'Of course. I hope that you can help your friend with her problems.'

We went out to her car. I opened the door.

'That was wonderful,' she said. 'I enjoyed myself.'

'I'm so glad.'

'I like your view,' she said, looking towards the road and the mist-covered mountains in the distance. The magpies in the wood were clattering angrily and there was a faint smell of turf smoke in the air. She stood beside the car as if about to be photographed for a motor advertisement. It was an unreal moment.

'Is something wrong?' she asked.

I reached out and touched her arm.

'I'm missing you,' I said.

She got into the car and rummaged through her handbag, looking for keys, produced them with a flourish and smiled at me. She drove out the gate without saying anything else.

In a morose humour I tidied the room, taking the sheets off the bed, throwing out the flowers and the empty champagne bottle. This stripping seemed to have a ritualistic purpose but when I had finished and everything was back to normal, I could still smell sex in the room and, more elusively, the hint of her perfume as if she were hidden away behind some piece of furniture. The bathroom was completely tidy. When I looked in the bin I discovered three or four rolled-up pieces of tissue paper. They were all that were left from those cathartic moments of passion, things to be discarded or hidden. I felt sad that one could not write a relationship like a book and have it there to browse over when the inspiration had passed. Already some details of what had happened were smudging and assuming a slight feeling of unreality.

I went downstairs to the study and sat where she had sat, behind my desk. I imagined, in an uncharacteristic flight of fancy, that I could feel her presence there, approving of me.

The telephone rang. Rachael's voice sounded near to me and breathless as if she had just run in from outside. She had lots of news. Jack had taken her out to lunch and had been sweet and she thought that she had been a little unfair in what she had said about him. They had great plans for the next few days and here was Mum.

I dreaded hearing her voice. I would have to avoid sounding guilty or abject or false. At least Ingrid had gone; the conversation would have been agony if she had been listening.

Laura sounded relaxed. They were having a lovely time. They missed me. Yes, her parents were in excellent form. She hoped that I was looking after myself. The irony of this was so great that I almost laughed with embarrassment.

'I feel so much more relaxed,' she said.

'You've reverted to childhood?'

She laughed.

'It's true. I even had rock buns and fairy cakes this afternoon.'

'No honey?'

'Rachael told you she's having a good time?'

'Jack has featured?'

'Yes. That was very nice for her.'

In the background I could hear a radio playing and her father's distinctive voice. I was afraid that I was going to blurt out some indiscretion, like someone who has telephoned a late-night radio show. She was waiting for me to say something intimate, to define a need, and I wanted to but feared that she would detect the false note in my voice. I loved her and needed the core of truth that she brought to our marriage but I also needed the redefinition that I was finding with Ingrid. There may have been an air of unreality about it, an unnerving softening of focus but it still provided something new and important.

'I miss you both,' I said. 'The house is like a morgue.'

'Are you looking forward to our holiday?'

'Very much.'

'We miss you. Here's Dad. He wants to have a word with you.'

Her father's emphatic voice appeared to hold some note of rebuke.

'Pity you couldn't come over,' he said. 'It's glorious here. We could have played some tennis.'

' I'd have liked that,' I said. 'How's Audrey?'

'She's very well. She's just visiting a friend.'

'Please give her my love.'

'I'll do that. When are we going to have another book from you? It's been far too long!'

'Soon I hope.'

'I re-read one the other day. The one where they go to Algiers. Very clever.'

'Laura and Rachael are both enjoying themselves?'

'Indeed they are. Indeed they are. I'll put Laura back on to you now. Good to talk to you.'

'I hope you're getting some work done,' Laura said.

I thought she sounded a little reproachful. She would have liked me to be there as a part of the family holiday, flying the flag of domestic contentment.

'I love you,' I said and the words came out sounding right.

'I love you too. I can't wait to be with you.'

'Me too. Tell Rachael I love her.'

When I put back the receiver, I felt threatened by the silence in the house. Then a floorboard creaked, contracting after the warmth of the day and I became aware, in an almost sensory way, of all the empty rooms filled with fading light, the imperceptible moving of boards, the stillness anticipating something about to happen. It was as if I could see the trapped heat caught in corners, see the furniture tensed, be aware of a special quality of stillness. I don't know how long I remained there, open to this experience before it vanished like a dream. I poured myself a whiskey and watched light change the colour of the mountains from an intense blue to a pale violet. I felt contented, as if the day had been without complication and my conscience was clear.

FIFTEEN

CROMER TELEPHONED the following morning and suggested that we go for a walk. I could think of no graceful way of refusing. I arranged to collect him at his house in the hope of having some contact with Ingrid but when I got there he was standing by the side of the road, dressed as if going for a shooting weekend in Norfolk: tweed cap, tweed jacket, twill trousers and polished brown shoes.

'Is there something I don't know about?' I asked when he got into the passenger seat.

'What's that?'

'Your clothes! Has some member of the gentry invited you to a shoot?'

'I'm not that open to humour about it,' he said abruptly then, after a pause, 'Do I look totally bloody ridiculous?'

'Not totally. But you're a little overdressed.'

'Fuck it!' he said with surprising emphasis and I realized that he was not going to find any humour in the situation. 'I knew it was wrong.'

'Perhaps the cap most of all,' I said, a little meanly.

'It's Ingrid,' he said. 'She bought the entire outfit in London. She described them as "comfortable country clothes". Nothing could be farther from the truth but she insisted I wear them today. I feel a proper prick!'

'I was exaggerating,' I said. 'I'm getting used to the new image already.'

'It's ridiculous!' he said. 'A working-class lad dressed up as a toff!'

'Come on,' I said. 'It's a long time since you've been working class. You changed class on the day you first went to college.'

We had been driving along a narrow road that bordered a state plantation. The tall pine trees were too evenly planted to be beautiful, yet the wood looked impenetrably dark and rather interesting. Then we turned a corner, away from the trees and towards a valley where I knew he had never been.

'I don't think anyone ever changes class,' he said. 'Upward mobility is little more than an optical illusion. You can assume the characteristics of another class as easily as putting on a suit of clothes but you can't really fake the attitudes.'

He sounded so serious about this that I thought it would be tactless to get into an argument about it. I knew, from his work, that he liked to assume that the class to which he had once belonged had a certain rugged individuality that added depth and strength to his writing. He had a sentimental attachment to his roots, yet his success was the result of his rejection of them. Now he sat beside me in his tweeds and twills, as uncomfortable as a boy dressed up for a party, perceiving himself as a parody of something that he usually professed to despise.

We drove downhill along a dusty road, then I parked in a space before a rusting gate that led into an unkempt field.

'Come on,' I said. 'We walk from here.'

He got out of the jeep a little reluctantly, as if the walk had not been his own idea.

'It's lovely here,' he said.

We climbed a wall and followed a path down into the valley towards a small dark lake in which the water appeared to be motionless. The path ended and we walked through bracken and ferns. On the other side of the valley there was a holy well and I could see a thorn tree with ribbons on its branches. The air was filled with a suggestion of recently sawn wood.

'Let's walk around the lake,' I said.

'What's it called?'

'I don't even know if it has a name. I'd have to look at the Ordnance Survey map at home. It's supposed to be very deep but who knows?'

After we had walked for about ten minutes he turned and looked back towards the road.

'Good Lord,' he said. 'It's a much steeper path than it appeared. Look at how far we've come!'

The jeep seemed to be tiny; the climb upwards more sheer than our brisk descent had suggested. A hare bounded from grasses in front of us, turning its pale, startled eyes towards us for a moment before vanishing into ferns.

'It's years,' Cromer said, 'since I saw a rabbit.'

We reached another narrow pathway near the edge of the lake and walked along it in single file like pilgrims. It occurred to me that there was something shrine-like about the lake. As we got closer to it I could see that there were movements on the surface, small, slow undulations of water that appeared to be moving across an icy stillness. If it were a place of worship – as the holy well on the other side still was – it would belong to some threatening God who would need to be pacified rather than praised. There was something hypnotic about the darkness of the water. Nothing was reflected in it and even the reeds that grew along its edges were dark and threatening.

'All those rags on that bush over there,' Cromer said, 'how did they get there?'

'There's a holy well here. Pilgrims used to come in big numbers in the second week of August but it doesn't happen very much now.'

'You're never very far from the pagan in Ireland, are you?' he said and I wondered if he were getting back at me for my remarks about his clothes.

'How do you mean?'

'Your customs,' he said vaguely, then a bullet whined past us and landed with a loud clump somewhere in the undergrowth.

'Jesus!' Cromer said and we both flung ourselves to the ground and the inadequate protection of the grasses that lined the path.

The second bullet sounded louder than the first and this time I could hear the report of a rifle. Cromer and I were facing each other. He was grimacing with pain and sweat was beaded on his forehead. He looked at me with something like an appeal for help as if unaware of my own fear. I heard, from the distance, the cawing of disturbed rooks. Then there was total silence.

'It's my ankle,' Cromer said.

I did not know what to do. I wanted to remain there, motionless, and wait for something to happen. I feared the idea of movement more than I feared all ideas of the unexpected.

'We can't stay here,' Cromer said. 'We're sitting ducks.'

I turned slowly and looked towards the hill on the other side of the lake. It was steeper than on our side and the vegetation was even more profuse. There were no obvious paths upwards. Near to the summit there was a thick growth of gorse bushes in which someone could be hiding. The calmness of the valley and the deep inscrutability of the lake were difficult to comprehend.

'Maybe,' I whispered, 'it was someone shooting rabbits.' I wanted to believe this. 'That could be it.'

'Then they're a fucking bad shot! And where the fuck are they?'

I looked along the line of gorse bushes for any sign of movement but there was nothing.

'There could be some fucking madman out there,' Cromer said. 'What the hell are we going to do?'

I looked around again. The valley was suffused with stillness.

'I'm not staying any longer,' I said, surprised by my decisiveness. I resented his helplessness and the burden of his injury. 'How bad is your ankle?'

'Not too bad.'

'Another possibility,' I said, 'is that the IRA are training near here. They use the mountains for that. Those shots could have been warning us off.'

'The IRA!' he said. 'That's everything I need. I bet that old cunt is behind this in some way. You wouldn't listen when I told you.'

I stood up, facing the lake. Nothing happened.

'Let's go,' I said.

I reached out to help him get to his feet but he ignored the gesture. I started walking up the path, resisting the temptation to look back. After a few minutes I stopped and looked around. He was fifteen or twenty yards behind me, walking with an elaborate limp that irritated me. His new clothes were dishevelled.

The quality of the light had changed. The colours had softened in tone so that the land looked more gentle and even the lake was less dark. Cromer came up beside me.

'What are you looking at?' he asked, red-faced and exasperated.

'Just where we were,' I said 'It all looks so peaceful.'

'Fuck that!'

He pushed past me.

'We haven't far to go,' he said, as if in encouragement. 'Let's keep up the pace!'

I could see the jeep. A woman, riding a bicycle, looked curiously at us.

'Nothing's going to happen now,' I said, following him and for a few seconds I feared that this foolish expression of confidence would precipitate some disaster.

Cromer stopped at the gate.

'Only in Ireland!' he said emphatically.

I felt humiliated by what had happened to us. We got into the jeep. Cromer rubbed his forehead with a handkerchief.

'Whose idea was this walk?' I asked in an effort at humour.

'Nobody knew where we were going,' he said. 'You didn't mention it to anyone, did you?'

'No.'

'So when you think about it that way, it can't really have been planned specifically for us. The same would have happened to anyone who went walking there.'

'Perhaps.'

'It's important to think about,' he said. 'It means that it doesn't necessarily connect with anything else that's happened.'

'Probably not.'

I could sense that we would be bound by a reluctant camaraderie, like soldiers who have survived some hazardous mission. I drove quickly along the narrow road, passing the woman on the bicycle and a boy carrying some books.

'I don't know about you,' I said, 'but what I want most in the world is a stiff drink.'

'The stiffer the better,' he said. 'If you'll forgive the expression.'

Barbara was in the pub and waved us over when she saw us. Mr Moore's niece brought us our drinks.

'Do you remember asking me about strange calls?' Barbara said to me. 'Had you some kind of inside information?'

'What do you mean?'

'I got a call last night. Quite bizarre. Asking me if I had adequate fire insurance on my house!'

'What did you say?'

'I told her to bugger off.'

'Her?'

'Yes, it was a woman. An aggressive bitch as well.'

'Just wait 'til you hear what happened to us!' Cromer said with the instinctive need of the good storyteller to outshine a rival anecdote. He told her, with already embellished detail, about what had happened in the valley. I noticed that he emerged rather well from this version; he kept his head and even displayed a sense of humour while I dithered. I resented this only a little, knowing that Barbara would change the details to suit her own storytelling purposes.

'How awful!' she said when he had finished. 'Why on earth would anyone want to shoot at you two? Do you think,' she added, turning mischievously to Cromer, 'that it might have been your clothes?'

I could see that he didn't know if she was being serious. He stared at her, looking a little resentful and she stared back at him, eyebrows raised.

'You don't seem very concerned by that call,' I said, breaking into the tension between them.

'Listen, darling,' she said emphatically, 'I don't want to give you a lecture about your own country but in my opinion it has more mad men and women per square acre than anywhere else I've ever been. So what's the point of worrying?'

'I've been thinking about a possible explanation,' Cromer said. 'Something more simple. Suppose someone was out hunting, legally or illegally as the case may be? There are deer around here, aren't there? And rabbits and birds and God knows what else. So they've been concentrating on a spot somewhere in the valley and they see something move and they blast off at it. They miss but when they take a better view they see that they've frightened the shit out of two men who think they've been shot at. So, whoever it is wouldn't exactly jump up and down and say sorry, would they? They'd lie low and avoid the implications.'

'Maybe,' I said, finding it difficult to take much interest in his theory.

'I'm disappointed with you both,' Barbara said. 'Why turn drama into ineptitude? There's quite enough of that around as it is!'

'Would you excuse me for a moment?' I said. 'I'm supposed to ring the garage about a service for the jeep.'

I went over to the telephone. It was being used by an elderly and irascible man.

'What? You what? You won't until Thursday? You won't what?'

I felt a surge of irritation and attempted to look disapproving but his sight was probably as bad as his hearing for he just stared at me without any reaction.

'The bus? What bus? On the corner? What corner?'

His interrogative shouting sounded as if it could go on for hours; so pointless a conversation had no logical need to end. Then, abruptly and without any word to signal the decision, he hung up.

'There's something wrong with that bloody phone,' he said to me.

I dialled Cromer's number, willing her to answer, still irritated by the delay. The elderly man was sitting at the counter, holding a glass of stout and muttering to himself. Her voice was like a deliverance from absurdity.

'I've only got a minute,' I said. 'I'm actually with Bill in the pub.'

'It's good to hear you.'

'I wanted to say that I love you. Will I see you soon?'

'I think so.'

'Can you be more definite than that?'

'Maybe tomorrow.'

'Tomorrow would be great.'

'You know that it depends on things?'

'But you'll try.'

'I'll try.'

'I love you.'

'I love you.'

'We had an eventful walk,' I said. 'Bill will tell you about it.'

'Did he tell you about his reprints?'

'No.'

The elderly man at the counter looked across at me and said, 'It was never there on a Thursday.'

'Some publisher wants to bring out six of his books in a uniform edition.'

'Are you serious?' I said enviously. 'He never mentioned it.'

'He'll have to write introductions to them. He'll be going to London to discuss it. That's why I'm telling you.'

'I see.'

I hoped that she didn't detect the envy in my voice.

'We'll talk about it tomorrow.'

'If I can,' she said.

When I went back to the table, carrying drinks on a tray, Barbara was well into a story that I hadn't heard before. It concerned the manner in which she had lost, or abandoned, her virginity and was replete with humorous detail that may even have been based on the truth. The momentous event had happened during the Easter term in her grammar school. She was sixteen years of age, the only one amongst a group of friends who had yet to sleep with a boy. Someone called Pendleton was selected for the initiation in a room behind the gym. His excitement was so great that he came on her stomach before she was fully undressed. Half an hour later, he managed to enter her.

'I said 'Well done, Pendleton!' Barbara said. 'I never knew his first name.'

Cromer laughed so much that his face turned red and then he coughed so violently that we feared that he was in danger of choking. I got him a glass of water and, as Barbara watched with an expression of mock horror, his mood calmed to a chuckle.

'It reminds me so much of myself,' he said and suddenly we were telling each other stories about our adolescent sexuality.

It was strange to feel so relaxed and comfortable after what had happened in the valley. It was another world; the thought of lying on the grass, filled with fear, one's life apparently threatened for the very first time, became, in some unlikely way, as farcical as the stories of youth which had, in their own time, been filled with anguish. I wanted Ingrid to be there. Even if Cromer had been demonstrative to her, I would have enjoyed the secret of our intimacies and the knowing glances that neither of us could have resisted. I wondered about her adolescence. Had she been pretty or beautiful, precocious or shy? I wished that I could share old photographs with her and memories of cousins and aunts and former next-door neighbours. I imagined her dressed in black leggings and a jumper, wandering around the rooms of their house, planning to be with me. It was a nice thought.

'One for the road,' Cromer said.

While he was getting the drinks, Barbara leaned towards me conspiratorially.

'Is someone putting pressure on our friend?'

'You mean today? And the calls?'

'Yes.'

'It's quite possible that his explaination is right. I'm totally confused.'

'That's not like you, darling. You're usually such a clear-headed old thing.'

Cromer came back with the drinks.

'Have either of you holiday plans?' I asked.

The words sounded so stilted they might have been from a phrase book for foreign students. I looked towards Cromer, hoping that he would mention going to England but he was pouring a mixer and did not react.

'I've been invited to Malta of all places,' Barbara said. 'A friend of mine has just bought a house there. Have either of you ever been?'

Both of us shook our heads.

'I'm going to London next week,' Cromer said. 'I got rather good news. They're going to bring out a uniform edition of my stuff with new introductions. They want to discuss the project.'

'Great!' I said but I felt envious again and unimportant. 'Isn't that what we'd all like? A reassessment of a body of work?'

'Speak for yourself!' Barbara said. 'I'd hate it! I don't even have copies of some of the books I've written! But it's great for you, Bill. You know as well as I do that you've been underestimated.'

'Do you think so?' he said. 'Well, maybe. Compared with some of the others. And anyway, as John said, a uniform edition is something of a milestone. And it's not all that common any more. I just hope that I can write decent introductions.'

'Tell them the facts behind the fiction,' Barbara said. 'That's what people want to know.'

'It's not always easy to tell the difference,' Cromer said.

I looked at him with dislike. Fact is making love to Ingrid, I thought. Fiction would be the thought of abandoning everything to start a new life with her somewhere. Fiction would be discovering that I was the best lover she had ever had or the most interesting companion. Fact is I envy you and your success.

'It's been a long journey,' he said. 'I've had to work really hard for everything. I was brought up with a kind of grimness that destroyed every relationship I've ever had except with Ingrid. That's rock solid.'

'Isn't that just a bit too convenient?' Barbara said. 'To blame your childhood for your inadequacy in relationships? Isn't that just a way of transferring a sense of failure on to someone else's head?'

'I don't have a sense of failure!'

'Of course you do!'

'Good God,' Cromer said. 'All this started with my telling you that six of my books are about to come out in a uniform edition.'

'Old work!' Barbara said and I realized that she was a little more drunk than I had perceived. 'Why haven't you six new books? Why has John written nothing since God knows when?'

I was oddly hurt by this rhetorical question. It brought out into the open something that was seldom mentioned, like a family secret. At this point in her drinking, Barbara was capable of total indiscretion and this worried me. I wondered if she suspected anything about my relationship with Ingrid.

'Actually,' I said, to distract her, 'I have an idea for a book. It just needs a little more thinking about before I settle down to work.'

I sounded to myself like some drunk in a bar, earnestly attempting to be plausible.

'I've heard that before,' Barbara said. 'You sat here in this pub more than a year ago and said the very same thing. A person either writes or they don't. There's no in between.'

'With the greatest of respect, Barbara,' I heard myself saying, as if I were a detached observer, 'your own work is hardly of a standard that allows you to make definitive artistic statements.'

I wished that we weren't having this conversation and saying things that would rankle long after we had forgotten the circumstances in which we had drifted towards this talk. Almost nothing marked the exact point at which conviviality had turned into antagonism.

'And your work is of a standard that allows you to pontificate?'

'I wasn't pontificating! I was challenging something you said.'

Barbara stared at me, her lower lip trembling, and suddenly she was very drunk. Her eyes filled with tears and she tried to say something but failed.

'Bloody hell!' Cromer said. 'I didn't realize you were so far gone.'

'We can't let her drive,' I said. 'I'll give you a lift, Barbara.'

I expected some protest but she acquiesced tearfully.

'Just finish my drink,' she said.

'Are you all right there?' Mr Moore called over to us.

'We're fine,' Cromer said. 'Has our friend been here long?'

'Twenty-five to eleven.'

'Good grief! No wonder she's blotto!'

'Speak for yourself,' Barbara said. 'Drink you under the table.'

'We'll leave your car here,' I said to her, speaking slowly, as if to a child. 'You can collect it in the morning.'

'Just finish my drink.'

She looked old and sad and her face appeared to droop as if some support had been removed from beneath her chin. There was something like despair in her expression, as if she had been cornered and knew that there was no way to escape from danger. She lifted the glass, unsteadily, to her lips; as she drank, some gin dribbled down the front of her dress.

'What a day!' Cromer said ruefully. He was standing behind her like a bodyguard. He looked as if he might pick her up and carry her to the door. She put the glass back on the table.

'I want to go to sleep,' she said, standing up with difficulty. 'There's nothing over the rainbow, is there, except for more of the same.'

I took her handbag and the three of us walked to the door.

'Good luck now!' Mr Moore called cheerfully. He would have ignored us if we had not made so bedraggled a group.

I opened the passenger door of the jeep and helped Barbara to get in. She sat with her legs wide apart, propping herself up with one rigid arm and gave me a meaningless smile. I put her bag beside her and unintentionally slammed the door loudly as if expressing some disapproval. I got into the driver's seat,

'It's good of you,' Cromer said, getting into the back seat.

I drove carefully out onto the road. A girl, riding a black pony, waved to us.

'Do you know her?' I asked him.

'Never saw her before.'

'She's the daughter of a doctor in the next village,' Barbara said with unexpected clarity but when I turned and looked at her she was almost asleep. I stopped outside Cromer's house. Barbara woke and attempted to get out.

'Not here,' Cromer said as if he were speaking to a child. 'John's just dropping me off.'

'I know that,' she said. 'You don't have to spell out everything as if I'm a total fool.'

'Thanks for everything,' he said to me.

I envied him going into the house, envied each minute that they would spend together.

'What's the matter?' Barbara said. 'Are you not bringing me home?'

I drove quickly to her house.

'I'll give you a lift to your car tomorrow,' I said.

'I should think so!'

I felt angry with her when I stopped outside her house. She made no attempt to move.

'You're home, Barbara,' I said.

'You'll have to help me out. My legs are weak.'

I got out and opened the passenger door. She moved hesitantly.

'I won't let you fall,' I said in what I intended to be a cheerful tone.

She got out and leaned heavily against me. I picked up her handbag and we trudged slowly to the front door of her house.

'I hope I have my key,' she said.

I opened her handbag and found a bunch of keys.

'Which one is it?'

'The yellow one.'

I opened the door. It was gloomy in the hallway and the air smelled stale.

'Get a good rest,' I said to her.

'You can't just leave me here! I wouldn't make it across the hall. My bedroom's there.'

She nodded towards a door across the hallway from her living room. We staggered towards it and I opened the door. The room was large and much brighter than the hallway. Its wide window looked out on an unkempt field. The double bed was unmade; a breakfast tray had been pushed to one side and a number of paperbacks were scattered across the rumpled blue duvet. The bedside light was on. There was a collection of phials, some glasses and an icebucket on the bedside table. The doors of the built-in wardrobe were open. Coats and dresses hung listlessly; a number were bunched up on the floor. The surface of the dressing table was almost entirely covered by jars and bottles of cosmetics, rolls of cotton wool and boxes of tissues. It reminded me of a theatre dressing room. All across the light blue carpet, strewn in a pathway, were magazines from Sunday newspapers. Their arrangement appeared deliberate.

'The inner sanctum,' Barbara said, as if we had arrived at the end of a quest.

I helped her over to the bed and she fell onto it, pulling me on top of her. For a few seconds I assumed that it was an accident and was preparing to apologize when she pulled me closer and kissed me, her hot, dry tongue moving urgently in my mouth. I was so surprised that I remained passive in her embrace, then realized that I was becoming excited by her kisses and by the pressure of her warm, soft breasts against me. I was about to respond when the dangerous incongruity of what we were doing occurred to me. I pulled away from her.

'Come on, Barbara,' I said. 'This doesn't make sense. We've both had too much to drink.'

She looked at me with watering eyes. Her face was red from exertion and she was breathing heavily. I wondered how things had gone so wrong.

'I couldn't do it to Laura,' I said dishonestly.

'Don't give me that crap!' she said. She appeared to drift in and out of a state of drunkenness. She sat up on the bed. Her clothes were dishevelled. 'Now get to hell out of my room!'

'I didn't ask to come here.'

'I said get to hell out of here. And don't give me that stuff about Laura. As if I didn't know that you're fucking that Kraut!'

'My God, Barbara! You mustn't say things like that! You couldn't be more wrong.'

She lay down heavily on the bed. I wanted to go, yet needed to persuade her that she was wrong.

'I can say what I like!' she said, childishly. 'You wouldn't care if it weren't true.'

'That makes no sense!' I resented the power over me that she had suddenly attained. 'You could cause such trouble by saying that.'

I could hear a tone of self-pity in my voice and disliked myself for it.

'Don't worry,' she said unexpectedly. 'I won't say anything about it. I like Laura too much.'

I was as unprepared for her reasonable mood as I had been for everything else. I waited for her to change again but she remained calm.

'Let's just forget about it,' she said.

'Of course,' I said, moving towards the door. I wondered what it would have been like to sleep with her. There was something provocatively sluttish about her posture on the bed and her legs spread wide and about the disorder in the room. It was as if we had experienced some unusually deep carnal knowledge. The reality was so different that I had to smile, and Barbara, interpreting this as a sign of affection, smiled back at me.

'I'm going to sleep like a baby as soon as you're gone.'

I went out to the jeep and drove home. The telephone was ringing. I hurried to it but didn't get there in time. I went into the study and poured a large whiskey. The telephone rang again.

'Why didn't you tell me?' Ingrid asked without any opening remark.

'I said that we had had a dramatic time. You must remember that we were together in the pub. I couldn't risk him finding out that I was talking to you.'

'All the same!'

'These things happen,' I said, 'when you go walking in the mountains. There are inexperienced hunters.'

'You don't think that it was someone trying to kill him?'

'Why would anyone want to do that?'

The words sounded more dismissive than I had intended.

'I don't know,' she said,' but he seems very worried.'

'Well it was worrying at the time,' I said, 'but it was a freak accident and nobody was hurt.'

'It's not like him to be so worried.'

'I love you,' I said, jealous of her concern for him. 'I'm longing to see you.'

'Now he says that he doesn't know if he'll go to London.'

'Persuade him,' I said, enjoying this moment of conspiracy against him. 'Remind him of how important it is to his career.'

'I suppose,' she said vaguely.

I loved her voice, her difficulty with some words, the care she took with several vowels.

'Well, anyway,' I said, unnerved by what had become a long

silence and an electronic sighing on the line. 'I wish I could be with you.'

The silence went on until I thought that she must have left down the phone and gone into another room.

'Hello?'

'I'd like that as well,' she said.

'It's not fair,' I said self-pityingly.

'But we'll see each other soon?'

'Soon.'

SIXTEEN

THE SHRILL RINGING of telephones echo through the pages of this journal. Listen: the telephone in the bedroom is ringing. I am in the bathroom, shaving, and my face is bearded with foam. I rush into the bedroom, hoping that the call is from Ingrid.

'He decided last night,' she said. 'He's going this evening.'

'Excellent!'

'What will we do?'

'We'll see as much of each other as possible.'

'It might be better if you come over here. You don't have to bring your car or anything.'

'Whatever you like,' I said.

'I'll get back from the airport at about seven. Do you want to come here at eight?'

'It's going to be an incredibly long day,' I said, 'but I think that I can just about manage.'

'I'll see you then,' she said, without, or so it seemed to me, much warmth.

I wiped shaving soap from the receiver and went back to the bathroom. A woman was complaining about something or other on the Gay Byrne show. Her unmistakeable Meath accent was like a sharp and sudden evocation of my childhood; the women on the

223

streets who would complain to my mother about the behaviour of their husbands. I had always been disconcerted by their frankness.

I drove to Barbara's house, uncertain of how I might be received. She opened the door before I had even knocked. She looked rested and well.

'Hello!'

She was dressed in a yellow suit that I had not seen before.

'Don't even try to talk to me!' she said. 'I'll confess to a certain amount of blurred detail but that's about it! I just know that I was completely over the top and I'm sorry. Only for you I'd probably have been ravaged by some village lout.'

'I hope you'll forgive me,' I said and she laughed. I felt most of the old affection for her and she appeared to have forgotten or forgiven my crassness. She kissed me on the mouth; her perfume was new and elusive.

'Will you come in and have a drink?'

'I don't think so.'

'You're right,' she said. 'I'm off it for at least a day. The hair of the dog never worked for me.'

'I thought you might like a lift to your car.'

'That's awfully good of you. I'm going on into Dublin. Hang on a minute and I'll get my bag.'

When she got into the car the sweetness of her perfume appeared to intensify.

'Do you know something rather extraordinary?' she said. 'Do you remember my young admirer?'

'Aidan?'

'The very one. He had a temporary job in a bookshop. I heard on the radio news this morning that he had been arrested for the possession of arms.'

'You're not serious.'

'No, I am! They gave his address in Finglas. He was one of three men arrested and charged at a special sitting.'

'Had you suspected anything about him?'

'Not really. I mean I knew that he had political opinions. He was from a Republican family but I never heard him say anything about the IRA. To be absolutely honest with you, I thought that his politics, such as they were, were fairly facile.'

I pulled into the carpark of the pub and turned to her, anxious for more detail.

'You don't think that he was on some kind of Republican assignment down here?'

'No way. He was here only because I picked him up!'

'I couldn't help noticing that you had an Ordnance Survey map on your bedroom wall. Was that his?'

'What? No, of course not! I was using it for my new book.'

'I'm just being paranoid,' I said.

She opened the door.

'You were good to collect me,' she said. 'And yesterday is totally in the past?'

'Totally.'

I went to the shop and bought the *Irish Times*. There was a two-paragraph report of the arrests in Dublin. At a sitting of the Special Criminal Court three men had been charged with the possession of firearms. It gave their names, their addresses and their ages. Aidan, who was twenty-seven, was the oldest of the three. Had he been one of the men at the back door? I attempted to remember their faces and his face at the party but failed. I put the paper aside and drove to a village on the other side of the lake where there was a large supermarket. I bought three bottles of Piper Heidsieck champagne and a bottle of Dow's port. The girl at the checkout was friendly and interested.

'You must be having a party?'

'In a kind of way, yes.'

'Well for you! The kind of parties they have round here you'd be lucky if they brought a six-pack of Guinness.'

She was surprisingly good-looking, despite the petulance of her expression and the shapeless supermarket uniform she was wearing.

'You deserve much more than that,' I said.

She tossed hair back from her face; her large green eyes were challenging. I was disconcerted by her directness. She looked at me appraisingly and I was oddly pleased that she was not immediately uninterested. She had a dimpled chin and a small mole on her right cheek. Her sallow skin was unlined except for a single vertical stroke above her nose. She was wearing too much eye make-up but her lips were entirely natural and as she tossed back her hair again I became aware of the perfume she was wearing. It was much more subtle than Barbara's. She looked at the name on my credit card but it obviously meant nothing to her. That was good. I had travelled away from local shops to avoid any speculation about my purchases. She watched as I signed the docket and I could have persuaded myself that there was some sexual interest in her expression. Another customer, a stout woman wearing a blue tweed coat, came to the checkout and when the girl handed me back my card the spell was broken.

I took my purchases out to the car. The village street was narrow and long and oppressive. I had parked, without noticing, beside a small Celtic cross that marked the spot where a local man had been shot during the War of Independence. Like so many others in this county, his name was Byrne; the name was displayed above several of the shops, including the supermarket.

I drove home. The house had an abandoned feeling as if no one had lived there for months. I saw, for the first time, the dust that had settled on surfaces like the onset of decay. I phoned Laura. Her mother answered. Her friendliness filled me with guilt and I talked too much to cover this feeling, enquiring about everything that came to mind, her golf, her cats and her reading. Laura wasn't there. She had taken Rachael into town for a shopping spree. I lied to her: the telephone was out of order. Although a caller heard what appeared to be a ringing tone, it was actually dead. I had reported the matter and the fault would be corrected in a day or two. In the meantime, I would keep in touch.

When that shoddy conversation was over, I poured myself a drink. The telephone rang. I was about to answer it when I remembered that it was supposed to be out of order. If it were Laura, ringing to tell me about their day in town, my lie would be exposed. I let it ring, watching it, feeling miserable, wondering if it were Ingrid. It stopped with an abruptness that was almost shocking. I phoned her but there was no reply.

I had been invited to write the preface to an Edwardian novel of suspense. I had welcomed this task enthusiastically and then neglected it. My notes were on the table. I looked, again, at the book. The opening chapter described a world of certainty: a house in a London square, servants going about their early morning tasks, a bath being filled. It was a serene world in which even adultery could be conducted according to a set of rules, a world that could be disrupted only by murder. I made some additional notes and then the telephone rang. I looked at it, feeling impotent and miserable. I imagined a mocking note to its ring as if I were listening to shrill, derisive laughter. It stopped ringing. I threw the book and my notes into a drawer, another small defeat.

When I had taken a shower I put on a suit that Ingrid hadn't seen before. The jacket seemed to be a little tight. Was I gaining weight? This was entirely possible. I was drinking too much and had no proper exercise regime. This was a further cause for self-pity, my transmogrification from author to overweight nobody. Looking at myself in the mirror, I was reminded of the kind of commercial traveller whom one has seen hanging around humbly in shops waiting for the customers to go so that he can solicit some modest order. I undressed and put on grey trousers and a brown sports jacket. The effect was better. I packed black jeans and underwear and a sweater into an overnight bag. I put in the bottles and arranged the sweater around them to stop them from clinking. These preparations cheered me a little; it was as if I were taking some control of my future instead of being at the mercy of continuous acts of chance. I packed some shaving things, then zipped the bag with difficulty and looked around the room as if I were not going to see it again for a very long time.

I locked the front door, then drove the jeep around to the side of the house where it could not be seen from the road. I walked down the drive and closed the gate behind me. Apart from Laura's car, the house had an unoccupied air. I hoped that Barbara would not attempt to investigate or, worse, see me walking with my bag towards Cromer's house. The fact that she had driven to Dublin gave me some hope that she would not be back until much later. Despite this, I felt uncomfortable as I walked along the familiar road, listening for the sound of an approaching car, wondering what I would say. Two magpies hopped away from me towards a hedge.

The roof and upper windows of the house came into view. It looked as deserted as my own and I thought of the telephone calls that she may have attempted to make to me, explaining that she had been delayed somewhere.

Throughout this journal I have attempted to describe my feelings with as much truth and objectivity as I can find. I don't really know how successful I have been. I have thought, often, of Daumier's assertion that photography describes everything and explains nothing. It is possible that in attempting to describe my emotions I have overlooked their true implications. What was I thinking as I approached the house? I wanted her, yet I was filled with unease. There is another quotation that has influenced me as a writer and as someone who enjoys looking at paintings. It is from a book by Gombrich. He wrote that artists have never painted what they saw. They paint what they have learned to paint. That clear-eyed recognition of limitations, the idea that craft liberates or narrows vision, is salutary. No matter how accurately I attempt to describe my feelings, I know that there are limitations that are beyond my control.

I certainly felt a turbulence as I approached Cromer's house. I kept looking around as if expecting accusing voices to come from somewhere. Then I looked at the inhospitable house and concluded that she was not there. The feeling of disappointment was like an ache. I didn't believe that I could survive the evening without her. This feeling transcended a sexual longing. I craved the reassurance of her company. As I approached the gate I heard the sound of a car. Absurdly and without premeditation, I pressed up close to the overhanging branches of a tree, knowing that I wasn't fully hidden but gaining some comfort from the attempt. The car was being driven very fast. As it came around the corner it had to slow down, with a protesting shriek of its wheels against the dry surface of the road. It looked familiar and then it was gone but its invasion continued for minutes. The evening was redolent of trapped heat; the tree that I was standing beside had a sharp and bitter smell. I became aware of the absence of birdsong, although there were many trees around the small, locked Church of Ireland whose grounds adjoined Cromer's garden. The quiet of the evening assumed a peculiar heaviness and even the cloud formation had swirled and twisted into thick, upright pillars as if supporting the pressure of the sky.

I stepped back onto the road and walked around the corner. The front door to Cromer's house was open. I couldn't see a car but assumed that Ingrid had parked it in the small garage behind the house. The thought that she wasn't there, that she had telephoned to cancel an arrangement that she had regretted, came so forcibly that I stopped on the driveway as if to postpone the moment of truth.

Then I walked slowly to the door and knocked. It swung back so that I could see the familiar stairs leading to the room that I could remember so well.

There was no response. I stepped hesitantly into the hallway, calling her name, wondering what I would do if Cromer came out of his study. The incongruity of the bag I was carrying was like a bad joke.

'Ingrid!' I called again, and my raised voice sounded unfamiliar and distorted. 'Can I come in?'

There was no response. I assumed that the house was empty.

I went outside and walked around to the garage, believing that her car would not be there. The door was unlocked. When I rolled it upwards I saw her car. I touched its warm bonnet and felt an unease that was much greater than my own self-protective sense of disappointment. I went back to the house and standing in the hallway I called her name again. Then, after a few seconds, I opened the dining-room door. The light was dim, because of the drawn curtains, but everything appeared to be neat and in place. There was a bottle of wine on the table as if she had taken it from somewhere to serve later. It was a friendly sight so that when I opened the door to the kitchen, I expected a similar experience, the evidence of food being prepared, the scent of garlic. Instead, I saw something much worse than I had ever feared.

SEVENTEEN

I HESITATED before going closer to her. I was certain that she was dead. I wanted to deny the experience. I wanted to leave the house as quickly as possible and get away from the body and the chaos and the blood. I stood there, staring at her, the body that I had so desired, appalled by its ugliness.

The room was a shambles, chairs overturned, utensils scattered across the floor.

A large bottle of olive oil had been spilled and the air was heavy with its pervasive smell. The oil had flowed from the broken bottle beside the kitchen table to join and mix with a pool of blood beside her twisted body. She was shockingly still, her face unnaturally pale except for a purple bruise across her forehead and a deep red weal beneath her closed left eye. She was lying on her side and her right arm was twisted oddly like the arm of a discarded doll.

Her wrist was bruised and swollen. Her dress, apart from an area close to her shoulder where blood had congealed, looked incongruously neat. It was very quiet in the kitchen and when I realized that I couldn't just turn away and leave, I went cautiously over to her. She seemed to smell of oil. I saw another bruise close to her ear and there were scratch marks above her breasts. A nipple was exposed.

I could see no evidence that she was breathing.

I was surprised at how calmly I was assessing her wounds until I realized that I was weeping. I heard a sob, a gasp for breath and then felt tears moving across my cheeks. I have no idea of how long I spent there, looking at her lovely body broken and discarded, knowing that I was in some way to blame. The marks on her face were terrible. The mixture of her blood and the oil seemed to suggest that some obscene ritual had taken place. I could see now that the blood had seeped from a wound at the back of her head. I reached out to touch her cheek with the tips of my fingers and she moaned, a small but anguished sound, filled with pain and helplessness, and I was so shaken that I stepped back from her and slipped and fell. I got quickly to my feet, holding onto the table, leaving bloody fingerprints on its polished surface.

She moaned again as if in protest at my ineptitude, but she was totally still. I reached back and felt the mixture of blood and oil on the seat of my trousers. I wanted to run from the kitchen and get away as far as possible from the house. I went over to the sink and washed my hands and dried them on a tea towel. There was a phone on the wall near to the porch door but, as if anxious not to be overheard, I went into Cromer's study. The letter from his publisher about the new edition of his work was open on his desk. I telephoned the guards.

The man who answered was either bored or uninterested in what I was saying. I had to give him my name, address and telephone number several times, then Cromer's address and then the name of the victim of the assault.

'You're still at the scene?' he asked me.

'Yes. I've told you that.'

'Don't go anywhere. Don't touch anything.'

'For Christ's sake,' I said. 'What about an ambulance? She's in a very bad way!'

'No time is being lost,' he said slowly. 'Just remember not to touch anything.'

When I went back into the kitchen I needed to know if she were still alive. I felt her cheek. It was very cold. I waited for her to moan, like a child squeezing a toy, listening for a reassuring squeak. She made no sound. The colour of the blood on the floor appeared to have darkened and her bruises were more vivid.

'Ingrid!' I said and using her name brought back my love for her. 'Ingrid! Please! I love you! Ingrid! Please! I'm sorry!'

Her left eyebrow stirred, a small, almost imperceptible movement, but I knew that I had not imagined it. I needed her to hear me. 'Ingrid, can you hear me? It's all right. Can you hear me? Please! It's all right!'

I knew absolutely nothing about her religious beliefs. If, like me, she had been brought up as a Roman Catholic, should I say an Act of Contrition? I could probably remember the words but the thought of whispering into her ear contrition for the sins that she had committed with me was too hypocritical.

I had loved our adultery and had no desire to atone for this sin.

I noticed my bloody finger marks on the table top, found a dishcloth and rubbed and rubbed until the surface was clear. It occurred to me that I was behaving like a guilty man, involved in some futile effort to remove evidence. Where were the guards? She needed help. She needed anyone but me.

'Ingrid!' I almost shouted again and from the distance I heard the wail of a siren.

I went out to the front door and the sound came nearer and when the garda car stopped in the driveway I was waiting with a fixed expression, not really knowing how I should behave.

Both the guards were young and wearing uniform. They walked slowly to the door as if reluctant to get involved.

'Is the ambulance coming?' I asked them.

'It should be here any minute. Are you the man who made the call?'

'Yes.'

'So what exactly happened?'

'I just called to the house and found her on the kitchen floor.'

We were standing in the hallway. I was surprised at their bulk, the space they occupied.

'The kitchen?'

'It's just here,' I said.

'Christ!' one of them said when they saw Ingrid. He looked at me with open dislike and I realized that, in my bloodstained clothes, I was an obvious suspect.

The other guard knelt beside her and felt for a pulse.

'This is terrible,' he said. 'You say that you found her like this?'

His voice suggested incredulity. His manner was certainly hostile. He looked at his colleague in a knowing way as if drawing his attention to some detail that might otherwise be missed. I resented the way they were looking at her.

Her body, although clothed, lay there with a greater vulnerability than it would have if she were waiting for a lover. I longed to be holding her, feeling the texture of her skin, tasting her.

'Do you know where her husband is?' the second guard asked me, as if emboldened by the secret that he shared.

'In London I think. I know that was his plan.'

'There's no reason to believe, is there, that he had anything to do with this?'

That idea had not occurred to me. I thought about it now with a kind of appalled fascination. Had Cromer found out about us and lost control? I couldn't believe it.

'It's just not possible,' I said.

'How can you be so sure?'

'Because I know both of them well.'

It was then that I thought of the speeding car.

'Do you know how we can get in touch with him?'

'No.'

'How come you were here?'

'I noticed that the front door was open.'

'Did you now?'

We heard the ambulance in the distance. I wanted to weep for her.

'Well, at least when she comes around,' the first guard said, 'she'll be able to tell us what happened.'

He stared at me meaningfully as if expecting me to break down and confess.

'Good,' I said aggressively. 'I can't wait to find out.'

I was impatient with myself. I noticed that I was developing a shifty manner. I couldn't look directly at either of them and my voice had a hollow falseness.

I looked at Ingrid and then looked away, appalled by her predicament.

'So you can't think of anything else that would help?'

'No.'

I heard the ambulance stop outside.

I went out to the hall. A black car had pulled in behind the ambulance and two men who were unmistakably plain-clothes policemen were walking towards the house. The ambulance men pushed past me and went into the kitchen as if they had been directed there. Both knelt beside Ingrid.

'How long ago did this happen?'

'I don't know. I found her about half an hour ago. She's lost a lot of blood.'

'It's not quite as bad as it looks.'

The two men from the car joined us. The older of the two, a tall, cadaverous man with a bald head and a cold air of authority was carrying my overnight bag.

I saw that he had opened it and had pulled aside a sweater to reveal a bottle of champagne. The indignity that I felt at having my property so casually examined was tempered by my discomfort. He put the bag down without comment and looked, without much apparent interest, at Ingrid. The second guard whispered something to him and they both stared at me. Then he came across to where I was standing.

'I'm the local Superintendent,' he said.

I held out my hand and he shook it a little reluctantly.

'You're a friend of this lady?'

'And of her husband,' I said with unnecessary emphasis.

'You live close by?'

'Just up the road.'

'I didn't see a car outside.'

'I walked.'

'I see.'

We all watched as the ambulance men lifted Ingrid with impressive gentleness onto a stretcher.

'We're taking her to Loughlinstown,' one of the ambulance men said.

'I'd like to go with her,' I said.

'It would be better if you stayed here to help us,' the Superintendent said. 'This is a serious criminal assault. I'm determined to find the person responsible for it.'

'Of course.'

Now that they had taken her away – did I think of her as a body rather than as a living person? – the evidence of the assault seemed to have an additional pathos. The blood was congealing in the oil and there was another stain where she might have urinated. I looked away, longing for the nightmare to end.

'Could we talk somewhere else?'

'Of course,' I said again.

He followed me into the dining room and closed the door. I switched on the light. A small candelabra above the table cast a soft glow on the polished wood.

'You have some blood on your clothing,' he said.

'I slipped in the kitchen.'

'I saw some evidence of that.'

He sat at the table and took a notebook from his pocket. I remained standing.

'I know who you are,' he said. 'I've read one of your books.'

'Thank you,' I said foolishly.

'Tell me how you happened to find Mrs Cromer.'

I described going for a walk, seeing the front door open, finding her.

He took scanty notes. Perhaps, like a novelist, he chose the smaller facts that he knew, instinctively, would hold the greater truths. He pressed me for exact times and I found that I was vague about these. There was a knock on the door and the other plain-clothes policeman came in.

'Can I talk to you for a moment, sir?'

They went out to the kitchen. When the Superintendent came back he stood at the other side of the table, stroking his face with long, pale fingers.

'I understand that Mr Cromer is in England?'

'That's my understanding too.'

'Would you know if Mrs Cromer was expecting a guest?'

'Possibly. I couldn't really say.'

'One of the bedrooms upstairs is prepared for a guest. A very special guest. Somebody particularly well known to Mrs Cromer.'

'I don't understand,' I said but I knew exactly what he was saying. I could picture the spare bedroom prepared for our love-making, the Leonard Cohen tape ready to be switched on, the ice-bucket on the table by the bed.

'Did you happen to notice a bag, a kind of carry-all article, in the hall?'

'That's mine,' I said unhappily.

He didn't pretend to be surprised.

'I thought that it might be. So it was you that Mrs Cromer was expecting?'

'Now listen,' I said, in a kind of pleading way that I despised myself for, 'I feel that I'm being cross-questioned like a suspect. I just happened to find her in the kitchen and the first thing that I did was call the guards.'

'But it was you that she was expecting?'

'I suppose so.'

'I'd rather if you gave me a yes or no answer.'

'Not all questions are open to yes or no.'

'Surely this one is?'

'Yes,' I said, defeated by my inability to extricate myself from the logic of his questioning. 'She was expecting me.'

'I'm only concerned with this, you understand, in so far as it's relevant to the assault on Mrs Cromer.'

'You'll find that it has no relevance!'

'With respect, sir, I'll have to be the judge of that.'

'Superintendent,' I said, noticing that my voice had taken on a disagreeable, mendicant tone, 'I hope that details which have nothing to do with the case can remain private.'

I was suddenly haunted by thought of the headlines in evening newspapers:

WOMAN SAVAGELY BEATEN IN LITERARY LOVE NEST

'I've told you where my interest lies,' he said ponderously. 'Relevant facts.'

I had no doubt he believed that I was guilty.

'I saw a car,' I said, ' just before I got here. I heard a car being driven very fast and I stepped off the road. It went past me at a crazy speed. I think it was a car that I noticed here before. It was once parked near to my house. And the driver was walking near to my gate.'

'You're suggesting that there's a connection between the car and this crime?' he asked sceptically.

'I can't think of anything else.'

He sat down and opened his notebook again. I told him what I remembered. Even to myself it sounded unconvincing. When he shut his notebook, he made a point of ostentatiously putting the cap back on to his ballpoint pen.

'The scene will be preserved,' he said, 'but fortunately this isn't a murder enquiry. The chaps in the ambulance were of the opinion that although she's badly concussed, she'll be capable of talking to us soon. So at this point I'm not certain that there's anything to be gained from any more discussion.'

'Really?' I said, suddenly reluctant to be alone and out of touch with the thrust of his enquiries.

'Unless there's something else that you'd like to tell me?'

'No, we've covered everything. I can't think of anything else. I just wish that there was something I could do. I mean, I hate to think of her there by herself and her husband not even knowing.'

'We'll make every effort to trace him.'

'I can tell you the name of his publisher. The office will be closed now but there may be some way of finding someone who knows where he's staying.'

'That's helpful,' he said in a more friendly tone of voice. Looking at him closely, I noticed that he had very pale, pendulous lips and unusual vertical crease lines on his cheeks. He wrote the name of Cromer's publisher in his notebook, then looked at me expectantly as if I had something else to tell him.

'Well, I'd better be going,' I said, moving uneasily towards the door.

'I know where to contact you. I'm sure we'll have another talk.'

'And if there's anything I can do...'

'Thank you,' he said formally.

There were many questions that I would like to have asked but I knew that I had been dismissed. It was a relief to be out in the fresh air, away from accusing eyes and voices, to have nothing to prove. The day had become cooler; a breeze was coming from the direction of the lake. My house, square and solid, looked empty and inhospitable. When I got inside I poured myself a large whiskey and sat in my study feeling lonely and isolated. I longed to hear that she would recover but knew that nothing would ever be the same again. I was not without self-pity. I thought about our first meeting and the lovely frankness of her sexuality.

I suddenly remembered my bag. I drove back to Cromer's house. The police had gone but the door was locked. I looked at the broken window but knew that if the bag were there and I took it, they would know immediately what I had done. I kicked the door and felt an irrational surge of resentment against Cromer as if he were responsible for my problems. I wish that you had never come here, I thought; you've been nothing but trouble. Please get better, Ingrid, please be well.

I was crying in the car as I drove home.

I was suffused with worry and more than a little drunk when Laura called. I had picked up the telephone before I remembered that it was supposed to be out of order. I think that I had gone to sleep, sitting in the study behind my bare desk. I had picked up the receiver, hoping, foolishly, that it was Ingrid or even the Superintendent to say that everything would be all right. Instead, Laura, sounding pleased, said 'Hi! I just tried on the off-chance that it might be repaired. How are you?'

I told her, as undramatically as possible, about Ingrid. When I had finished she said 'I'm coming home tomorrow.'

'There's no need to do that,' I said.

'Of course there is.'

'Why spoil your holidays?'

'I could hardly enjoy them now, could I? Thinking of her and all that she must have gone through. Suppose you hadn't noticed that the door was open. She'd be dead, right?'

'I suppose so.'

'So, in a way, you saved her life.'

'I wouldn't put it like that.'

'I know you wouldn't but you know what I mean.'

My hand was shaking. The receiver bumped against my lips. I could hear Laura saying 'Hello? Hello?'

'I'm sorry,' I said. 'It will be great to see you. Let me know about your flight.'

'I'll leave it up to Rachael as to whether or not she wants to stay here.'

'She's well?'

'She's fine. I'll tell you everything when I see you. I still can't believe that this has happened in our sleepy little district.'

I was glad when the call ended so that I could sit down and consider the days ahead. It appeared inevitable that Cromer would learn about our affair. I dreaded the series of confrontations, the apologies, the attempts to explain. I telephoned the hospital but they refused, politely, to give me any information. That could be provided only to identified close relations. The term excluded me into some squalid zone of petty curiosity. Please God, let her be all right, I prayed, as if prayer were a sudden irrational appeal from the mind rather than from the heart. I had lost the child's ability to pray with conviction and concern.

In the old church in Kells, cruciform and austere, I had knelt often and believed that the light in the sanctuary lamp was witness to a real presence. Please God, please God, please. There was nowhere else to turn. It would require some remarkable intervention to prevent my world from toppling, piece by piece. I was ashamed that so much of my time was being devoted to my own predicament when Ingrid's plight was so terrible. I wanted to be with her, amongst the technical anonymity of intensive care, be there when her eyelids flickered, when she looked up with curiosity, when she first smiled. I'm sorry, I thought, I'm sorry, I'm sorry, remembering the faint scar line and the small tattoo, the intimacies of her body, the wonderful things that we had experienced. I think that I cried again, filled with self-pity but with a genuine regard for her well-being, a disinterested desire for her to be well. I knew that I loved her intensely, but the fact that I also loved Laura and Rachael was unbearable. It was possible, I knew, that I would lose all of them but I was too confused to think my way through the intricate maze of that possibility. I was filled with premonitions of loss. The thought of her death, the yielding body that I had held so closely as cold and remote, filled me with panic.

The telephone rang. Who could it possibly be? Had she died? Was I some kind of accessory before the fact to her brutal murder?

Cromer's voice, instantly recognisable, trembled down the line. 'Thank God you're in!' he said. 'I had to talk to someone! What's going on?'

'What do you know?' I asked.

'Thanks to you I at least know something. The Superintendent told me that you gave him Tim's number. The office was closed when they rang but one of the editors was working late and she knew where we had gone to dinner.'

'So you know about Ingrid?'

'You found her? It was you who found her? What if you hadn't called?'

'Somebody gave her a terrible beating, Bill,' I said. 'You're going to be shocked.'

'I know all that. I was talking to her.'

'Talking to her? Where are you.'

'I'm here in the hotel in London. I'm booked onto the first plane in the morning. But they let me talk to her for a minute.'

'And she was able to talk?'

'Well she's very medicated and obviously in shock. But she was able to say some things.'

'I'm so pleased to hear that. I didn't even know if she'd live.'

'The list of her injuries is pretty dreadful. They read them out to me. It goes on and on like something from a coroner's inquest.'

'But she's going to be all right?'

'That's what they've told me. They're tough, you know, those Krauts,' he said with an attempt at levity, to which, ridiculously, I felt he had no right. 'I'll ring you in the morning. Thanks for everything that you did.'

I imagined him in his hotel room, restless and eager to get going, discovering, perhaps, that he loved her more than he had thought. He could have no suspicion of what awaited him in the house, the evidence of her infidelity laid out before him like crudely planted clues. Listen, I wanted to say to him, just before you go, there's something that I want to say to you. We didn't intend to hurt you, we hardly ever thought about you or talked about you. We were just two lonely people, you understand, don't you?

'All right,' I said. 'I'll talk to you then.'

I had another drink and was just about to go upstairs when the telephone rang. I assumed that it was Cromer with some afterthought but the voice was unfamiliar.

'Listen very carefully,' the man said. 'What I have to say I'm only going to say once.'

'Who is this?'

'Never mind. Just listen.'

The voice was unfriendly and impatient as if already tired of my interruptions.

'Pull back from what happened at Cromer's house. Don't have anything to do with it.'

'But Mrs Cromer is my friend!'

'Are you not listening to me? Have nothing more to do with them. They're not friends of this country.'

'I don't know what you mean.'

'You know exactly what I mean.'

'Are you threatening me?'

'Of course I'm fucking threatening you!' he said with exasperation.

'But I don't know who you are.'

'You don't have to know who I am. You just have to behave sensibly, okay? Do what you're fucking told!'

'You can't just talk like that,' I said, hardly knowing what I meant but hating the weakness I could hear in my voice.

'Just do what you're told and nobody else will get hurt.'

'My wife and daughter?'

'Will be fine if you don't fuck up.'

'How can I be sure of that?'

'You're not listening to me.'

'I need more information.'

'You already know too much.'

'Please, just—'

'Goodnight.'

The conversation ended with a shocking abruptness.

'Hello?' I said, although I knew that there was no longer anyone there. 'Hello?'

I knew that I would have to behave in some cowardly manner and was already ashamed of how easily I could be threatened. I went to bed but lay awake for hours, thinking back on the worst possible of days, unaware that something even worse lay just ahead.

EIGHTEEN

I CUT MYSELF while shaving; the demoralizing scar, a small crescent beneath my left nostril, seemed to indicate decline. I liked nothing that I saw in the mirror.

My face looked weak and crumpled and old, my eyes were shifty and undependable. It was the face of a man in a bar who was attempting to borrow money for more drink, tentative and humble.

The news on the radio was of a Loyalist lorry driver in Belfast who had been shot in the head as he left his terraced house on the way to work, watched by his wife and two children. A neighbour described him as 'The nicest man on the street. He was the one that everyone went to if they were in any trouble. It didn't matter what religion you were. He was just a decent man.' Her voice rose towards incredulity and hysteria before a catchy jingle prefaced an advertising break. I switched off the radio and the bathroom seemed to close in around me, as cool and clinical as a threat.

Laura had telephoned to say that her flight would arrive just before lunchtime.

Cromer, I assumed, was already on his way to the hospital. Despite my involvement, I was the only one with nothing in particular to do.

I dressed slowly, putting on a suit as if its sober, protective colouring might provide some illusion of reassurance. I thought that I still looked shifty, a well-dressed confidence trickster with a practised story and too plausible a manner.

I could see see something of my father in the shape of my face and in my stance.

I went downstairs and made coffee and some slices of toast. Outside, the morning light was celebratory, the mountains violet, the grass a vivid green beneath a melting dew.

The telephone rang.

The Superintendent's voice was measured and almost without any regional accent, as if he had been coached in some special, anonymous way of speaking.

'The news about Mrs Cromer is good,' he said. 'She's already provided me with a brief statement. They've patched her up very effectively,' he added incongruously, and I attempted to imagine Ingrid swathed in bandages like a figure in a cartoon.

'So she's going to make a good recovery?'

'I have no reason to believe to the contrary.'

'Good.'

'The story you told me about the two men in the car.'

'I was thinking about it,' I said. 'I don't know if it's of any importance.'

'Let me be the judge of that. Mrs Cromer has confirmed that she was assaulted by two men. They were strangers to her. Before she opened the hall door, she had heard the door of a car being slammed outside. So your evidence is of considerable importance.'

'Do you really think so?'

'Absolutely. We need to talk again.'

'I have to collect my wife at the airport,' I said as if this excuse made a meeting impossible.

'At what time?'

'Before one.'

'You can drop into the station on your way. You have to pass it in any case.'

'All right,' I said unhappily. Then an idea occurred to me.

'I accidentally left a bag behind yesterday. In the Cromers' house. Would it be possible for me to collect it this morning?'

'Do you have a key?'

'No.'

'I think it might be best to wait until Mr Cromer is home,' he said.

His office was small and shabby. Its only window looked out onto a concrete walled yard that contained a number of dustbins and a large, old-fashioned bicycle. He sat behind a green steel desk that was piled high with papers and a collection of coffee mugs in which dregs had congealed. A calendar advertising a local veterinary surgeon hung on the wall behind the desk; the other walls, chill areas of grey distemper, were entirely bare. The guard who had shown me into this office was older but noticeably deferential.

'Is there anything else, Super?'

'Not at the moment.'

The chair on which I sat had grey stuffing protruding like entrails from cracks in the false leather seat. I refused the cigarette that he offered me. He appeared to be distracted by one of the papers on his desk, his eyes drawn back to it again and again. He held out a match.

'I appreciate you coming here,' he said. 'I don't want this thing to mushroom. I don't want it reported stupidly. There are quite a few non-nationals living in this area and I don't want them frightened unnecessarily.'

'Of course,' I said, without any conviction.

'When I spoke to Mr Cromer on the telephone last night, he mentioned something about being shot at in Glennua a while ago. He thought that there might be some connection.'

I had not prepared for this. I stared at him, foolishly, as if he had made some accusation.

'You remember the incident?'

'Yes, of course I do, but I'm not convinced that there's any connection.'

'Nor am I. I explained to Mr Cromer that there've been a number of complaints of careless shooting in that district. Only the other day we managed to catch two young fellows at it; they'd borrowed a shotgun from one of the fathers and went hunting for rabbits. It's the mercy of God that they didn't shoot someone.'

I was so relieved at what he had said that I began to relax. He was leaning back in his chair, swivelling it a little. He had put on a reassuring expression like a mask, but I knew that I didn't want to trust him.

'I can have a cup of tea or coffee made if you like?'

'No thanks, I'm fine.'

'I'm trying to cut down myself. When you're here in the office it keeps on coming.'

He looked again at the paper on his desk then stared at me as if surprised that I was still there.

'Tell me everything you can,' he said, 'about the car.'

'It was just a car,' I said. 'I've told you everything that I remember.'

'What sort of car?'

'A big one.'

'Can you not be a little more precise than that?'

'I'm not very good at identifying cars. It was blue I think.'

He continued to stare at me but the reassuring expression had been replaced by one of disapproval.

'I'm almost certain,' he said, 'that when you told me about this yesterday you mentioned the make of the car. Am I wrong?'

'I think that you must be.'

'And you don't know anything about the registration number?'

'Why would I? I wouldn't even remember having seen a car if I hadn't gone into the house and found Ingrid the way I did.'

'Didn't you tell me that you had seen the car before?'

'I think that I might have.'

'How could you think that if you're so vague about what kind of car it was?'

'It looked like the same big, blue car.'

He sighed elaborately and the crease lines on his face deepened. I knew that I was shifting uneasily on my chair like a restless child.

'What about the driver of the car? Or the passenger?'

'It went past so quickly,' I said, 'that I just had the impression of two men.'

'The impression of two men,' he repeated sardonically. 'Would you recognize them again?'

'Probably not. Look,' I said, 'I know that I must seem unhelpful but everything has been so shocking.'

He looked at me doubtfully. Outside, in the corridor, somebody was laughing.

'If any other details occur to you,' he said, 'you know where to get me. Anything at all.'

I got to the airport early. I had a drink in the Arrivals bar, feeling lonely and irritable. I was not looking forward to seeing Laura and the guilt about this added to my unease. I wondered if Cromer were still at the hospital or if he had gone home. Perhaps he wouldn't see the bag at first, perhaps he wouldn't look in the spare room. I knew that these were foolish hopes.

The arrival of the flight was announced. I finished my drink and went down to the gates. Small groups of people stood around anxiously, speaking in subdued tones as if anticipating bad news. She came out, wheeling her baggage on a trolley and I felt a lurch of love for her and guilt and annoyance at the predicament in which I found myself. She did not see me at first and looked anxious, peering in the wrong direction, small and vulnerable. Then, as I waved, she saw me and smiled expansively like a girl greeting her lover.

When we kissed, I wondered if she sensed something different for she seemed tentative. Then her body slowly relaxed and she kissed me with such force that I almost stumbled backwards.

'It's so good to see you,' she said. 'How is Ingrid?'

This juxtaposition of ideas disconcerted me. Why did she assume that I would have up–to–date information?

'She seems to be doing very well. Much better than expected. Bill was getting home earlier so I'm sure that he's with her now.'

'Have they any idea who did it?'

'Not really. I saw a car but I'm hazy about the details. I was talking to the local Superintendent this morning. He thinks it might be important.'

We were walking towards the exit doors. I took her bags from the trolley.

'You saw a car?'

'Yes. Driving away from the house.'

'So that might have been the man who did it?'

'Men,' I said. 'Apparently there were two of them.'

'Did they take a lot of things?'

'I don't think they took anything.'

She stopped walking. We were standing in the carpark. There was something oddly bleak about the rows of deserted cars, left there while life went on somewhere else.

'Was she raped?'

'There was no sign of that.'

'Then why did it happen?'

'I haven't the faintest idea.'

'There must be a reason.'

'Maybe there is, but I don't know anything about it.'

'That's awful,' she said. 'If it could happen to Ingrid for no reason, then it could happen to us as well!'

I didn't want to think about that or to have the conversation. Laura would know the details soon enough.

'There's no point in worrying,' I said, sounding facile and evasive. We reached the jeep. I put her bags in the back.

'You don't think it was the IRA?'

'What makes you think that?'

'The fact that they're English. Could it be some sort of anti-English thing. It's happened before, hasn't it?'

'But Ingrid's from Germany.'

'You know what I mean.'

'I doubt it.'

We drove for a while without speaking.

'How is Rachael?'

I was embarrassed at how long it had taken me to enquire about her.

'She's okay now,' Laura said. 'Jack turned out to be a bit of a bastard.'

'I'm not surprised to hear it. What happened?'

'They went out together a few times, then he dumped her.'

'He dumped her?'

'Yes. He told her that she was immature compared with girls he knew in London. He took her to a party where everyone there seemed to have gone out of their way to be bitchy to her. Then his girlfriend turned up.'

'Poor Rachael! Is she shattered?'

'Not really. She was for a while but then she made friends with a girl who lives near to Mummy's house. They play tennis and go to things.'

We were driving through Drumcondra. The traffic was surprisingly light. Laura talked about the family of Rachael's friend and, for a while, it was almost as if everything was normal. Then, after we had left the city and were on the way home she said, 'I still can't believe what happened to Ingrid! It just doesn't make sense. When do you think we can see her?'

'I have no idea. I suppose Bill will get in touch with us.'

'Did you send flowers?'

'There hasn't really been time. I spent half the morning in the bloody barracks!'

'It's good you were able to help,' she said vaguely, as if reassuring a child.

'I don't think I was any help whatsoever. I wish I had never mentioned that car! He acted as if I were withholding information.'

'I'm sure he didn't, darling! Why would he do that?'

'It's the way they're trained,' I said.

We were driving towards the mountains but the sight had lost its usual power to heal. I felt increasingly agitated as we came closer to home and deliberately avoided passing Cromer's house.

'It's lovely to be home,' Laura said when our own house came into view. 'What a pity there has to be such sadness!'

'It's great you're back,' I said, wanting to mean it but feeling real apprehension.

'The house looks lovely,' Laura said. 'I really missed it. And I missed you!'

We kissed, lightly, then got out of the jeep. I carried her bags into the house and up to our bedroom. I heard her going from room to room as if to reassure herself that nothing had changed. I attempted not to think of Cromer doing the same thing.

I went downstairs and poured us drinks. The study was untidy. I gathered magazines from the floor and and put them into the bin in the kitchen. When I went back to the study, wondering what we would say to each other next, Laura was looking out of the window, the glass of gin and tonic in her hand.

'You don't think they'll come here?' she asked.

'Of course not! That wouldn't make any sense.'

'It doesn't make any sense now.'

'This isn't Belfast,' I said. 'It's an isolated incident. A terrible one but isolated.'

'But what if all that violence is about to cross the border? It could so easily. It's all happening just up the road!'

'I don't know why you keep on thinking that the IRA were involved.'

'I can't think of who else would have any kind of motive. What a pity you can't remember anything else about that car.'

'I wish I had never even mentioned that car!'

'Was he a nice man, the Superintendent?'

'Not particularly. Not at all, in fact.'

'Did he know who you were? Did he know that you were a writer?'

'He said he had read one of my books.'

We sat beside each other on the sofa near my desk and there was something really sad about the subdued nature of her home-coming. We were like strangers in the lounge of some hotel, wary about getting to know each other, keeping to ourselves. Laura looked tired and strained and the suit she was wearing was wrinkled from the journey. She finished her drink.

'I'm going to take a shower,' she said.

'I thought that we might go somewhere for a meal later?'

'I'd be just as happy with something here. Is there anything in the house?'

'I'll take something out of the fridge.'

'Something simple.'

She went upstairs and I finished my drink, saddened by the constraint between us. When I heard the splash of water in the shower I found it was Ingrid's naked body that I was picturing.

I went into the kitchen and prepared a salad to go with the meats that I knew were in the fridge. It was pleasingly distracting to mix the ingredients in a large wooden bowl that we had bought together at some craft fair. The holiday smell of the olive oil evoked mixed memories. The telephone rang. I picked it up.

'Hello?' Cromer said.

I didn't know how to reply. I could hear his breathing as if he had rushed to make the call.

'Hello?'

'Bill,' I said.

'I'm glad you're home. Is it all right if I call around?'

'Of course. What's the word on Ingrid?'

'She's making good progress. I'm just leaving the hospital now.'

'You haven't been home yet?'

'Not yet. I'll drop off my stuff, then come round to see you.'

'That's fine.'

'I have so much to tell you,' Cromer said. 'And I want to thank you as well.'

'You don't have to thank me.'

'Of course I do! I'll get to you as soon as I can.'

I wanted to get drunk, to replace responsibility with stupidity, to drift away from the facts and hide behind some fantasy. I wanted to pretend that none of this had happened, that I had made it up, creating a work of fiction out of the mundane facts of my life. I poured another drink and heard Laura move from the bathroom to the bedroom.

When she came downstairs she was wearing blue jeans and a black top.

'What's wrong?' she asked. 'Who was on the phone? You look dreadful.'

'Bill Cromer.'

'Has something else happened?'

'No. He's calling by soon.'

'Good. Maybe he'll be able to make sense of it all. How did he sound?'

'As you'd expect.'

I felt disadvantaged by her concern and by her post-shower vivacity. Her remark about my appearance was disconcerting. Did I really look dreadful? Yes, I probably did. She was sitting on an armchair near to the window, her legs bent beneath her buttocks, looking, suddenly, young and provocative and ready for love. I felt old and sour and dismayed by the violence I had unleashed.

'I don't think that you've recovered from the shock yet,' she said with a sympathetic smile that really annoyed me. Some criticism was implied. I sat down beside her and we chatted in a desultory way. All time I was waiting to hear the sound of Cromer's car. We talked about Rachael again.

'I never liked Jack,' I said, too emphatically.

'Didn't you? I don't remember you ever saying that.'

'I'm sure I did.'

'She bounced back,' Laura said. 'It could have been much worse.'

We had our supper of ham and the salad that I had made and a white wine that was disappointingly sweet and some of the brandy that Laura had bought at Heathrow. If things had been different, we would then have gone upstairs and made love but I knew that there would have been something different about my performance, a diminution of conviction, and that she would hate me even more when she learned about Ingrid.

We brought the brandy into the study and I forced a conversation between us, asking question after question about her parents and the details of her travel.

She was talking about a boring West End play of brittle, over-articulate inter-relationships when I heard the car. It came slowly up the drive, its sidelights faint in the twilight. I recognized it immediately and felt actual nausea, the physical symptom, I suppose, of cowardice. I looked helplessly at Laura but she was pleased that Bill had arrived. The thought of his company must have promised a welcome relief from my evasive intensity.

'How awful!' Laura said suddenly. 'Why didn't we think? We should have made some supper for him.'

'I doubt he'll want anything after all that he's been through.'

Cromer got out of his car and walked briskly to our front door. I went, reluctantly, and opened it.

'How is Ingrid?' I asked before he had a chance to say anything.

'Still very shocked.'

He kissed Laura.

'You must be very shocked yourself,' she said. 'Come in and have a brandy. Have you eaten? I can easily fix you some supper.'

'No, please don't,' he said as we went into the study. 'I'm not hungry. But I wouldn't say no to that brandy.'

I poured him a large measure and the three of us sat, a little uneasily, as if each was waiting for one of the others to speak first. He didn't appear to be hostile. He held the brandy glass between his hands like a priest about to elevate a chalice. I asked him if he had been home.

'Yes,' he said, without looking at me. 'I've just come from there.'

'But tell us about Ingrid?' Laura said.

'The wounds on her head are the worst. She was concussed for quite some time. She has several broken ribs and wounds all over her body that I could hardly bear to look at. She remembers two men.'

'Who were they?'

Laura was leaning towards him as if physical proximity could help her to empathize with what he was saying.

'That's the question,' Cromer said. 'People determined to destroy a world. That's for sure.'

'And nothing was taken?'

'No, it wasn't a robbery. They came to harm us.'

'I told you,' Laura said to me, 'that it must have been the IRA.'

'There's the additional disadvantage,' Cromer said, 'that Ingrid is even worse than me at differentiating between one Irish accent and another. But she was able to give reasonably good physical descriptions.'

'That's good.'

Cromer placed his glass on the table.

'I wonder if you'd mind, Laura,' he said to her, 'if John and I were to take a short walk. It would help to clear my head.'

'Please do,' Laura said. 'I was actually going to suggest it.'

I stood up, reluctantly, holding my glass. I had no idea what to expect. His mood, subdued but not noticeably unfriendly, made it impossible to predict what he was likely to say or do.

We went outside. The evening air had cooled but was filled with the pungent essence of late summer. A startled bird was protesting in a bush near the road. We walked down the drive in silence, then Cromer said 'I'm not going to waste any time. I want us to be upfront about this.'

'Of course,' I said, although I didn't yet know what I was agreeing to or why we were walking side by side in so apparently companionable a manner.

'One of the first things I saw when I got home,' Cromer said, 'was a bag left in a corner of the kitchen. I didn't think it was ours, so I looked in it and found champagne and port and overnight things. I was quite certain that it must belong to one of the bastards who had attacked Ingrid, so I telephoned the guards. The Superintendent told me that it was yours.'

'That's right,' I said because there was nothing else that I could say. We stopped at the gate.

'It's yours,' Cromer repeated as if he were still working out the implications of the fact.

'Then, later, I went upstairs and saw that the spare room had been turned into some kind of love nest.'

He wasn't looking at me. He stared in the direction of his own house, his back against a gatepost. He appeared calm, although I could see a nerve beating above his right cheek. I looked away from him, back towards the house where Laura was outlined in the study window, grey and insubstantial, like a haunting. The silence intensified into something almost tangible, as if it were a third presence. I knew that I had to say something but could think of no response that would match the mood of his words. I thought that I might be able to cope with anger or bitterness more easily.

'I take it that you had nothing whatsoever to do with what happened to her?'

'Please,' I said, 'you must at least know that.'

'I'd do my very best to kill you if you had!'

He still appeared to be calm, even withdrawn, but his tone of voice suggested that these were qualities of strength. He was totally in charge of the conversation. He sighed and looked at me.

'I thought you were a friend,' he said.

He said this with a tone of genuine surprise as if he had never before encountered betrayal. His definition of friendship, to which I could no longer aspire, excluded me so totally that I felt a kind of shame.

'I wouldn't have done that to Laura,' he said.

Something about that stung me into replying.

'Why do you speak about it as if Ingrid were entirely passive? Waiting to have something done to her?'

That was more hostile than I had intended but the words came out like a weak and unconvincing defence.

'Because adultery usually takes a fair bit of pressure from the man, doesn't it? Are you trying to say that Ingrid persuaded you into it?'

'No. Not at all! We were attracted to each other. You were away. Laura was away. It just happened naturally.'

This lie was so unconvincing that I was embarrassed by it. It lay between us like a blatant falsity, something contemptible when compared to the things that he had been saying. I wondered what Ingrid would think of me if she could see me cutting so poor a figure. In attempting to deny the reality of our love, I was betraying her with the same carelessness that I had shown towards Laura.

'The truth is, I have no excuses.'

'I wouldn't want to have heard them. Does Laura know yet?'

'Not yet. Are you going to tell her?'

'No. You're going to tell her.' It was the first time in the conversation that he sounded angry. 'You're going to tell her!' For a moment or two I thought that he was going to throw a punch. I tensed, waiting for the blur of his fist, the scuffle afterwards as we swayed together like a couple engaged in some crazy kind of waltz. He was bigger than I was and broader and probably stronger but I knew one or two foul blows that he would not anticipate. Then he turned away.

'I might have guessed,' he said, 'that the only thing that would concern you is Laura finding out.'

'That's not true! Of course I'm concerned about Ingrid.'

'What right have you to be concerned about her?'

'As a friend.'

'You couldn't just have settled for friendship, could you?'

He was beginning to sound more bitter. It was as if the strength and composure he had shown had become too great a burden and anger and wounded pride were breaking through.

'How long has it being going on? And no bullshit! I want to know the truth.'

'Not long.'

'That's not an answer.'

A teenage girl on a mountain bike came down the road at considerable speed. She braked when she saw us, the wheels of her bike grating against the road, then pedalled forward again, her head in a bright, red helmet bent low over the handlebars, her legs in tight white trousers moving as if entirely separate from the stillness of her upper body. The effect was entirely sexual and might have been arranged in some kind of ironic contrast to our conversation.

Cromer stared after her then said to me, 'What will your daughter think about it?'

'Look,' I said, 'I'm sorry that it happened, I really am, but it happened.'

'How often?'

'Just twice.'

'Is that the truth?'

'Yes,' I lied. 'It is.'

'I don't think I can believe you.'

'And anyway,' I said, 'your son treated my daughter very badly.'

'What does that have to do with it?'

'Nothing, I suppose.'

'I've nothing more to say at the moment but you better tell Laura before I do.'

He walked back to his car. I followed a few paces behind him like a poor relation, aware of my place. When he reached the car he turned and said, 'I was going to hit you but what's the point? I don't think I'd get any satisfaction from it.'

He got into the car and turned it before the front door. Then he accelerated quickly towards me. There was plenty of room on the drive but he made no attempt to swerve so that I had to step back very quickly, stumbling on the edge of the grass and falling backwards. The wheels of the car went past very close to my outstretched legs. The car slowed a little at the gate, then drove quickly towards the crossroads.

I got up slowly. My left wrist ached a little. Laura came hurrying from the house.

'What happened?'

'I tripped,' I said. 'I must have stumbled over something, though I can't see what it was.'

'Why did he leave so quickly? He didn't even say goodbye. Why did he drive away like a madman?'

'He's very stressed,' I said. 'It's not surprising.'

We walked back to the house. She had turned on the lamps in the study so that part of the room was framed by the window like a painting of a country interior. There was a glimpse of books on shelves, real and accessible, the back of an armchair, a lamp on a drum table. I longed to enter the safe and tranquil world that it suggested, to move from reality to this fiction.

I followed her inside.

'Please!' she said. 'I'm not a fool. What exactly is going on?'

We went into the study. Cromer's brandy was on the table beside our own glasses.

'I told you. He's very stressed. He's not rational.'

'He was perfectly rational ten minutes ago.'

'I'm just telling you what I observed.'

'Just tell me,' she said. 'I saw that you were arguing at the gate.'

I noticed how tired her eyes looked, their colour faded. I was touched and longed to reassure her but knew that this was impossible. The face that I had known for so long was beginning to show signs of age: a dryness beneath the eyes, vertical lines above the nose, a slackness of skin at the corners of the mouth. If I could have reached out and embraced her, I would probably have wept with guilt and loneliness and a longing for the easy emotions that we had shared. Instead I felt, hopelessly, that nothing would ever be the same again.

'All right,' I said, 'I'll tell you. He believes that I was having an affair with Ingrid.' She sat down on the sofa.

'And were you?' she asked.

'Laura,' I said, 'please let me try to explain.'

'Is that a yes?'

'I suppose so. No, I wouldn't call it an affair. We just got involved.'

'Jesus!' she said, 'I can't believe that you're standing there so calmly telling me this. Why would you get involved with Ingrid? We had a lovely relationship. Why would you want to destroy that?'

She was staring at me, bewildered at what I had done to her world.

'It wasn't like that,' I said weakly, not even knowing what I meant. I sat down on the armchair and reached out for my glass.

'Leave that glass alone!' she said. 'Talk to me. What do you think you were doing, you stupid bastard?'

'Let me try to explain.'

Her face was distorted with anger, her eyes narrowing, her lips clenched tightly. This was the worst moment we had ever shared.

Her hostility and contempt were like forces pressing against my chest as I attempted to speak. We appeared to be locked into a stopped moment. I noticed that she wasn't blinking and that one wrist was frozen into an awkward angle that looked too difficult to maintain for long.

'I'm sorry,' I said. 'I just don't know why.'

'Has it being going on for long?' she asked in a tone that was more controlled but no less hostile.

'Only since you went away.'

'I don't believe you. I *know* you're lying. I bet you've been fucking her for ages.'

'Not at all!'

She looked at me contemptuously.

'How did he find out?'

'I left an overnight bag in their house.'

'So you were planning to fuck her the night before I came home!'

'I'm sorry.'

'You're sorry that you've been caught! I'll never be able to believe anything that you say! How often has this happened before?'

'Never.'

'I don't believe you! I think it's pathetic that you've behaved like this. There've been times in the past when I wondered but I always gave you the benefit of the doubt! What a fool I was!'

She began to cry, her shoulders moving convulsively. This was even worse than her anger.

'If I could make things different ...' I said.

'But you can't, can you? This is what you've made! This wreckage of everything that we've built up together.'

Her face was bloated and streaked with tears. I hate the detachment with which I make this observation, as if I were out of the scene, looking in on it, but that is how it looked.

'I'll try to explain,' I said.

'Don't bother! Why should I listen to some self-serving rant?'

'Please forgive me.'

She looked across at me and, although her eyes were blurred with tears, her expression was cold.

'If it had been some casual encounter I might. But someone we know! A friend? Someone who lives just down the road! No wonder Bill Cromer tried to drive into you!'

'That was an accident.'

'It didn't look like an accident to me. Was she here? In this house?'

'No.'

'Of course she was! You fucked her in our house! You fucked her in our bed!'

'I swear ...'

'Don't swear anything! Why should I believe you? Will you be happy when Rachael hears all about this?'

'I'd hate that!' I said sincerely.

She walked out of the room. I looked at the empty doorway. The house became very quiet, as if absorbing some stillness from the darkness outside. It was immensely uncomfortable to be there with her in an atmosphere of such hostility. Looking back on it now I suppose that what I hated most was being so totally in the wrong. I know that my account is accurate and so am shocked by my own crassness. I was thinking only of myself and taking very little responsibility for my actions. It took several weeks for me to confront the hurt that I had done to Laura. I had no real sympathy for Cromer and, in truth, I have little enough sympathy for him now. Nothing in his work suggests that he would regard sexual fidelity as an admirable male quality. I have no actual evidence for it but I'm sure that he himself had many affairs. Last Sunday, I read in one of the British newspapers that his first novel in almost ten years will be published in the autumn. I will read it with considerable interest and look for my shadow in it.

Later, when I went upstairs, unsteady from having had too much to drink, I found that the door to our bedroom had been locked. This had never happened before. Standing there, I felt that I had blundered into somebody else's life. The situation was so clichéd; I had seen it in innumerable bad movies. Was I supposed to rattle the handle in protest or rush at the door using my shoulder as a battering ram?

I went into the room in which Ingrid and I had made love. I imagined that I could sense her presence there like some sexual expectation. Perhaps a trace of her scent remained. I lay on the bed and thought of our time there, desiring her, remembering the urgency of her kisses. I longed to know where she was, what she was thinking, what she knew. I heard a car drive down the road and slow down near to the gate. I wondered if it were Cromer but the car drove away.

I didn't want to spend any more time in that room. I went down to the study and smoked a cigarette while half-listening to something on the radio. I wondered if Laura had gone to sleep. It seemed improbable. I imagined her in our bed, curled up on her right side, her knees against her stomach, her eyes open as she considered what had happened to us. I wished that I were with her, drawing strength from the precious familiarity of a loved body. It seemed so wrong, regardless of what had happened, that we were separated in a house that we had fashioned into a symbol of our unity. I considered going upstairs and tapping on the door, acting out the least violent of the familiar clichés. Perhaps she was as lonely as I was and would welcome my presence. It took me only moments to know that this would not be so.

At some stage, with the radio still playing and a half-finished glass of brandy on the table, I fell asleep.

NINETEEN

IN THE MORNING, everything seemed to be a little worse. I woke abruptly, immediately aware of the discomfort that I felt from having slept on a chair.

My shoulders and arms ached and there was a sharp pain in the small of my back as if I had pulled a muscle. The air in the study was stale.

It was fourteen minutes past eight. Outside, the day was already bright and exhilarating, sunlight reaching one corner of the lawn, leaves stirring in a breeze. When I went to the window I immediately noticed that Laura's car was not parked outside. She usally left for work at just about this time but since she was still officially on holidays I was surprised by its absence.

I went upstairs. The door to the bedroom was open; there was something reproachful about the unmade bed. The jeans and the top that she had been wearing were bundled into the open laundry basket. Nothing else in the room had changed.

I ran a bath and felt some of the tensions in my body dissolve in the embracing heat. The day stretched ahead like some kind of unfamiliar threat; hours to be put down, nothing to do except worry about consequences.

I wished that I had some word from Ingrid and knew what

Laura was doing. The monotony of the day was overpowering, tedium and tension replacing each other at irregular intervals. Even the countryside seemed boring; paths that I had walked, hills that I had climbed were places where I did not want to be.

I thought it would be a good idea to seek distraction by driving into Dublin for lunch and spending time in the bookshops or in the National Gallery. This germ of an idea cheered me in the way, I suppose, that distractions must cheer the days of the old. I wished that I had work to distract me and for a while I looked through a file in which I had noted down ideas that I had once thought might be developed into something. One of these, a two-page portrait of a man whom I had known when I had worked in Belfast, appeared to be of some interest. He had come from the North of England at a time of particular unrest in Belfast. A sniper had shot a number of British soldiers in the vicinity of the Divis Flats. Coincidentally, or, more probably, in retaliation, four Roman Catholics had been shot on their way to their jobs on a building site on the outskirts of the city. Rumours of greatly increased action by both sides were being fed, nightly, to the journalists in the bar and lobby of the Europa Hotel.

He had come into this hothouse world full of urgency and a need to talk. He had created a complex narrative about himself which some thought to be fiction and others accepted as true. One evening, he claimed to me and to three of my colleagues that he had acted, for five years, as an agent of British intelligence in Dublin. Throughout that time, he told us earnestly, he had not only gained the confidence of a number of relatively unknown but important Republican leaders but had also collected invaluable information from a prominent government minister with whom he had had a sexual relationship. I knew the minister in question and had heard some speculation about his proclivities but had never seen unassailable evidence about it. And the story just didn't seem convincing. I told him this and added that to make claims like this, in Belfast, was inviting a death sentence.

'Well I don't tell everyone!' he protested.

'But you've just told us and you hardly know who we are.'

'I know your by-lines.'

'That doesn't tell you enough!'

'I've got to talk to someone,' he said. 'I've got to get a voice. The buggers have cut me off completely now that I'm no use to them.'

He stuck to his story for several weeks; one had to concede that he believed in it passionately. Then his confidence visibly deteriorated. He seemed to live in real fear that his bosses, whoever they may have been, had formulated plans to harm him. I remember his fear like a kind of sickness; he changed and weakened as the days went by. Then, one afternoon, his naked body was found in a ditch beside a country lane outside the city. A black plastic bag had been pulled down over his head and he had been shot, once, in the back of the neck. None of the paramilitary groups claimed responsibility for his death, so, after a while, I had to concede that, in some crazed way, he may have been telling the truth as he understood it.

I had often thought about him since then as a possible central character in a novel, a man of complex loyalties, punished for a fact or for a fiction. I sat at my desk and wrote a possible opening sentence, 'This is an attempt to discover the truth about Davis.' I paused, wondering how I could go on to describe his humble and imploring eyes, his slightly sycophantic manner, his accent, which changed, perceptibly, under stress, his unusually pale skin. I liked the directness of the sentence that I had written and, suddenly, it seemed possible that I would begin writing again. 'I can picture him as he was that day in the bar of the Europa Hotel, small and apologetic, looking at me with his imploring eyes, wanting me to believe him.'

I thought about the next sentence, then put the sheet of paper that I had been writing on back into the file.

The telephone rang. I stared at it as if dazed. When I went across to answer it, the ringing stopped. I was filled with apprehension. A post van came up the drive and there was the satisfying, normal sound of letters falling onto the hall floor. Three were for Laura; I recognized the handwriting of two of her English friends.

There was a letter for Rachael from the Belgian penfriend with whom she had corresponded for years. The rest were household bills or direct mail pieces.

The telephone rang.

I ran into the kitchen and snatched up the receiver.

'Hello!'

'Hi, Dad.'

She sounded very young and flustered and I knew that she would be twisting a strand of her hair between her left thumb and forefinger.

'How are you?' I said. 'It's lovely to hear you.'

'Is Mum there?'

'Not at the moment.'

'Will she be back soon? She's not at work, is she? Not until next week.'

'I'm not quite certain when she'll be back. I was out when she left.'

'I see.'

'Are you at Granny's?'

'Yes. I've just got up.'

'Can I help?' I asked uncertainly.

'Well not exactly,' she said after a pause. 'Well, maybe.'

'Tell me about it.'

'I lost all my money.'

'Darling,' I said, 'I thought something terrible had happened!'

'It's terrible for me!'

'I'm sorry. It's just that I thought you might be in real trouble.'

'I must have left my purse in a taxi last night. I had about seventy-five pounds in it.'

'I'll post you a cheque today. Papa will change it for you tomorrow.'

'Do you mind?' she said, sounding so relieved that I wished that our other problems could be so easily solved.

'I'm only delighted. I really miss you!' I said, remembering the fierceness of her determination when she was small. The force of her will had been a feature of her childhood.

'I miss you! But I'll be home in less than a week.'

'That'll be lovely! Won't you ask Papa for money until your cheque arrives?'

'I won't have to do that. I had some in another jacket.'

'I love you.'

'Love you. Give my love to Mum.'

'I'll do that.'

I felt drained by relief that she hadn't yet heard about the troubles to which she would be returning. I was also glad to have something to do. I wrote the cheque and a short, affectionate note. I copied her address from a notebook on my desk. Years before, I had written dozens of letters to Laura at that same address, letters filled with excitement and expectation. I made myself a coffee, more interested now in going to the Post Office than in spending the day in the city. I was looking out of the kitchen window when the telephone rang. 'Yes?'

'I can't stay long,' Ingrid said.

'Jesus!' I said. 'How are you? Are you all right? I had no idea I'd hear from you.'

'I'm still in the hospital. But I'm much better. Battered but better. We're going away tomorrow.'

'How do you mean? Where to?'

'I don't know. Somewhere. They asked me to be available for a while, so I can't leave the country.'

'I wish I could see you. What happened to you? Who did that to you?'

'I don't know. They just pushed their way into the house, shouting. I couldn't even understand most of what they were saying. They said we shouldn't be here. That Bill was a spy.'

'You know that he knows about us?'

'What do you mean?'

'He knows that we were lovers.'

'How do you know that?'

'He was here yesterday. He tackled me about it.'

'I didn't know that,' she said without any evident concern. 'But it explains something.'

'What?'

'He wants us to get married.'

'You can't be serious!' I said, surprisingly hurt. 'I'm longing to see you.'

'It's better not,' she said.

'Are you going to marry him?'

'I haven't said yet but I don't see why not.'

'That doesn't sound very positive.'

I could hear, in the background, a doctor being summoned over a public address system. There was so much that I wanted to say to her but I couldn't say it.

'Does Laura know?'

'Yes.'

'Does she mind?'

'She minds a lot.'

'What a mess!'

'Well it all seems to be working out for you,' I said bitterly.

'You think so?'

'I'm sorry,' I said. 'I'm just confused. I miss you. I hardly know what's happening. I think Bill tried to drive into me when he was leaving last night.'

'No,' she said emphatically. 'He wouldn't do anything like that.'

It irritated me that she came so quickly to his defence.

'If I hadn't jumped aside…,' I said.

'He wouldn't. That's not like Bill.'

'I love you,' I said inadequately. 'I really love you. I'm so sorry that it's turned out so badly. It's all such shit. I wish that we could talk about it.'

'I'll have to go,' she said. 'There are people waiting to use the phone.'

'Just another minute! Please! Do you love me?'

'I don't know. So much has happened.'

'But you did, didn't you?'

'What's the point in saying that?'

'Are you going to marry him?'

'Oh please!' she said. 'Maybe.'

'I miss you,' I said after some time had passed. I felt pangs of jealousy, loss and envy. Silence stretched between us like an intimation of loss. Even the hospital sounds, the hints of other people's routines, had dulled into a faint background presence.

'I'm going to have to go,' she said.

'Do you miss me?'

'Yes, I do,' she said but in a tone of voice that was oddly without emotion.

She sounded like someone repeating a phrase in a language lesson.

'I hope that it all works out for you.'

'You too. I really have to go now. Bill will be here soon.'

'I understand. I love you.'

'Goodbye,' she said before hanging up with a shocking abruptness. The dull day surrounded me like an endurance test.

I walked to the corner and posted the letter to Rachael. On my way back I bumped into O'Dalaigh. He lifted his walking stick in a kind of gruff greeting.

'There was an ambush there once,' he said, pointing back towards the corner with his stick.

'Really? I thought that it was down at the crossroads.'

'No. There,' he said emphatically, as if correcting a troublesome child. His hands trembled and a small trickle of saliva came from one corner of his mouth. There was a shaving cut on his chin. Despite his pallor, his eyes were bright and cunningly alert.

'We had the word about them,' he said. 'We had a man in the barracks in Bray. We knew to within half an hour when they'd be coming around that corner. Eight of us were behind this wall here and four were in that ditch up above. It was higher then. It divided the field. We all had rifles and thirty-five rounds. Joe Byrne had a Mills bomb. It was a cold day, nothing like this, and we came here early to get into place. There was good cover. Plenty of local people went by on the road and not a single one of them saw us. John Fahey, who was inside that wall, beside myself, heard his own brother talking about him, saying he was a stupid man. I had gone to confession the evening before. The priest wasn't with us but he wasn't against us either. "Mind yourself!" he said to me after I had said my Act of Contrition. I never forgot that.'

He spoke in a monotone, looking back towards the corner all the time, yet there was something hypnotic about the story. I was repelled to be standing so close to an old scene of violence, yet fascinated by it. It was almost like taking part in some experiment with time. I had a sense that, at any moment, the Crossley tenders would come around the corner, dust spurting from beneath their wheels, the sound of their engines echoing around the empty countryside.

As if to mock at this conceit, a very old blue van owned by a local builder came around the corner and drove noisily towards us. The builder pressed the horn twice as he passed us.

'We heard them when they were nearly a mile away, two of them, like we'd been told. We were all in our positions. One of the lads put a bit of an old log out onto the road. It wasn't blocking the road or anything. It was just a nuisance. They were singing when they came around the corner, some rubbishy old song. They walked right into it. The first driver slowed when he saw the log and Joe Byrne let them have the Mills bomb. That killed the driver and two of the Tans and the tender went off the road just there. We picked the rest of them off no bother and the lads above in the ditch gave it to them in the second tender when they tried to drive past. We had been told to take no prisoners; to give them a taste of their own medicine. Well, they got plenty of it I can tell you! One boyo got out of the second tender and went legging it down the road but we used him for target practice. It was a comical sight!

You wouldn't believe the noise. Deafening! And he screamed like a pig!'

I turned away from him and looked up the field to the ditch. In the stillness of the day, the singing of a blackbird seemed to be imbued with a certain alarm.

'We got every single one of them!'

He was leaning against the wall. The effort at telling his story had taken its toll.

'It took us a while to clean up,' he said unexpectedly. 'We gathered up their weapons and their papers. We threw the bodies in a heap over there and we burned the tenders.'

'Were any on your side injured?' I asked. He looked vague for some moments as if this were an aspect that he hadn't considered for many years.

'My side?' he said, looking at me with his old, red-rimmed, bright eyes. 'We had some losses. There are always losses! But remember they were entirely wiped out. Fourteen of them. The bastards got Tom Traynor. And John Fahey. Michael Russell was wounded in the side and he died in Arklow a few weeks later.'

'I'm surprised there isn't a cross here,' I said.

'I think that there used to be and something drove into it. I hear that your friends above in the Old Rectory had a spot of bother?'

'Who would have done that?' I said, hoping that my abruptness would take him by surprise. 'Why would anyone want to do that?'

'There's all kinds of strange boyos going these days,' he said. 'We're none of us safe in our own beds!'

'I think it had a political dimension.'

'What had politics got to do with it?'

'What have politics got to do with any act of aggression?' I asked, knowing that this theoretical question was beyond his grasp and was, in any case, rhetorical. He leaned heavily on his stick.

'What are you talking about? Ours was a glorious revolution.'

He was too old to have his bloodthirsty memories subjected to any critical appraisal. Having lived his life as a local hero, a man

with contacts, real if remote in the upper echelons of the Fianna
Fáil party, he was n ot going to reconsider inglorious moments.

'These things can go wrong,' I said vaguely, wishing that I
hadn't met him.

'Glorious!' he said, banging his stick against the road. 'Glorious.'

'How are you getting home?' I asked him, for he lived three or
four miles away.

'No bother to me,' he said. 'I'll walk home the same as I always
do. I cut through the fields in no time.'

As if to demonstrate his agility, he crossed the road and scram-
bled through a narrow gap in the hedge and set off across the field
at an unexpectedly fast pace. I watched until he was out of sight.

I walked home slowly, determined at some future time to
research the incident and discover how accurate his memories
were. When I got to our gate I hoped to see Laura's car but it
was not there. I wished that I knew where she were. Who would
she go to at a time like this? Whom did she trust? I knew little
enough about the actual details of her professional life. I think
that I assumed, rather than knew, that she was good at her job but
when she talked about it, usually when we were having our evening
meal, it was because she was upset or amused by the minutiae of
hospital politics. If she confronted important ethical issues, she
never discussed them with me. I think that we may have evaded
questions of career because of my own ongoing failure to write.
There were other doctors, male and female – a psychiatrist, a paediatrician, an oncologist – with whom she was friendly and whom I
had met but I didn't think that any of them would be the recipient
of important confidences. A certain reticence may also have been
imposed by the checks and balances of medical politics. It was difficult to imagine her with any of them today, taking up their time,
telling them about the shock of my infidelity. The need to appear,
a few days later, cool and unemotional at a departmental finance
sub-committee would preclude an honest exposure of the extent
of her hurt.

The house enclosed me with its newly acquired air of reproach. My study smelled of stale tobacco and I resolved to give up smoking soon. The thought of being without cigarettes filled me with a sudden panic, so that I lit one and inhaled deeply, relishing it.

The telephone rang. When I answered it, Laura said 'It's me.'

I could hardly contain the excitement that I felt on hearing from her, even though the call from Ingrid had been equally welcome. Her voice humanized the situation; she was not the injured party or the affronted wife. She was the woman whom I had loved for almost twenty years. I hardly trusted myself to speak to her, afraid that even one syllable of what I might say would betray the complexity of my feelings.

'Where are you calling from?' I asked, attempting to make the question appear concerned rather than inquisitorial. Before she replied, it occurred to me, for the very first time, that she might have a lover. The special recipient of important confidences about whom I had speculated earlier would almost certainly be a man, someone mature and reliable and reassuring. I attempted to imagine him and discovered no jealousy until I imagined her naked in his reassuring arms. But it would mean that she would lose moral superiority and could no longer criticize my own unfaithfulness. In a sense, any prospect of future happiness for us could depend on the existence of this lover.

'I'm at Catherine's,' she said.

Catherine? The paediatrician. I had once sat beside her at dinner, a small, sallow-skinned woman with big teeth and dark-brown, ursine eyes. I remembered wondering if her hugs would be as rib-challenging as her broad shoulders and muscular upper arms suggested. Her smile had been disarming. It was sudden and unexpected and it illuminated her face, making her look younger and more sexually alluring. Her husband, a successful businessman who imported or exported machine parts, was a bore.

'Have you been there all the time?'

'Yes,' she said, not appearing to detect the jealousy inherent in the question. 'I came here early this morning. Before you woke up. I just had to get out of the house.'

'I'm sorry,' I said. 'Please tell me if there's anything I can do. I don't expect you to trust me but if there's something …'

'I've talked to Catherine about it. I had to talk to someone.'

'Of course,' I said, insincerely, resenting the poor figure that I must now cut in Catherine's eyes. Yet I remembered when, after the dinner, speaking to her in a corner of our living room while the others were arguing about the health service in the way that one does when just a little too much wine has been enjoyed, I, also a little drunk and discussing some book that we had both read, had spoken to her flirtatiously and she had responded in a manner that may have been amused or polite or even interested. Her professional knowledge, her skill with the complex workings of the body, had added to the allure.

'She's been a real help.'

'I'm glad.'

'I'm going to stay here tonight.'

'I miss you.'

'I don't want Rachael to know,' she said, 'so I'll be back before she comes home.'

'She was on the phone earlier. She had lost her purse, so I sent her a cheque.'

'You didn't say anything?'

'Of course not!'

'It's not for your sake,' she said. 'It's for hers.'

'I'm so relieved that she's not going to be involved.'

'I still have lots of thinking to do.'

'I understand that completely.'

I think that we had been closer on our very first date. I seemed to have lost the ability to decode her tone of voice, to fill some meaning into her silences. The telephone receiver was unpleasantly hot in my hand and I was angry at myself for having nothing appropriate to

say. To be honest, although I was manifestly in the wrong, I none-
theless resented having to make these efforts towards reparation. I
wanted to be back, unpunished, into the old, easy relationship in
which I played a part that was unquestioned, good husband and
father. If, as now seemed at least possible, we were going to work
at some kind of possible future, I welcomed that, but resented the
thought of the long climb back, the measured progress, the cur-
tailments of freedom.

'It's not just Ingrid,' she said, 'although that's bad enough. It's
also the thought of the others that there might have been when I
thought that we had everything.'

'But there weren't others.'

'You'd have to say that!'

'It just happened,' I said, despising my own tone of voice
which was helpless, as if seeking sympathy.

I could hear another woman speaking in the background – I
suppose it must have been Catherine – and Laura became distracted.

'I'll phone you tomorrow,' she said.

She hung up without saying anything else. I knew that we had
made a start of a sort, an inch of the journey towards reconciliation, but that there would be much bitterness and anger along the
way. It would erupt in moments of apparent calm, revealing new
aspects of how broken trust can fragment into hostility. I pictured
her face, the young woman whom I had met on Grafton Street, the
curve of her cheeks tightening, interesting lines appearing on her
face. She seldom spoke when we made love, her eyes closed, her
lower lip trembling, her fingers moving restlessly along my back
until, at the moment of orgasm, she would sigh, with an exhalation
of air that seemed to have been held in her lungs for longer than
one might have thought possible.

The room was darkening and suddenly chilled, as if absorbing
my regret and my self-pity. I stared out at the dim shadows on the
lawn, remembering the details in O'Dalaigh's story, and it was as
if I could hear the lorries coming down the road, driving towards

my gate, the men singing. The sound of the Mills bomb must have been shocking as the rifles barked.

I believe that I saw my estrangement from both Ingrid and Laura as a kind of violence, as if it had been imposed by some independent, tyrannical force. I know that later that evening I wept. Perhaps it was with regret or perhaps I was like a child wishing this was merely a pretence that had got out of hand and that everything would eventually return to normal.

I sat there in the darkening room, like a figure in a Victorian novel, invested with some kind of symbolic role, the miser or the sleepless cuckold.

I attempted to remember anything positive that Laura had said or anything that could be cherished about my relationship with Ingrid. I kept on expecting the telephone to ring yet again and an unknown voice to make some kind of sense out of all the disparate pieces. Had the foolish journey to Belfast precipitated all the events that had followed? Had that old, bloodthirsty man intervened in some brutal way? Had Cromer any connection with espionage services? Was there a pattern to be found and imposed upon all these events as might be done by the omniscient narrator of a book, or was the summer a collection of fragmented pieces that had no connection with one another?

The summer was coming to an end, the days getting shorter, the nights cooler.

It was a melancholy time of year, those uneasy weeks between seasons that are characterized by small decays, the deaths of insects, the wilting of flowers. I liked the maturity of autumn but that was still some weeks away. In the meantime there was this time to be coped with; shortening days, unhappy nights, regrets. I sat there with a feeling of apprehension as if something even worse was yet to happen.

At dawn, distressed and hung over, I went to bed in the spare room, in which Ingrid and I had made love, and remembered the curve of her hip as she turned to me and the taste of her nipples and the texture of her tongue. I went to sleep and dreamed that I was back in Belfast watching pieces of a car bomb victim, twisted and charred beyond recognition, being placed carefully into a body bag.

TWENTY

LAURA CAME HOME two days later. I was in the kitchen, waiting for the kettle to boil, a coffee mug held in my hand, when I heard the wheels of her car scatter gravel on the drive.

I did not know what to expect. She had not telephoned again. When Rachael had called to confirm that she would be taking a flight on the following day, I had invented some story about a crisis in the hospital and an early return to work. She had believed this because she wanted to believe it; she had no reason to doubt the truth of what I was telling her.

I went out to the hallway, a space in which I had once taken such pride but which now seemed dull and austere, just as Laura pushed the front door open.

She stood against the afternoon light that shimmered around her like water.

'Hello,' I said.

'Hello.'

I could see that anger had been replaced by something more cool and considered, a compound of disappointment and disapproval. She had probably concluded, with the assistance of Catherine, that it had all been only too predictable, that men's immature egos depended on the sad and cynical challenge of getting their penis into something, anything, new.

'I was just making coffee,' I said. 'Would you care for a mug?'

She nodded and followed me into the kitchen. I made the two mugs of coffee, adding a spoonful of sugar to hers. We sat down at the table opposite each other.

'Do you want us to continue?' she asked.

'In the marriage?'

'Yes.'

'Yes, of course I do, if you do.'

'That's what I've been thinking about. I do as well. But in a different way.'

She was stirring her coffee. The spoon rattled against the sides of the mug in a more frantic way than was suggested by the graceful movement of her wrist.

She left the spoon on the table and held the mug between her flattened palms.

'Here's what I'm offering,' she said. 'We'll do everything the same because of Rachael but only what she can see. What she can't see has to be different. No,' she hesitated as if searching for the correct word, 'no intimacy.'

The choice of word made the decision seem particularly desolate.

'All right.'

'We'll just have to see how it goes,' she said, holding out some hope. 'Time will tell.'

'Of course.'

We were embarrassed with each other and awkward. We drank the coffee. Even small talk became difficult because of the unspoken assumption that any personal question could transgress the new boundaries. After a few minutes she said good night and went upstairs.

Rachael was in high spirits when we met her at the airport the following afternoon. She had gifts for us, bought at Heathrow, perfume and a silk scarf for Laura and a bottle of brandy for me.

'Papa and Granny insisted on giving me money,' she said. 'They were so sweet.'

I hated the way I had threatened her world. Her energy and humour rebuked me. She assumed that nothing was different and this faith was in marked contrast to my shifting moods and furtive misadventures.

I parked in Stephen's Green and we had afternoon tea in the Shelbourne Hotel. A colleague of Laura's joined us for a while, a tall, florid-faced oncologist. I noticed how relaxed she became in his company, talkative and happy. Later, Rachael spoke frankly about Jack. She had been hurt but not as much as one might have feared. Her resilience was encapsulated in her humour. She was able to parody the pretensions of some of his friends and explain how the age difference, which had seemed to be unimportant in Ireland, had become more and more marked in London. It was the kind of experience that could have caused heartbreak, but she had survived and I was very proud of her.

When she asked about Ingrid, I found it difficult to say much but Laura described the assault without any evident difficulty and then related, with equal detail, a fictitious meeting between the four of us where they explained that they would almost certainly return to England.

'For good?'

'I'd guess so.'

'Ah! You'll miss him, won't you, Dad?'

'I certainly will.'

I stared unhappily out the window at the traffic on the Green. I thought about Ingrid and for some reason remembered, vividly, her tattoo, innocent against her skin like a symbol of youth that has survived the passing of the years.

'That's sad,' Rachael said.

She seemed to have matured in the weeks she had been away. There was a more confident note in her voice and she was more relaxed than she would often have been when she was with us in public.

'I'll soon be going back to school,' she said.

'Has it been a good summer?' I asked, suddenly remembering that Laura and I were supposed to be going away to Amsterdam. That now seemed to be an unlikely prospect.

'One of the best! Really, one of the best. I kept a diary,' she said, 'the first that I've kept for ages and I wrote in it every day.'

We drove home. Passing Cromer's house I felt upset and embarrassed and wished that I had taken the other route. From the corner of my eye I saw that Laura's expression was as rigid as a mask but Rachael, reflected in the rear-view mirror, looked out with interest and even turned to look back at it.

'It looks empty already,' she said. 'I wonder who'll live there next?'

Our house was bleached in late-afternoon light, some of its windows reflecting the sky. It looked like a house in a child's story book in which someone good, like a granny, lives and into which one could escape from the giant who was roaring at the crossroads.

Later, when Rachael had gone to bed, I finished a drink, completed the nightly ritual of checking doors and windows, and went up to our room. Laura was reading a paperback novel by a writer who was so inept that I had to suppress some irritated comment. I undressed and got into bed, careful to stay on my own side.

'It's nice that she's home,' Laura said.

'What do you think it will be like here when she's gone for good?'

She was still staring at the pages of the novel but could hardly have failed to notice that this was a contentious question.

'Who knows?' she said.

She put down the book but didn't turn to look at me. The cover showed a young woman being caressed lasciviously by an older man.

'Sometimes I wonder,' she said, 'if Rachael was the cement that kept us together over the years. I suppose there's at least a possibility that we won't have much in common after she's gone.'

'I can't believe that,' I said but I suspected that my voice lacked conviction.

'I hope you're right,' Laura said as if she had gained some minimal reassurance from what I had said.

'What about Amsterdam?' I asked.

She turned to look at me with genuine surprise. I would like to have kissed her.

'I had completely forgotten about that,' she said.

'I suppose it's not a good idea any more?'

'I suppose not.'

'It's a pity, though.'

'It's not my fault.'

'I know that. But I can still be disappointed!'

'You could always go by yourself if you like,' she said, opening the book again.

'That would be pointless. I wanted to be there with you.'

'Do you mind if I read for a while?' she asked, holding up the book as if offering it for sale.

'Of course not! But do you really find it readable?'

'It's trash,' she said. 'But it's relaxing trash. Who wants Tolstoy at this time of night?'

'I still can't understand his success,' I said, with what might have been a hint of jealousy.

'He churns them out,' she said and this must have been a criticism of me.

I switched out the lamp on my bedside table and settled down self-consciously.

I could hear the rustle of the pages as she turned them and the gentle persistence of her breathing.

Long after she had turned off her own lamp and went to sleep, I lay awake, wishing that the world hadn't shrunk to such loneliness. I went to sleep and dreamed about Ingrid and woke and lay there until light invaded the room.

TWENTY-ONE

OVER THE NEXT few days, Laura returned to work and Rachael went back to school. I didn't even pretend that I was writing in a notebook.

When Rachael left, I moved into the spare room. It was something of a relief to be there. I could, at least, read throughout the night or listen to the radio. In the spare-room bed, where sex with Ingrid had been so intense and joyous, I could seek solace in masturbatory fantasies. This added to my general feeling of wretchedness. Like a furtive schoolboy, I was both ashamed and guilty to be so unloved. The house became a place of internment.

Laura returned home in the evenings much later than had been customary.

Sometimes she said that she had been to a seminar or to a conference or to dinner with a friend. At other times, she gave no explaination at all. I never asked. I didn't really want to know, although sometimes, alone in bed at night, I imagined her being expertly fucked by the florid-faced oncologist. I could dismiss these thoughts during the day but at night they were powerfully persistent. On only one occasion, close to midnight, a little drunk and a little more jangled than usual, I asked her where she had been. She looked at me coldly and said, 'I'm sorry but I don't think I have to answer that.'

In an attempt at some kind of retaliation, I started going out in the evening and not coming home until late. Those evenings were a kind of self-imposed ordeal. I had nowhere to go; there was no one whom I particularly wanted to see. I would usually drive into the city and go to some film. I often left the cinema before the film had ended, bored by the predictability of the action on the screen. Then I would go to a bar where I knew that I might bump into some old acquaintances. We would have desultory conversations. My books had built a barrier they were unwilling to cross, under the impression that I embodied some kind of success.

After closing time, with the impatient shouts of barmen ringing in my ears, I would sometimes go to one of the clubs on Leeson Street and sit by myself drinking expensive but not very palatable wine. On a few occasions I chatted to women and once or twice I could probably have gone home with them. I remember, in particular, a sad, stout, attractive girl who was even lonelier than I was. I was tempted, but shame and embarrassment for both of us overwhelmed my lust and with some unsubtle excuses I disentangled myself from her plans. I'm sure that I cut an odd figure on my visits to these clubs where the patrons always seemed to be the same. I would have been marked out by my air of not really wanting to be there. There was no one to whom I had to pretend that I was having a good time. I could be as morose as I wanted to be, the skeleton at the feast.

When I got home, Laura was invariably in the bedroom, sleeping or pretending to be asleep. She never commented on my absences or asked me where I had been, so the entire exercise was probably a total waste of time.

Sometime during those weeks, I was driving down to the local shop for my copy of the *Irish Times* when I came across a funeral approaching a laneway that led to the old Roman Catholic cemetery. I pulled the jeep into the side of the road and turned off the engine in a small act of respect to some unknown neighbour. The hearse came slowly towards me and, as it passed, I noticed, with some surprise, that the coffin was covered with a tricolour.

Three men were walking immediately behind the hearse. There was a family similarity in their faces and in their low-slung way of walking, arms hanging inertly by their sides. One nodded towards me and I suddenly realized that he was the postman, O'Dalaigh's son.

Behind the family there were seven survivors of the War of Independence.

They were very old; one was being pushed in a wheelchair by a girl who might have been a grand-daughter. They all wore hats and fustian overcoats, belted despite the mildness of the morning, and they all had medals pinned across their chests. They shuffled along, although one still managed a short, military strut and I realized that I was probably seeing the last survivors of the ambush that had been described to me in such detail. I looked at them with fascination as they went past, old men whose faces had caved in round bad dentures so that they all had similarly fixed expressions. It was difficult to think of them as active and merciless young men, fighting a war for a future that had stretched out to encompass this moment.

I couldn't feel any real regret about O'Dalaigh's death but I was glad to have heard his account of the ambush.

It was a big funeral; there were many priests. Car followed car into the narrow lane. I recognized two local Dáil representatives and a local doctor and Mr Moore from the pub. Near to the end of the procession, when I was about to start the car, I thought that I recognized the blue car that had stopped close to my gate and that had driven away at speed from Cromer's house. The driver was unfamiliar but beside him, in the passenger seat, was a figure who, at the very least, resembled the man whom I had seen limping from my gate to this car. A few children went past on bicycles, determined to extract some fun from the funeral and then the road was empty. It would have been easy for me to contact the guards. I thought about it for a few minutes before deciding against it. I could offer no proof of any kind.

As I write this I feel a certain shame at having made what was probably another shabby, subjective decision. I am well aware that I emerge from these pages as less than admirable, self-interested and lacking in moral courage. I have attempted to tell the truth about myself and others so there would be little point in attempting to avoid the implications of what I have written. But the process has been both instructive and humbling.

Some weeks went past in a kind of truce. Laura came home to dinner much more often and I stopped going to Leeson Street. One evening we watched 'The Late Late Show' together, then Laura, who had worked very hard during the week, took a bath and went to bed. I was reading an anthology of American short stories and stayed up quite late. Then I went to bed, listened to the radio and fell asleep.

I know that I was dreaming about something comforting, some sensation of warmth or of desire but when I woke, the body beside mine was real. I kissed her anxiously, urgently.

'Laura?'

'Don't talk,' she said. 'We've talked enough. Let's not talk it away.'

I was excited but, in some strange sense, timid, as if challenged by her desire.

Her body was familiar, yet there was something very different about her presence, about the force with which she moved onto me. We struggled in the darkness in a ritual of reconciliation, yet when it was over I felt that the act, although intensely pleasurable, had not brought us closer together. It was as if we had asserted our own separateness. In a sense, we had used each other, not speaking, as if emotionally and intellectually detached from the activity of our bodies. The reconciliation had been physical, a need satisfied, a re-enactment of past closeness. I wanted to say something generous or express some gratitude or love, but guessing that she had experienced the same psychic chasm, I remained silent, clinging to her damp body as if safety depended on it.

As our breathing calmed, she stirred a little in my arms, the movements of someone waking. It was still very dark but the lobe of her ear appeared to be translucent in some unnoticed source of light. I kissed her; the response was comforting but detached.

'I love you,' I risked saying, 'I want to make it up to you.'

In the pause before she replied, I imagined that I could hear both our heartbeats, dissonant and disturbed.

'Let's make the most of what we've got,' she said.

'Yes!' I said, although I couldn't suppress a memory of being in this same bed with Ingrid. 'Yes, let's do that.'

Later, we switched on the bedside light, and, without touching each other, we talked about Laura's time in England and about her parents and about Rachael. We avoided talking about our relationship. I can picture us now in the lazy bedside light, each propped up on a pillow. It is a memory as peaceful yet as charged with meaning as a Dutch interior and I cherish it, for I believe that it was then that I began to feel the need to make some sense out of all that had happened to us.

TWENTY-TWO

BY CHRISTMAS, the emotional osmosis of our marriage had reformed into a distinct and recognizable entity. It was different, yet oddly similar to what had gone before, like a clever forgery. This inevitably suggests something fake or contrived and I cannot avoid those implications. In a sense, we were counterfeiting certain emotions, drawing on memories of the past rather than on the reality of the present. We behaved to each other with an elaborate courtesy, as if each day had been choreographed by some expert on domestic conflict management. We knew each other well enough to avoid all possibilities of discord.

Barbara invited us to a party which, after some initial worry and hesitation, we decided to attend. I believe that both of us feared the ways in which Ingrid's name would come into the conversation. It was a hurdle that had to be faced, so, feeling a little paranoid and more than a little defensive, we turned up at her house.

'My drinking friends have deserted me! Even you!' Barbara said, pointing at me. 'When have you last been to the pub?'

'I seem to have got out of the habit,' I said, not wanting to allude to the number of evenings I had spent in Dublin.

'I hope you're writing something that will justify your defection!'

'Time will tell,' I said with deliberate vagueness. Any reference to writing made me uneasy but I found that I was thinking more and more about a book explaining what had happened to Ingrid. Although I knew that I would have to alter many details to avoid giving offence to some people, the first draft, at least, could be frank.

Since this was the last time that I was in Barbara's house, I look back at it with considerable nostalgia for it had been a pleasant piece of my world. I have already written about her death. The last moments must have intensified her loneliness into a passionate resolve. On the evening of her party she was wearing rather too much make-up and behaving with a little too much anxious gaiety; the good hostess under stress. The thought of killing herself had probably crossed her mind by then, so her use of the word 'deserted' may have been more than small talk.

Inevitably, there was talk about the Cromers. The topic was introduced by another of the guests, a tall, angular woman with a strong, rather masculine face and a manner that veered unnervingly between the uncertain and the assertive. She had been introduced as an old friend of Barbara's, a current affairs producer at the BBC. In a lull in the conversation, one of those uneasy moments that needs to be filled quickly, she turned to me and said 'Barbara's been telling me about that awful business! That friend of yours, the German woman. And you found her?'

'Yes,' I said, aware of a tremor in my voice. 'Yes, I did.'

'Those savages! And all for nothing, I gather.'

'You must read your history, Dorothy,' Barbara said. 'Beating up strangers is enshrined here as a national sport.'

'Come on, Barbara,' I said, 'it would be foolish to attribute any historical imperative to the attack on Ingrid.'

Laura was staring at me disapprovingly. I knew, at that instant, that I had blundered into an unnecessary conversation. I could have ignored Barbara's remark or even laughed at it.

'So you don't think it was political?' Dorothy said. 'You think it was personal?'

'I think it was psychopathic,' I said, attempting to distract attention from the more obvious implications of Barbara's question.

'I'll never feel safe in my own home again,' Barbara said, folding
her arms across her breasts. She looked at me in a way that I found
difficult to interpret. Was I being challenged or teased? If Laura
had not been listening I would have responded more directly but
knew that I should be cautious.

'But you don't think it was the IRA?' Dorothy persisted.
'Everybody else seems to think so. Otherwise, why would the
Cromers have left so abruptly? I understand that they've gone for
good. Don't you think they must have felt really threatened?'

'I really don't know,' I said. 'I wish that I did.'

'I'm sorry. It's just that I'm interested. And I liked his novels.'

I finished my whiskey. Barbara took my glass and poured me
another. I added lots of water, anxious not to get drunk and start
speaking in a way that I would regret later.

'I had a letter from Ingrid the other day,' Barbara said, then
turned to straighten bottles on a tray. I knew that she was deliberately challenging me to ask for details, to betray an interest that
transcended curiosity. I attempted to prepare a tone of voice that
would be polite or merely socially engaged.

'Really!' Laura said and I wanted to give her a grateful look.
'How are they? Where are they living? They never left an address.'

'Norfolk!' Barbara managed to invest the word with some
humour. 'A village in Norfolk!'

'Why Norfolk, I wonder?' I said.

'They saw a picture of a house for sale. A converted school-
house. A young architect and his wife lived there and apparently
they did a smashing job.'

I knew almost nothing about Norfolk. I couldn't even point
to it on a map of England. I would have to read about it and gain
some understanding of her new world. I wanted to know what kind
of landscape she would see when she pulled back the curtains on
her windows. Was it bleak or fruitful? Did the village rest uneasily

between mountains or was it the focal point of gently sloping fields?

'Is she working?' I asked, a detached question that I hoped might elicit more information.

'Yes, she is,' Barbara said matter-of-factly, looking around the room, checking the glasses of the other guests. 'She's working for something in a local theatre.'

She went across the room to the other guests and Laura saw someone she knew standing in the doorway. I was left with Dorothy. She cleared her throat uneasily, got ready to say something, then changed her mind.

'Have you known Barbara for long?' I asked her and she gulped like a fish before answering.

'Oh for donkeys' years!' she said. 'Absolutely! We worked together on *Reynolds' News*. You wouldn't even remember it but it had a good circulation in its day. They had really good writers. Negley Farson.'

She leaned towards me in a confiding manner.

'I've got to say again that it must have been awful for you!' she said. 'To be absolutely frank and I know that you won't mind my saying this but I couldn't live here. Absolutely not! I know that the tax concessions for writers are attractive and all that but are they worth it? I worry about Barbara.'

'I don't think that you need to. It was an isolated incident.'

'It got lots of coverage in England you know.'

'Did it? I mustn't have seen the papers.'

'Most of the coverage suggested that it was political.'

Laura joined us and introduced the woman who had been standing in the doorway. She was a doctor who practiced in Bray. The conversation became general and unthreatening. I relaxed and the next few hours were perfectly pleasant.

On the way home, Laura, who was driving, asked, 'Does Barbara know?'

'Know what?' I said, although I knew exactly what she meant.

'About you and Ingrid?'

'Of course she doesn't.'

'She certainly suspects something.'

'You know Barbara! She loves intrigue.'

'I hope I'm not the laughing-stock of the county.'

She stopped the car, leaving the lights on and the engine running.

We were near to the house but it seemed better not to go there. The light from the headlamps, reflected from the road, made the interior of the car appear ghostly. I reached across, touched her shoulder, put my arm around her and, instinctively, she leaned against me so that we were like a young courting couple. I kissed the top of her head, then realized that she was crying quietly.

'Please don't be sad,' I said. 'I love you with all my heart.'

'I feel like a fool,' she said, 'as if everyone were talking about me. It simply isn't fair.'

I held her closely, awkwardly, not knowing what to say. She was a little drunk but her unhappiness was real.

'What would Rachael say if she could see us?' she said. 'Let's go.'

She drove home slowly, as if we were carrying something fragile and precious, and parked just outside the front door. When we went inside I switched on the lights and Laura went upstairs. I sat at my desk. There was no work in progress, nothing to suggest that I had once lived a writer's life. Despite this, I felt much closer to the routine of working than I had done for many years. The urgent need to make sense out of experience is, I believe, a definition of inspiration. My feelings needed to be explored.

Almost six months have passed since I wrote the first words in a small red notebook. Now I have filled eleven more, writing on both sides of each page. They make a pleasing pile on my desk, their spiral bindings intricate as the spines of some small animals.

Nothing that has happened since has been as bad as that drive home. Barbara's death was horrific, of course, yet in some odd way it was more shocking than sad. It didn't hurt us.

When Rachael came home for the Christmas holidays, Laura and I were less cautious, less reticent, less extravagantly polite. We were talking again, telling each other some of what we felt, trusting each other a little. In bed, when we made love, although there was something different about it, some changes indicated by omissions that were almost impossible to define, it was good and satisfying and real. These omissions were never discussed. There was no language for them.

For a time it seemed that it might snow at Christmas, an unusual occurrence, but the cold spell passed after three days and the day itself was mild and a little disappointing. Barbara had gone to London to spend some time with Dorothy.

The day before she left, she called to our house with some brightly wrapped gifts.

We had nothing to give her in return.

One day, in February, I was looking through a book of the paintings of Edward Hopper. I was struck by the loneliness of his people, yet moved by the dignity of their anonymity. They occupied worlds viewed through windows as if seen from a passing train, people seated in isolation, contemplating their lives. That same day I drove to a local shop and bought the first notebook.

I reach out and touch one of the notebooks now, hesitantly, as if afraid of what I might rediscover in my familiar handwriting. The first words were written when I was alone in the house. Now, working down the pages towards a final sentence, I am alone again. Laura is attending a conference in Lisbon, Rachael is at school. It is a cold evening; gusts of wind rattle the windows and it has rained heavily.

I have attempted to tell the truth, yet I must confess that not everything I have written actually happened. I have invented incidents and details that helped my own understanding of the story. These embellishments have made it possible for me to analyze my feelings and they now seem as real as the rest. Some parts of every day are, in any case, a fiction; the hopes and aspirations, the desire to be loved, the ambitions that one might have for one's children, the plans to take revenge. We escape out of the reality of our lives to create dreams of what might have been or what should have happened.

I sit here in this room, the windows rattling, the sense of other people's lives beginning to fade away. I feel a detachment from these people, as if they have been exorcised. I am no longer the 'I' of this narrative, so full of opinions and judgements, so anxious to explain, so determined to appear reasonable. They would tell their stories differently and from their point of view I might be a peripheral figure who, after some involvement in their lives, sits in a darkening room with nothing left to say.